MOON BEAM

by

Steven Burgauer

MOON BEAM

Steven Burgauer

© Steven Burgauer 2018

Battleground Press
P.O. Box 2327
Lady Lake, FL
32158

FOR FURTHER INFORMATION:
steven.burgauer@gmail.com

ISBN 978-0692105351 (sc)
ISBN 978- (e)

To My Children, Scott and Kate, Who Stood by Me In A Time of Great Need

The woman sat, half-naked, shivering in the cold, sterile air of the lunar habitat.

She sat, legs crossed, finger poised on the trigger of her automatic pistol. Her gaze was fixed, her hand steady. The barrel of the snub-nosed weapon was pressed firmly against the taut flesh of her right temple, its metal rim carving out a round indentation in her throbbing, tension-filled skin.

The woman had a wild look in her eyes. Flaming red hair. Strong, muscular arms. Savage, feral eyes. Bone-handled hunting knife sheathed at her waist. Tattoo of a rising Phoenix splayed in full color across her neck, shoulder, and upper arm.

This was not the first time the woman had been here, in this desolate place, on the cusp of ending her life with a bullet to the head.

But, would this be the day, the day when she finally did it, the day when she finally pulled the trigger and ended it all?

She found that it took a lot of nerve to end one's life, more than she cared to admit. Each time before, when the gun had been in her hand pressed up against the side of her head, doubts had crept in.

Was this really how she wanted to end it? Or would she be leaving behind unfinished business?

No, not yet! she suddenly thought, relaxing her trigger finger. *First, make them pay! First, make the bloody bastards pay!*

That's when she decided — *Revenge first, suicide after.*

Once she had her revenge, then she could dictate the terms of her own demise and finally put an end to her wretched life.

But, revenge first . . . .

CHAPTER ONE

Day One, 1400 hours

Chief Engineer Clay Flynn was in the married quarters, a place he had no business being, not at this time of day, not without a guest pass in his hand or a work order in his pocket. Being in bed with this woman could only court trouble. — It had once before.

Rules were important. They kept order. They helped prevent accidents and they kept people safe.

Rules were meant to be obeyed, not flaunted. Yet, every time the two of them slipped beneath the sheets and went one on one behind closed doors, Chief Clay Flynn was breaking one of the moonbase's strictest rules of all, the rule against a male officer fraternizing with another man's wife.

Rules were written for a purpose. They were written for a purpose by exacting people with orderly minds. Every accident produced a new rule or procedure designed to prevent the same accident from happening again. Every mishap. Every death. Every dismemberment. Every near miss. Every work stoppage. Every air leak. Every severe burn.

Living and working in space was dangerous. Aside from the inherent risks attendant to close confinement, space could kill a man in a thousand different ways. Radiation. Micrometeorites. Loss of cabin pressure. Ruptured fuel tanks. Oxygen deprivation. Carbon-dioxide poisoning. Dehydration. Starvation. Extreme cold. Extreme heat. Micro-gravity. Loss of power. Unseen hazards.

Confinement to a space hab, even one as large as this one, brought with it a unique set of problems. More problems meant more rules. Strict adherence to a twenty-four-hour clock. Three eight-hour shifts. Mandatory exercise periods. Limits on alcohol consumption. Regimented activities. Psychological testing. Command structure, even for the civilian population. Prohibitions against fraternizing. Single men were not to consort with married women, nor single women with married men. The casual mores of Earth had no place in this tightly controlled bubble.

Chief Engineer Clay Flynn rolled over in the bedsheets and stared at the mottled ceiling. *What was it about this woman anyway?*

Ouida was attractive, of that there was little doubt. Some might even say the woman was fetching.

But good looks were hardly enough of a reason, not for him to risk so much, not for him to break so many rules just to be with her. Ouida was married; he was the hab's chief engineer, a senior officer in the facility's command structure. *What was it about this woman anyway?*

Availability. That was the short answer. In a place as remote as this one, the moonbase, any woman who signaled her availability by whatever means, regardless of age, social status, or looks, was bound to attract takers. As always and forever, men were dogs, women were kibble.

But with this woman the magnetic attraction was more than simple availability. It had to be. He was a senior officer. She was one of the more qualified medical officers on-station. He had a lot to lose if they were found out. So did she. There would be hell to pay, a censure at least.

Ouida Baldwin was one smart and beautiful woman. Plus, the two of them had history. Back in the day, ten years ago, seventy-two torrid hours that began in a zero-g room aboard the space station. She was in the service, finishing medical school on the military's dime. He had just graduated from the Academy near the top of his class. A tragic accident had brought them together. But, for three glorious days, the length of her leave, they had been unable to keep their hands off one another. Then, a decade later, wonder of wonders, they met up again for a second time, here at the hab. By then she was on her second marriage trying to bring up a boy from her first.

Flynn pushed aside the bedsheets now and caressed her hair. "I have to go," he said quietly, admiring her tattoo.

"Just like the old days, Flynn. Cum and go. Do the deed and leave."

"Crudely put."

"But true."

He shook his head. "You want we should be found out by Doyle?"

"Oh, I think Doyle already knows."

Flynn sat bolt upright in bed. "Don't play games with me, Ouida. You want I should lose my job?"

"Even Hanrahan isn't stupid enough to fire his senior engineer over some mislaid sperm and an unauthorized lay."

"Don't be so sure. Our Mr. Winston Hanrahan prides himself on establishing a reputation as a hard case. He would like nothing better than to make an example of me, of us. We could help him make his bones as the new commandant."

"The man is going to cashier his best surgeon and most senior moon engineer just to make his bones? I seriously doubt that," Ouida said, pulling the sheets up over her breasts. "Six months here on this rock will smooth out the man's rough edges."

"Your husband can make trouble for us."

"You should have thought of that before you unzipped your trousers. Besides, Doyle is too busy stümping Nora Goldman to be jealous of my afternoon workout."

Flynn was just about to answer her, when there was a loud — *Bang!* — from somewhere down the corridor or perhaps the next module over. Sound traveled a great distance in the culvert-like corridors.

Suddenly, the direction of airflow in the room changed. Chief Flynn felt it in the whiskers of his unshaven face. The slight fluctuation in cabin pressure presented as an outward force against his inner ear.

He swallowed hard, tried to neutralize the pressure imbalance in his eustachian tubes. Then he heard it, the faint whistling of rushing air as it was sucked out of the room and into the network of corridors beyond.

"Shit. I know that sound," he said, his face darkening. The pressure inside his eardrums became more pronounced.

Then came a resounding bang as the first in a series of heavy compression doors clamped shut, one after the other in rapid succession.

"The pressure doors are closing," Flynn said in an urgent panic. He launched himself from the bed in the general direction of his clothes.

"What does that mean?" Ouida asked, wide-eyed with fear.

"What that means is that there has been an accident somewhere in the hab."

"Oh, my God. My son Adam is at the learning center with the rest of the young people. School lessons, then calisthenics, then some sort of vid."

"The explosion didn't come from that direction."

"Explosion?"

"Too loud to have been much of anything else," Flynn said. "Besides, it came from the opposite direction. Near the waste treatment plant, perhaps. Or down in the area of Lava Tube One somewhere. I need to get over to that side of the hab right away. You need to round up Doc Runyon and the rest of the medicos and get up to the infirmary. If there's been an accident, there are bound to be casualties. You folks need to be prepared for incoming."

Flynn slipped on his pants. His beeper chirped urgently. "They are already paging me. I have to go, Ouida. I have to investigate."

"I'm not going to the infirmary with Doc Runyon or anybody else until I've first had a chance to check on my son," she said, hastily pulling on her scrubs. "Once I know that Adam's okay, then I'll go to the med."

"Forget about Adam. The boy is okay. Do as I say. Track down Runyon. Get to the med right away."

Flynn's rushed movements were awkward in one-sixth-g. He dressed and was in the corridor. Red emergency lights were flashing in both directions. Audible alarms were ringing. Ouida was now sobbing in the background.

"Since when do I take orders from you?" she cried. "Adam first. Then the infirmary."

"Pull it together, woman!" he shouted from beyond the doorway. Handholds in the corridor helped him move swiftly along.

Flynn turned right and strode rapidly down the passageway in the general direction of the recycling and waste treatment facility. He shouted back to her as he ran.

"If you have to go to the activity center, then be quick about it. Go there; pick up your boy; then straight to the medical center."

Then Flynn was gone, a serious man facing a serious situation.

CHAPTER TWO

Day One, 1410 hours

"The pressure doors close automatically," Lou Santini said. "That is just a fact of life."

Lou Santini was Chief Flynn's top tech. Santini was an older man, older than Flynn anyway, highly intelligent and with hundreds of hours on the job. Lou Santini possessed a litany of skills and was considered by most to be well briefed on virtually every hab subsystem — production and storage of electrical power, comm, solid and liquid waste treatment and recycling, heating and cooling systems, crater ice processing, farm irrigation, pumps and filtration.

Santini continued in his instructive way. "It is a longstanding safety measure. The pressure doors close automatically. That protects the integrity of the rest of the facility against catastrophic blow-in. If the sensors measure more than a one-eighth-pound change in air pressure, the doors shut tight. They will not reopen automatically. It has to be done manually, either from a panel beside the door or else remotely from the Command Center."

"So, what are we looking at here, Lou?" Chief Flynn asked, as they both squeezed into the tiny control booth on the third level. Office space was at a premium inside the hab. "A major breach in Tunnel One?"

"Take a look at the schematics on the upper screen," Santini said, pointing.

Flynn drew closer and squinted at the screen. "Make this bigger, will you? Picture's too small for old eyes."

Santini nodded and enlarged the image as he explained. "Tunnel One runs underground from the rim of the GAPS Crater, past a series of pressure doors and into Node A. Node A is arguably the most important of the five lunar nodes. It connects tunnels leading to waste processing, the married quarters, comm, water processing and . . . "

"Yeah, I get it, Lou. We lose Node A, we lose everything, the entire hab."

"Yep. That is about the size of it, Chief. The breach is in the terminus section of Tunnel One. That's the section closest to the surface exit at the rim of the Gravity Assist Power Station Crater."

"Lou, I think what you're trying to tell me is that forcing our way into the tunnel from the rim side of the Crater is particularly dangerous. The terminus is the oldest section of tunnel, isn't it? I mean besides the lava tube."

Lou Santini looked up and nodded quietly. He had but four months remaining on his current contract. As soon as he clocked out on his last day, Santini's plan was to go see the Paymaster, collect his bonus, then raise anchor for home. He had been setting aside money for a while now and had banked more than enough to afford a six-month leave of absence, time he could use to try and patch things up with his daughter. Money bought freedom. After all, nobody in his right mind signed on to work at the moonbase unless it was for the money. Certainly not for the beautiful scenery or a chance to go hiking or sport fishing. Those were earthly pursuits. Prestige, yes. Line on a resume, yes. Great fun, no.

"Do we think anyone was in that section of tunnel at the time of the rupture?" Flynn asked.

Santini nodded again. A sad look filled his eyes.

"Do I want to know?"

"No, Chief. You do not want to know."

"Tell me anyway." Flynn leaned back against the poly-cement wall of the control room. The concrete walls were cold to the touch, as they always were. Such was life inside a metal can surrounded by porous rock and lined with ceramic concrete. Cold walls. Flash-frozen sterility. Bone-crushing darkness. Mind-numbing boredom. — Except, of course, for today.

"It is possible that there are — were — two children trapped in that last section of tunnel," Santini said. In his estimation, the Moon was no place for children, and never would be. Too damn dangerous. He had argued against it at every turn. But the answer from the higherups had always been the same. Skilled scientists often came with baggage — children and wives — baggage that could not be left behind for long stretches of time, certainly not for months or years. In the eyes of the company, children were a necessary evil.

"Christ! Children? That is the worst possible news."

"Indeed. Doyle and Ouida Baldwin's boy — Adam. Also, Nora Goldman's daughter. The girl's name escapes me."

"Kyra," Flynn exclaimed. "The Goldman girl's name is Kyra."

"The two missing children were at the activity center along with the other youngsters. Fourteen children in all. Various ages. The counselors took the lot of them on a field trip to the waste treatment center."

"Field trip? What the hell?"

"You approved it," Lou Santini said defensively.

"I did?"

"Yes, I have your signature right here on the form. Tour of Waste Treatment Plant on a date to be determined. Approved by you. The missing children must have wandered off the tour without the counselors noticing."

"Bloody hell. I did approve that tour. I just didn't make the connection. The counselors assured me there would be adequate adult supervision. Sarena something or other."

"Lopez. Sarena Lopez. That is the name on the form," Santini said, pointing.

"Shit . . . and Ouida Baldwin's boy is one of the missing? . . . Have the parents been notified? . . . Are we even sure the children were in that section of tunnel when it blew?"

"Pulling up vid now," Santini said. "As it happens, the supervisors are notifying the parents as we speak."

"Run the vid," Flynn ordered.

The small computer room suddenly felt uncomfortably warm and crowded, though it was just the two of them. Flynn was stone-faced. Three years ago, he had left his post at Field Station Six because of the constant danger and turmoil. This place was supposed to be more serene, a good place to add luster to an already impressive resume, perhaps wind down a long career, while also taking home a darn good paycheck.

Lou Santini touched an icon on the screen, slid it aside, adjusted two settings, tapped the screen. "This is four minutes prior to the explosion."

"We know for certain, now, that this was an explosion?" Chief Flynn asked his number two. "Do we have any shrapnel? A bomb casing? Explosive residue? Confirmation of a propellant? Do we have any concrete evidence whatsoever?"

"Nothing concrete, no." Santini said it like a little boy taken to the woodshed by his father.

"Then let's not get ahead of ourselves, Lou. Until we know different, call it an event. Or call it an anomaly. Call it any damn thing you want. But do not call it an explosion. Next thing we know, panic will set in and the residents will be talking nonstop about terrorists."

"Roger that," Lou Santini said. "Like I was saying, this is the tape approximately four minutes prior to the . . . event.

Tunnel cams are motion sensitive. They start recording anytime there is movement within its range. The cams are also auto-tracking. They follow the movements of whatever woke them up to begin with."

Santini continued. "Now watch carefully. The cams show two children entering that section of tunnel at three minutes fifty-two seconds prior to the event. That's Adam on the left, Kyra on the right. The camera tracks their movements for about two minutes thirty. They laugh, play some little peekaboo game, engage in some harmless horseplay. Then Kyra points to something out of range of the cam and they trot off in that direction. Seventy-two seconds later — *Bam!* — lights out. We never see them on camera again. Whatever caused the . . . event . . . took out the cams as well."

"So, we don't know for certain whether or not the kids even survived the event," Flynn said flatly. "How can we be certain that the two of them are even still alive?"

"We can't. All we know for certain is that the two children entered that section of tunnel."

"What was she pointing at, do you think?"

"I'm having one of my people pull up blues of that section of tunnel," Santini said. "Maybe you and I can figure that one out for ourselves."

"Damn. This is the Kobayashi Maru."

"Chief?"

"The Kobayashi Maru. The no-win scenario."

"Sorry, but I do not follow."

"Ancient science fiction. But do the math, Lou. Say we mount a rescue effort. Say we suit up people and send them out there? Say we risk more lives, perform some heroic act. What are the odds? Do we dare make a concerted effort to rescue two children who are almost certainly dead already?"

"Odds be damned, Boss. There is absolutely no math to do here. We have no choice but to try and save them. People will expect us to try. They are children, for God's sake, children of colonists."

"I thought you hated children?"

"Don't hate them, Chief. Got one of my own. Just think the moon is no place for folks too young to properly assess the risks. By definition, that means all little ones. The dangers are many, the risks far too great. All the same — we have to try and save the little bastards."

"And try we will. But make no mistake about it, Lou. This rescue op we're cooking up is an extreme longshot. No one survives a sudden decompression event like that, not without a pressure suit. The human body is too fragile. Explosive devices cause devastating compressive forces. Highly compressed air has the force of a rock-hard battering ram. It breaks bodies, shatters windows, busts concrete."

"Please don't tell me we are going to stand by and do nothing," Santini entreated.

"No, we are not," Chief Flynn said as he started issuing orders. "I need a minimum of four men in pressure suits, two teams of two men each. I need a rover with full charge standing by, plus a driver and a medic with full kit. Kick it into gear, Lou. Let's make this happen. Like pronto."

Lou was scribbling notes on his handheld e-pad as fast as he could. Chief Flynn continued. "Get a sealant bot on the rim of the GAPS Crater. Arm the bot with a comm package. Also, software protocols *epsilon* and *mu*. Set the bot on auto-roll until it locates the source of the breach. Then have the bot drop the comm package into the hole, lay a sealant patch in place, and glue the hole shut with a poly-aluminum cap. As soon as the comm package is in the hole, get me a live feed on this screen so I can see what the hell is going on in there. Move, move, move!"

Clay Flynn already had a bad feeling in the pit of his stomach about the outcome of this effort. The words of doubt didn't leak out of his mouth. But he thought them nonetheless.

A new voice broke in upon his thoughts. It was one of the team captains from the volunteer Rapid Response Force, a young man from Santini's department, Junior Mate Gunderson.

"Chief Flynn. I have both mothers here in the Command Center with me, both of them. Nora Goldman and Ouida Baldwin. There won't be a moment's peace with these two women unless we can give them some answers. Do we have any to give?"

"On-screen please, Gunderson. One mother at a time. Nora Goldman first. Private feed."

There was some movement in the background, then a tear-filled woman's face filled the screen.

"Nora?"

"Chief?"

"I wish I had better news."

"Is my Kyra dead?"

"Nora, the honest to God truth is that I simply do not know. But you and Mitch have to prepare yourselves for that possibility, just in case. The cameras show the kids entering that section of Tunnel One. After that, we just don't know. We have men and bots on the way. But it will take time."

"How much time?"

"Hours."

"They don't have hours, Chief."

"I know that, Nora, I really do. We are moving just as fast as we can. *Allegro.* At a quick and lively pace. Just like we practice most nights in our jam sessions. *Allegro.*"

"The Clay Pigeons?"

"You're a mad hatter on that electric banjo," Flynn remarked with some amusement. "Truly you are."

Nora laughed, and the tension was broken. "Not a banjo, a guitar."

"Thanks for clearing that up," Flynn said. "Now can you please put Ouida Baldwin on? Private feed, if you don't mind."

The tear-filled face left the screen a bit more relaxed than before. A door opened and shut in the background. Then another face, not tear-filled but creased with worry.

"Are we on private feed?" he asked.

"Yes." Ouida choked out the words.

"I am not entirely sure what to say here, Ouida. You and I are . . . well, you know what we are, what we once were. We are lovers and Adam is your son."

"He is yours too, you know."

"He? Who? Just what are you saying here?" Flynn stammered. He could feel the blood in his head begin to throb.

"Adam is your son."

"Since when is Adam my son? . . . What in blinking blazes are you talking about? . . . How is that even possible? . . . I always thought that in zero-g, one couldn't get in a family way . . . And why in bloody hell are you sharing this with me now? . . . Just so that I'll conduct a more thorough search and rescue effort? Is that what you're after?"

Ouida began to weep. The tears seemed manufactured. "Ten years ago . . . when you and I were together . . . that night . . . those days . . . I was already pregnant by the time we broke up and went our separate ways."

Chief Flynn sat in front of the screen, mouth agape. "Ouida . . . why didn't you tell me?

Before she could answer, Lou Santini charged back into the small room. "Sorry to barge in, Chief. But this is important. I have news."

"News? What news?" Flynn barked.

Then he turned back to the screen. "I have to go, Ouida. We will talk again later. In the meantime, one of my people will get back to you with any developments. Flynn out."

Flynn abruptly disconnected the feed and turned back to Santini. "This better be important, Lou. What have you got?"

"I was just looking at the blueprints and I may have found something."

"Damn it, man, are you going to tell me or not?" Flynn roared.

"This is ancient history, Chief. But if I'm reading this blue right, it's something that dates back well before your time or even mine. Remember when we last saw Kyra on tape, she was pointing into the distance towards the crater airlock?"

"Yes, do go on. You have my attention."

"I was looking at blueprints that date to when the original astronaut team bored that first section of tunnel. What about the pressure closet?"

"I'm sorry, Lou, but I don't know what the hell you are talking about."

"The pressure closet. It is an old side tunnel the original colonists burrowed into the regolith after the ceilings of the lava tube section were reinforced. This was still years before the current base was built, about the same time the cyclotron was dug. The folks back in those days used the pressure closet for storing supplies, dry goods and such. It is pressurized and to this day should still have an earth-normal atmosphere inside."

"And you think this is what Kyra was pointing at?" Flynn asked. "The bulkhead door leading into that side tunnel? How would she even have known about that side tunnel, much less have the proper access code to open the pressure door? That is assuming the door even still opens after all this time."

Santini went on. "If I remember my history correctly, all the original tunnels were lined with concrete and a lead-regolith amalgam, even the inner surface of the lava tubes. The idea was to shield the tunnels against cosmic rays and solar radiation."

"So much the better."

"No. So much the worse. A lead lining would mean that the children's thermal signature will be damn near impossible for us to detect with even our best instruments."

Chief Flynn fell silent, trying to recalculate their odds for success. Then he spoke:

"Can you tell from these blueprints whether or not there is an intercom feed into that side tunnel? Quickly now. Check the blues. Check the computer databanks. This is all quite troubling. How the hell would Kyra even have known about a side tunnel?"

Santini took a long moment to study the blueprints. "I don't see anything here about a comm system inside that room. For all we know, the intercom was installed much later."

"Check the computer."

Santini nodded his head and turned to the terminal. He enunciated each command slowly and deliberately.

"Computer . . . File search . . . Primary intercom system . . . Quadrant 1.1B . . . Pull up vid and sound."

A millisecond later, the input screen was spun-up and working. "I think we now have a live feed," Santini said. "We're up, Chief. No buttons to press. Simply talk into the mic."

There was an explosion of sound the instant the system went live.

"Help! Help! Get us out of here. Would someone please help us? We are trapped." It was a young girl's voice. She sounded desperate, her voice cracking with emotion.

Flynn spoke into the mic in low even tones. "Settle down, Kyra. We know where the two of you are. We know exactly, and we are coming to get you. It won't be long, maybe an hour, two at the most. Please try to be patient. Both of you. We are coming."

"Oh, oh, thank you, mister, for saving us. We don't have much light and Adam is hurt. He banged his head against the wall when the explosion . . . " She started to cry softly.

"Be patient, sweetheart. We are coming to get you, fast as we can. How badly is Adam hurt?"

Flynn turned to Lou. "They have light in there?"

"Probably emergency lighting. It likely runs off a battery, one of those old chemical batteries. The juice isn't going to last long, maybe an hour or two, less if the battery has leaked reactant."

"Then we must hurry. Get those men into pressure suits and onto the rover and down to the crater rim. Quickly! I am going down there myself. Someone needs to stay here and keep talking with the children over the comm. We need to keep them as calm as we possibly can."

There was activity in the corridor outside the control booth. A young lady, perhaps twenty years of age, stepped forward now from the corridor. "Sir, if you will permit me, I can handle a mic. I can keep the youngsters calm."

"And you are?"

"Sarena Lopez. One of the counselors from the activity center. Those two children are still my responsibility."

Chief Flynn frowned. "Don't be surprised, young lady, if the new commandant — Hanrahan — doesn't send you packing once this whole damn thing is over. What the hell were you thinking, letting two children you are responsible for out of your sight?"

"Well . . . I . . . "

"Do you even know how many different ways this is complete fubar? Do you know how many different ways a little kid can get himself killed in this place?"

"Fubar?"

"Military slang. Fucked Up Beyond All Recognition. You, my young lady, are the one who fucked things up."

"Please. I am begging you. Give me a chance to make this right, to fix things. At least allow me to help."

"Fix things? I hardly think so, Sarena. Until I can get an adequate explanation of how these two kids wandered off your field trip without you even knowing, consider yourself suspended. But, yes, for the moment, you can indeed help. Sit your ass down here and man the mic until I send someone to relieve you. Keep those two children calm," Flynn said as he turned away to speak with Santini and the others who had gathered at the doorway. They were all eager to help.

"I need a pressure suit, Lou. I'm going down there to the site of the — what did we decide to call it? — oh, yes, an event. I am going down to the site of the event myself. But I need you to stay up here and run overwatch while I'm gone."

"No way, Chief. I want to be on the scene, same as you."

"You're the best tech I have, Lou. I need you to remain here at the Command Center and run things. I can read a blue as well as the next man." Flynn pointed. "That old tunnel had an overhead pressure hatch. It led from the surface down into that storage area where the kids are trapped. Does your database show any emergency pressure suits in that chamber? It would normally be the case."

"Let me check."

Flynn continued to converse as he stepped into his Mag 10 pressure suit. The suits hung on the wall, zipped open, so a man could step backwards into the one assigned to him and zip up quickly. The suits were personalized and sized to fit a man snugly. The helmets hung on separate hooks beside each spacesuit.

In the background, as he dressed, he could hear Lopez talking to Kyra over the mic. "Don't cry, sweetheart. Are you hurt?"

"No," the child said softly.

"Do you have anything you can use as a bandage for Adam's head?" Sarena inquired softly.

"What do you mean bandage?" the child burbled.

"Maybe tear off a corner from your tee-shirt? No, better still, use one of your socks. It will make a perfect compress."

"But my socks are dirty," Kyra complained.

"It will be okay," Sarena assured her. "Take off one of your socks and press it gently against the bloody area on Adam's head. Have him hold the sock in place. The bleeding will soon stop . . . "

Smart girl, Flynn thought wryly, listening to the exchange. As he listened to Sarena handle Adam's first-aid long distance, Flynn completed putting on his pressure suit and readied himself to return to the job at hand.

"That overhead pressure hatch is a big mother," Flynn said, "big enough to lower KL-sized crates into the hole. Back in the day, the space agency used those gigantic crates to lower supplies and equipment down to the surface. Not so much now, since we learned how to raise our own kibble."

"Still checking on those emergency flight suits, Chief."

"I still don't understand how those kids knew to duck into that side tunnel for protection. They would have needed a valid passcode to enter the pressure closet from Tunnel One. Someone must have taught them how."

Lou answered. "Sheer speculation here, Boss. No facts whatsoever. But Mitch Goldman, Kyra's father, heads the Emergency Preparedness Team. The team does regular inspections of every tunnel and lava tube on a weekly basis. He may have taken Kyra along with him one day when he made his rounds, shown her how to enter a passcode on the keypad. You know how dads are."

"No, I actually do not. But I guess I will learn soon enough." The thought became a sentence and Flynn let them both drift off into mid-air, as if they should never have been said in the first place.

"Something I ought to know?"

"A story for another day perhaps," Flynn said. By this time, he had suited up and was ready to go. "Get those kids in spacesuits if the equipment manifest comes up positive. I would be willing to bet my stripes that a full complement of suits is stored in there."

"You ain't got no stripes. But I do get your meaning. What if there are no child-sized suits stored in the locker?"

"Then improvise. Figure it out. Call me once I'm inside the rover. I am out the door."

CHAPTER THREE

Day One, 1440 hours

"Boss, I think I may have found a solution to our problem."

"Inventory manifest come up empty?" Chief Clay Flynn asked, trying not to lose his grip on the rover's roll bar or bang his head against the metal frame of the eight-wheeled cart while he spoke into the headset. A hands-free comm unit was built into the Snoopy cap a man wore on his head inside his helmet as part of his spacesuit gear.

But the connection was iffy. Flynn was in the passenger seat and being bounced from side to side as the rover made its way along the rocky rim of the GAPS Crater at high speed. The two-man crew composed of him and the driver, Antoine LeClerq, was headed toward the pressure hatch. The hatch opened from above into the storage area below, where the two frightened children sat huddled close together.

"Slow down!" Flynn ordered LeClerq. Given the terrain, Antoine LeClerq was driving far too rapidly for Flynn's taste. "Damn it, man! You drive this rig like you play your bass guitar. — Too damn fast!"

"No joy on the manifest, Chief," Lou Santini reported as LeClerq and Flynn bumped along. "According to our records, at no time were suits of any size ever stored in that side tunnel."

"But you have already figured out a workaround, haven't you?" Flynn chortled. "Is that what you're trying to tell me? No good trying to deny it, Lou. I know how your mind works."

"My solution ain't foolproof, Chief. In fact, it is untried and rather experimental. I only mention it as a last resort."

"Is this the good news you are giving me now, or the bad?" The rover was slowing to a crawl as they neared the map coordinates for the pressure hatch. Despite the accuracy conferred by the lunar positioning satellite overhead — the so-called LPS — the exact location of the pressure hatch might still be difficult for the two men to pinpoint. They didn't need Santini to remind them that the hatch would likely be at least partially buried beneath a layer of regolith dust. The moon's surface was a gray carpet of corrosive dust.

"Not good news, not bad news — the only news. The way I see it, Chief, we have only one way to get those kids out of that hole alive. What I am about to suggest is our one and only shot."

"Then we best not cock this thing up, Lou. When you say untried and experimental, what are we talking about here?"

"The docking collar, along with a pressure tent."

"I thought that contraption was still in the testing stage? I thought the docking collar and pressure tent arrangement had not yet been approved for general use by the Space Council?" With the rover slowed to a crawl, it was easier for the two of them to converse.

"I take it you are not current on your technical reading."

"I guess not," Chief Flynn permitted. "But cut me some slack, would you? I may not be as blinking smart as you are, but my doctorate in A.S. ought to count for something. And let's not forget I have worked on one or two experimental gizmos in the past. You know that, right?"

"Yeah? Like what?"

"Jumpships. Lightcraft. That sort of thing. I did a stint at Field Station Six."

"Then you can appreciate the risks of working with something still in the testing stage," Lou Santini said.

"I have seen one accident too many in my time," Flynn observed.

"So, is that degree in A.S. engineering or A.S.S. engineering?"

"You know exactly what it is in, Lou — Astro Space Engineering. Now get serious. Do you honestly think this unproven tech of yours can be made to work or not?"

"I think so. — Maybe."

"You aren't inspiring much confidence here, Lou. How is this docking collar thing supposed to work?"

Santini explained. "Step One is to first place the hard rubber collar around the circumference of the closed hatch. You will need three, maybe four men working together to make this happen. Fix the collar in place with a reactive mixture of accelerant and molten glue adhesive. Inflate a poly tent over the collar and pump in a tank or two of compressed air. If you pump in enough air, you will create an overpressure condition inside the tent and above the pressure hatch. This way, when you unseal the hatch from the outside, compressed air will be forced down into the hole, instead of being evacuated into space."

"Okay, I see now where you are going with this. But poly tent or no poly tent, the kids will still need to be wearing pressure suits when they come out of that hole."

"Already thought of that, Chief. The children's suits have been collected and are on their way to you courtesy of the boy's father, Doyle Baldwin. Five minutes tops to your location."

"And how long for the collar?"

"I just got off the horn with some snot-nosed kid named Phelps in the QM. He says the guys in Capital Equipment are breaking their hump for you, Chief, so hold your water. Tent, collar, and sealed barrels of adhesive are being loaded onto the big rover as we speak. Best case? We are looking at a quarter of an hour before they can reach you at the rim with Rover Two. Worst case? I wouldn't want to hazard a guess."

"Roger that," Flynn said. "The kids' mothers will need to be told. Leave out the part about this being experimental and untried."

"You want I should lie?" Santini asked as LeClerq maneuvered the vehicle past a series of rock outcroppings.

"No, I don't want you to lie. Tell them the truth. Only don't tell them the whole truth. Tell the mothers that four men — maybe more — are about to risk their lives on a dangerous mission to try and save the lives of their children. Tell them that in this form of rescue we have only one shot for success and that there are absolutely no guarantees. Prepare them for the worst without scaring the living crap out of them."

"There is one more thing, Boss."

"Isn't there always?"

"Ouida Baldwin became hysterical after you signed off with her twenty minutes ago. Doc Runyon had to shoot the woman up with tranks to quiet her down. But the whole time, tranks or not, she has been babbling on and on about Adam being your son, not Doyle's, and about some guy named Jaxson, who I have never heard of."

"Jesus H. Christ. When it rains, it pours."

"There is more rain to come."

"Isn't there always?"

"Doyle knows. He heard his wife say that you are Adam's father."

Flynn grumbled something unintelligible into his headset. It sounded like a swear word. "Oh, that's just swell. And now you're telling me that Doyle is one of the men on their way out here to meet me in Rover Two with a pair of junior-sized spacesuits? Oh, this meet ought to be great fun."

"Yes, great fun. At least we'll have something new and interesting to talk about the next time we get the band together for a jam session."

"My good man, how can you possibly think about band practice at a time like this?"

"You would rather I'd not told you? Besides, we promised the planning committee that the Clay Pots would provide entertainment for next week's community dance. We have to practice sometime."

"No, you did the right thing by telling me, Lou. I'm not criticizing. Doyle did volunteer to bring me those suits, didn't he?"

"Now that you mention it, I think he did volunteer without being asked. Seemed quite eager to help in any way he could."

"I will talk to you again after Rover Two arrives. You'll probably have to talk us through the collar installation. Flynn out."

CHAPTER FOUR

Day One, 1530 hours

"Stand back kids, we are going to blow the hatch."

Chief Flynn's voice was crisp and clear as he spoke over the headset to the two children still trapped in the side tunnel underground. He didn't want them to sense from his voice the fear and dread he felt for them in his heart. This final step was going to be the most dangerous step of all — and that was even taking into account the terrible accident that had befallen them not one hour ago. If the seals failed now, the two children would surely die a most hideous death.

"Chief, we have to move quickly now," Santini said into his mouthpiece. He was still holed up inside the Command Center. "When you crack open the hatch, the overpressure inside may fall rapidly. Have your men prepared to pipe in more breathable."

"Roger that," Flynn said, his voice brusque and tired.

The last sixty minutes were mostly a blur now, a frantic race against time. Those sixty minutes had begun with a conversation between him and Lou Santini as the two rovers closed on the rim of the GAPS Crater at flank speed. It went like this:

"Now listen closely to my instructions," Santini said. "This is not going to be easy. The ring collar we have given you is made from a type of rubber-poly amalgam with threads of Zylon running throughout. The stuff is like Kevlar, though the makeup of the materials isn't important. What is important for you to know is that the craggy thing is stiff and quite unforgiving. Very tough stuff to move about without man and machine working in concert."

"Machine? What machine?"

"I thought I told you, Chief. To lower this beast into place requires a crane."

"And from where, pray tell, are we going to get a crane?"

"The winch on the back of your rover. I am sending you the details now," Santini said. "Take a look at your onboard screen."

"I'm looking," Flynn said, trying to focus. "But we are bouncing around so badly here, it's tough for me to read. Tell me what I should be looking for."

"Okay. Use the keypad. Key in software protocol 7BQ. That's Seven Bravo Quebec. I say again: Seven Bravo Quebec. That protocol places the winch in crane mode. The crane will take most of the weight."

"Hold up a second, Lou. We are almost there. LeClerq and I are pulling up to the site now. Call you back in five, once we get situated."

The rover rolled to a stop and the hydraulic doors rolled slowly open. In the low gravity and deep cold, man and machine moved slowly and awkwardly.

"Okay, Lou, we're out of the rover with boots on the ground. What next?"

"Keypad. Seven Bravo Quebec. Crane mode. The docking collar is heavy. The crane will take most of the weight, like I said. But it will take all four of you to position the collar properly around the hatch. Are the others onsite yet?"

"Rolling up now." Flynn used the stylus, thumped the keypad. "Okay, Lou, protocol keyed in."

"Once you have everyone's attention, put everyone on Channel Three," Santini said. "More bandwidth, less traffic."

Flynn motioned to LeClerq and to the two newcomers, Doyle Baldwin and Hank Pierce. He tapped his earpiece, held up three fingers with his gloved hand, waited while both teams spooled up Channel Three on their comm.

"Extend the boom," Santini said. "The crane's arm is articulated. It can extend quite some distance. Do that now."

"You heard the man," Chief Flynn said to LeClerq as he extended the boom to the full extent of its reach, some thirty meters.

Santini continued. "You will need to use the crane to raise the collar off the loading platform at the back of Rover Two. Then use it for a second time to lower the collar to within one or two meters of the surface."

"How the hell do we attach the collar to the boom?" Flynn asked. "It's darker here than all get-out."

"Yeah, I forgot to tell you about the metal loops," Santini replied from the control room. "Sorry about that. There are three metal loops on the docking collar. They are sixty degrees apart and together form an equilateral triangle."

"Tell Lou I found one," LeClerq said, sliding his gloved hand along the hardened ridge of the rubberized collar. He flashed his light twice in Flynn's direction to get his attention.

"Okay good," Santini replied. "Use the metal cable. Feed it through the three metal loops and onto the boom. Lower the collar like I said."

"Easy as pie," Doyle Baldwin said. He and Pierce had arrived minutes ago in the second rover with the kids' spacesuits in back.

"Don't get cocky, old friend. This mother can go south on us any old time she pleases." Pierce said.

"Forget about things going sideways on us. Hand me the free end of that cable," LeClerq said. He fed the free end through the third metal loop.

Flynn and his team worked feverishly while Santini doled out instructions from the Command Center.

"Okay, lift," Flynn said as Hank Pierce got behind the controls of the boom. "Lift the collar and swing it over."

"Don't lower it all the way to the ground," Santini reminded them sternly.

"We heard you the first time, Lou. Pierce is bringing it down to within about two meters of the surface, maybe a little less. But the surface ain't level, not like some glass tabletop. You got that, right?"

"Now comes the glue," Santini said.

"What kind of glue we talking about here?" LeClerq asked.

"Nothing like anything you have ever seen," Santini said. "It is a mixture actually. Glue adhesive and machine oil. There are two barrels of it on the steel loading platform at the rear of the rover. The goop must be spread on thickly to the underside of the collar. Once the collar is fully lowered, that is the side that will make contact with the regolith."

"Spread it how? What are we supposed to use to spread on this crap?" LeClerq asked as he pried loose the tight-fitting cover from one of the two barrels. When he removed the cover, it was dripping thick with goop. The goop had splashed against the barrel lid during the bumpy ride over from the equipment garage. Now, when he pried the lid loose, drops of excess goop dripped onto his glove and down onto the kneepad of his leg.

LeClerq ignored the spill and said, "Please tell me we're not going to be using a paint brush to spread on this goop? That seems like a lot of damn work for just four men short on time and breathable. We'll go through our oh-two in nothing flat."

"Oh, goodness, quit whining, will you?" Santini replied sharply. "Nothing so plebian as a paint brush. Slapping on the goop by hand would be physically exhausting. Plus, it would take far too long. No, the techs have developed a specialized form of bot for this kind of work. A paint gun bot, if you wish. Wheels, a caterpillar tread, and a long, flexible hose trailing behind. There should be a big metal case beside the two barrels of goop on the rover. Open it. Peggy is inside."

"Peggy, is it? You finally found true love on this rock, Lou? Is that it?"

"Yes, Peggy and I make sweet algorithms together every night. Wait 'til you see the size of her hose. The woman gives stupendous head."

"You are kidding, right?" Doyle chuckled.

Lou laughed hard. "I never kid about size or head. The job of you four gullibles is to connect Peggy's hose to that tank of goop and switch her on when everything is secure. Peggy will do the rest."

"So this glue goop is what makes the docking collar bond firmly with the regolith?" Flynn said.

"Yes," Santini answered. "Once the pressure tent is inflated, we need a near-perfect seal with the ground to capture and hold in the air. Doesn't have to be 100 percent. Ninety-nine point nine nine nine will do."

"Cute. How do we make that happen?"

"I'm coming to that, Chief. Mixed into the glue adhesive are lengths of primacord. Once the collar has been lowered into place and the crane moved safely away, the final step will be to light the primacord."

"Light it? You cannot possibly be serious," Antoine LeClerq exclaimed. "Primacord? We shouldn't be anywhere near that stuff, not now, not ever."

"You're right about that," Santini admitted. "Primacord is dangerous. It has a continuous core of RDX or similar high explosive bound by textile yarns, then sealed beneath a watertight layer of wax and plastic. The stuff will burn hot and bright, with or without oxygen present. The molten glue will harden in about thirty seconds and fuse a nearly unbreakable bond between collar and ground."

"And what about us, you pyromaniac?"

"I suggest you all stay clear of it. Otherwise, when the cord ignites, you'll be vaporized. And don't get any of that goop on you. It'll melt your suit and you'll burn up like dry tinder when the primacord is lit."

"Okay, good safety tip," Flynn quipped, looking at the others for confirmation that they understood.

"I didn't sign on for no suicide mission," Doyle said. "I have a wife and a kid."

"Yeah, no one said anything about a suicide mission," Pierce said. "I have two kids of my own back at home."

"Do you have any good news for us, Lou? Any good news at all?" Flynn asked breathlessly. "This is somewhat more than these fellas bargained for."

"One piece of good news, actually. Once the collar has been securely glued down around the hatch, the next step is comparatively easier. The poly tent is stored inside the collar. Enter the code and the tent will automatically unfold itself according to its own software protocols. As a precaution against micro-tears in the fabric, more of the glue adhesive will need to be applied afterward, only this time on top of the collar all the way around its circumference at the base of the tent where the tent material meets the collar."

"Glucinda, the paint bot again?"

"Be respectful. Her name's Peggy. Once the tent has been fully unfurled and the goop has been sprayed along the bottom edge of the tent all the way around, it is time to again light the primacord and allow it to harden."

"Won't the burning primacord damage the tent in any way?" Flynn asked.

"Aye, there is the rub," Santini admitted. "This sort of fire-induced damage has been seen more than once in the testing phase. That is why this rescue technique is still considered experimental. But I already told you that. We have toyed with various workarounds, but still one in five test-runs end in disaster."

While they talked, Peggy did her thing, spreading on the heavy, shiny goop to the underside of the collar still suspended in midair by the crane. When the light on her monitor shone green, she was done, the paint job complete.

"Goop is applied, Lou. What next?"

"Engage the boom and lower the collar to the ground. Disconnect the cables and back the equipment away. Then light her up."

They moved with dispatch and quickly did as Santini instructed and backed the crane a safe distance away. LeClerq looked at Chief Flynn, nodded to the others. "Lou says we have to light up this stuff. How exactly do we do that?"

Santini broke in on Channel Three. "Same way you light an outdoor barbecue grill back home — with a glow stick. There's one in the same container Peggy arrived in."

"Can't Peggy do this?" Flynn asked. "Why risk a man with primacord and a glow stick in his hand?"

"My girl Peggy's got a hose, not an articulated arm. If we'd had more time to prepare, I would have sent a second bot along with the proper architecture or a separate attachment for Peggy. Can't be helped — it'll have to be one of you four."

"Should we draw straws for who has the honors?" Flynn asked. "It is a bit dangerous after all."

"No straws," LeClerq said. "Time for a drum solo. I'll do this myself. You blokes all have children and wives. I'm a bachelor."

"That don't make you expendable."

"Oh, do shut up and hand me that glow stick already."

"Please be careful," Pierce said.

"Always." The two of them were close friends, had been for years.

LeClerq said nothing at all to the others about the earlier spill. Either he didn't understand the risk or didn't care.

When it happened, it happened extraordinarily fast. There was an electronic contact in the handle of the glow stick. All a man need do was put his gloved finger on the contact and hold it down for three seconds. The ignitor would glow hot, hot enough to start a fire.

"Stand back, boys," LeClerq exclaimed, his voice filled with bravado. "Time to light this candle."

No sooner had LeClerq pressed the contact, than the primacord ignited. First his glove, then his kneepad, then his entire body and suit. All engulfed in flame.

LeClerq screamed horribly once, for about two-and-a-half seconds, then fell sickly quiet. The fire raced around the docking collar, melting the glue, and sealing the collar to the regolith. His body was a charred stump.

"My God. What have we done?" Doyle cried. "LeClerq is dead. Lou, the man is dead." Then Doyle began to shake uncontrollably with dry heaves.

Lou Santini sat motionless in the control booth, unable to speak. Then finally he blurted out. "Say again."

This time, Chief Flynn was the one who replied. His voice was cold. "LeClerq is dead. He burned to death inside his suit."

"How can that possibly be?" Santini asked, his voice cracking with emotion. "Did he somehow get some of that goop on him before he lit the glow stick?"

"I don't see how," Flynn replied.

Pierce suddenly snapped to. "It could have happened that way. LeClerq was the only one . . . " His voice cracked. "Tony was the only one to directly handle those barrels. He was the one who hooked up Peggy's hose to those godforsaken tanks."

"Shit!" Doyle swore. "No way around it. There is going to be one hell of an investigation."

"That's what you're worried about?" Pierce swore, clenching his fist. "Whether or not there is going to be an investigation? Tony was my friend, you asshole."

"Knock it off you two," Flynn ordered. "We still got two children in that hole whose lives are literally in our hands here. Can we please set all this crap aside for a moment and stop pointing fingers at one another? Screw your heads on right, lads, and let's get back to the job at hand. Clock is ticking."

"Chief's right," Santini echoed. "We are running out of time to save those kids."

"Heartless bastards." Pierce said. "Both of you. Heartless bastards. LeClerq was my friend."

"Mine as well," Flynn said. "But what the hell do you expect me to do? Our friend is dead and there is nothing much you or I can do to change that. The man is dead; he'll never make sweet music with us again. But we still have two small children to save. Do what I ask now and you can ream my ass as much as you want later on."

"Okay, Chief, you have the conn. What next?"

The sun was low in the sky. It rose and set every fourteen days. The Earth was on the horizon, earth-rise as they called it. Blue and brown and green and white. Just seeing its bright visage made a man homesick for whatever home he came from. But when death was fresh in the air . . .

"Santini said that the poly tent was stored inside the collar. He said that it would unfold on its own once we enter the code. But he also said that as a precaution against micro-tears in the fabric, more of the glue adhesive would have to be applied, only this time on top of the collar. Do I have that right, Lou?"

"Yes. Peggy will know what to do. She will spread the adhesive all the way around the circumference at the base of the tent where the tent material meets the collar. Then, once the tent has been fully unfurled and the goop has been sprayed along the

bottom edge of the tent all the way around, the primacord has to
be lit and then allowed to harden."

"That shit again?" Pierce said.

"Yes, that shit again," Lou said. "Please do it now.
Assuming the tent isn't damaged by the burning primacord, the
next step is for all three of you to step inside the tent with your
equipment and the kid-sized spacesuits. Zip the tent shut.
Perform a pressure check and seal shut any leaks by hand."

"Okay, you heard the man," Flynn said to the other two.
"Hit it."

"Call me once it's done," Lou said.

"Roger."

Minutes passed without further mishap. The tent
unfurled. The goop was spread and lit. The pressure check was
performed and one small leak sealed.

"Okay, Lou. Tent is up and we are in it. Now what?"

"Release the bottles of compressed air. Keep pumping in
the air until you achieve an overpressure of 4 to 5 pounds inside
the tent."

"Won't that level of overpressure burst the seams?"

"For the last time, Chief, no promises. We've never
actually done this before, remember?" Santini was exasperated.
"Assuming the seams hold firm with the overpressure, then —
and only then — crack open the hatch into the chamber where
the kids are holed-up. If the air pressure inside the chamber is
low, the tent will start to collapse. So keep the bottled air close at
hand, capiche? You may need it."

"Yeah, I capiche," Flynn grumbled. "You from Sicily,
Santini? That why you speak to me in tongues?"

"Like I said: Keep the bottled air close at hand. If the tent
starts to collapse — which it almost certainly will — move quickly.
Release more bottled air into the tent so that it maintains its
overall general shape."

For the next ten minutes or so they didn't talk while the
three men executed the steps Santini had laid out for them.

"Okay, Lou," Chief Flynn said into the comm. "Collar in
place, tent inflated, ready to pop the hatch."

"Tell the kids to stand back," Doyle added. "We are about
to blow the hatch. I don't want Adam or Kyra hurt when we do."

Santini cut in. "Once the kids are suited up, leave the
tent by the way you came. And don't forget to reseal the hatch on
your way back out of the hole. We already have a sealant bot
working to patch over the original source of the decompression,

the tunnel breach. Once the kids are safe, we need to send in an investigative team."

"Looking for anything in particular?" Flynn asked, as he spun the wheel on the hatch to unseal the door.

"Put us on private feed, Chief. What I have to say should go no further."

Flynn fiddled with a few knobs. There was a sharp buzz in his ears.

"Too much gain," Santini yelped. "Turn it down."

Flynn fiddled some more and the feedback subsided. "Okay, Lou. Private feed. Go ahead."

"Tunnels don't explode for no reason," Santini said. "This level of damage took a serious amount of military-grade bang-bang."

"Yes, okay. I see where you are going with this. We will finish this conversation later on. But why do you think this stuff is military grade?"

"Two reasons, Chief. The entirety of Tunnel One is firmly underground, from the rim of the crater all the way back up to Node A, all underground. That whole section of tunnel — about three hundred meters from tip to tail — is buried beneath three or more meters of solid rock."

"You said there were two reasons."

"I did indeed," Santini agreed. "Word has been passed up to me from the Station that a terrorist group based in southern England has claimed responsibility for the explosion. A manhunt is currently said to be underway in Devon and in Cornwall for the ringleaders."

"So this was deliberate sabotage?" Flynn asked as the hatch was opened and the other two men descended into the hole.

"It is beginning to look that way," Santini said. "There are said to be Loyalists to their cause among our number up here."

"I find that hard to believe."

"Even so. That same group has apparently also threatened to blow up the lunar space elevator that Paddington Sinclair and his people are getting ready to build. Plus, there have been unconfirmed threats to topple the railgun and derail the electrical power storage system. Construction on the Moon Beam space elevator is supposed to begin this week, two days from now."

"But, Lou, surely you don't believe this malarkey about some terrorist group based in England. That is a feint. We both know this was an inside job. It had to have been done by someone up here. Hell, only a limited number of people have access. It would have to be someone who can get his hands on explosives, someone who can gain unfettered access to the tunnel system without raising suspicions. This is not the work of some random terrorist group."

"I have already begun to do the math," Lou Santini said. "The list of possible insiders is short, very short. I think I know who we are looking for."

"Who?"

"You're not going to like it."

"Spill."

"The most likely candidate is with you at this very moment."

Chief Flynn drew a sharp breath. "And those other facilities, the railgun, the power terminal? How do we protect them from this nutball?"

"You have to be the one who gives the order, Chief. I don't have the authority. What say we begin by doubling the guard at the tunnel nodes? Then, as soon as you return to base, you and I will need to start reviewing security tape and checking sensors."

"For now, keep this *entre nous*, yes?"

"Seriously? Frog speak? Does Santini sound French to you? If you must, the term is *tra noi*. Italian for 'between ourselves'."

"Yes, that is what I am trying to say. Keep it between just us two, Lou."

Santini chuckled. "Of course. I wouldn't have it any other way."

▲

Ouida sat now, finger calmly poised on the trigger of her gun. Red hair. Wild, animal eyes. Phoenix tattoo splayed across her neck, shoulder and arm.

She had been here before, on the cusp of ending her sad, pathetic life with a bullet to the brain. Now, as she pressed the business end of the steel weapon against the side of her head, the adrenaline rush made the tips of her fingers tingle with excitement.

But then, as before, she hesitated, a single thought freezing her into inaction.

Make the bloody bastards pay. Get your revenge first, then put an end to it.

Yes, that is what she would do, get her revenge first, then put the gun to her temple. She would end her life once and for all. The pain and suffering would finally be no longer.

Ouida did not know which was worse, the accident that had crippled her husband and partner? Or the icy stare he had given her that day, when he sent her away the last time they were together?

Jaxson had ordered her from his hospital room as if she were nothing. He had ordered her away from his bedside, directed her to leave the room and to never return. *But his manner!* Jaxson was dismissive, treated her as if she were a subordinate, a stranger, one of his jobsite monkey wrenches.

Was that it? Or was it the guilt she felt because she hadn't put up a fight, had not even argued with the man when he told her to leave?

Jaxson had told her what to do and like a sheep she had obeyed.

Is that what her anger was truly about, about her giving up without a fight?

CHAPTER FIVE

Day Two, 0600 hours

"For heaven's sake, Flynn, why the hell was I ordered to report to your office at the frigging crack of dawn?" Doyle Baldwin demanded to know. He was looking worn out and tired after a short night spent tossing and turning on a lumpy cot in the children's wing of the base hospital. "You have no direct authority over me."

"Please come in, Doyle. Sit down, take a load off. You are not under arrest. But, you are under investigation, same as everyone else on this rock."

"What do you mean, everyone else? I don't see a line of suspects standing outside your office door waiting to be questioned. The only one you have called in so far is me. And why is that, Chief? I thought you and I were friends. Don't you trust me? Or is there something else at work here that I know nothing about?"

"I'm coming to that."

"Are you making this personal, Chief? People ought to be treating me like a hero, not some grubby criminal. You, me, Pierce — we are all three heroes. We saved my son's life, Kyra's too. Where's the goddamn ticker tape parade?"

"This is not personal, Doyle. Why would you say such a thing?"

"Because it turns out that I have been living a lie. Yesterday I rescue my son from an almost certain death, and in the next breath learn that he may not even be my son."

"Doyle, how can you possibly blame me for something I didn't even know myself until just last night? That's when Ouida told me I might be Adam's father, right in the middle of our rescue operation."

"Might be? *Might be?* Are you suggesting Ouida fabricated the entire story, that she made up the whole thing? . . . Why in blazes would she make up such a ridiculous story?"

"Why do women do anything?" Flynn asked. "To get attention. Maybe she wants to make you jealous so you'll quit screwing around with Nora Goldman and pay more attention to her."

"She knows about Nora?"

"Apparently so."

"And why, exactly, would Ouida tell you about my love-life?"

"We talk," Flynn said.

"I bet that's not all you do."

Chief Flynn lingered a moment beside the tiny porthole of a window in his office and looked out upon the bleak lunar landscape. It was gray as always. No trees, no grass, no flowing water, no wind or rain, no sand dunes, no oceans. When the surface wasn't scorched by life-killing solar radiation, it was cloaked in utter choking darkness. *No wonder depression was legend among the Lunatics.*

"Is the boy yours?" Doyle Baldwin wanted to know.

Flynn shook his head. "I really don't see how. It's no secret. Ten years ago, over what amounted to a long weekend, she and I had a toss in the sack. But here's the thing, Doyle. The only sex she and I ever had was while we were in zero-g. You know the science as well as I do. Conception is a statistical impossibility in space."

Doyle smirked in disbelief. "So, what are we talking about here, Flynn? Immaculate Conception? Me and Jesus don't see eye to eye on that one."

"This isn't religion; this is science. It's not even science; it's biology. No way did my sperm fertilize your wife's eggs ten years ago. Just because the two of us had a passing fling a decade back, doesn't prove a damn thing about paternity. Besides, you are the only father Adam has ever known. Why would I want to interfere with that?"

"You were banging her back then. Are you banging her now?"

"Did she tell you that I was?" Flynn asked.

"She said no such thing. Anyway, I'm not asking her, I am asking you. Are you having sex with my wife?"

"Yes, I am most definitely having sex with your wife," Chief Flynn replied with cold detachment. "Does knowing the truth make you feel any better?"

"Geez, Clay, we have been friends for a long time, nearly two years, ever since Ouida and I first landed on this rock. How long have we played together in the band? Does my friendship mean nothing to you? I could easily have you brought up on charges, you know that, right?"

"Yes, Doyle, you could put me in hack, have me brought up on charges. But you won't. And do you want to know why?"

"Enlighten me, friend."

"Because your wife's career would be over, finished, flushed. Put me in hack and your wife ends up being brought up on charges as well. Plus, you may soon be going to prison yourself."

"Is that so?"

An unexpected knock came at the door and a new face peered into Flynn's office.

"I see that you have company," Doc Runyon said through the open doorway. "I can come back later on, if you wish."

"No, Doc, I don't wish. Please come in and have a seat. I have been waiting to hear back from you about the condition of the two children. I need your report for the record. I know Adam took a hit to the head in the explosion. But how were they otherwise? Did they both get a good night's sleep last night? I need to know when the two kids will be released from the med."

Doc Runyon remained standing, even though Flynn had offered him a seat. "The children presented with a few scratches, a little dehydration. Adam had a head laceration, like you said. But it wasn't serious. The girl improvised a bandage from her sock. I cleaned the wound and put on a new bandage. We fed them both, slipped a relaxant into their nighttime milk and cookies, and the two kids slept like babies. Both of them were still out cold when I left the surgery a few minutes ago to come here and have this chat with you. Doyle can attest to that. He spent most of the night on a cot sleeping beside his boy. Ouida, too."

"So, Doc, in your professional opinion, Adam and Kyra are going to be okay, none the worse for the wear? A bang to the head, a few scratches and a case of simple dehydration? That is your official diagnosis? None the worse for the wear?"

"Look, Chief, they had a bad scare, no doubt about it. Who wouldn't have? But both sets of parents spent the night in the hospital alongside their child, including — like I said — this basted turkey wing right here." Doc Runyon pointed to Doyle Baldwin, still in the hot seat. "He your prime suspect?"

"I'm coming to that. Lou Santini has accumulated some rather strong evidence, although at this point, all of it is circumstantial. Every bit of it, however, points to our Doyle Baldwin as being the tunnel saboteur."

"What evidence?" Doyle jumped to his feet.

"Lou spent half the night on it. He has evidence that suggests you supplied the detonation cord and ignitors used in the tunnel sabotage. The chemical signature of the residue left behind by the explosion matches the batch of explosives you signed for last month. This is the same batch of explosives you personally requisitioned in order to open that new vein of ore two craters over. Now sit the eff back down.”

“But I reported that lot stolen,” Doyle declared, “just like the Base Manual says to do when explosives go on walkabout. I have the paperwork to back that up.”

“Perfect cover story for a man who stole the munitions himself. After Santini makes his report to Hanrahan, don’t be surprised if the rumor mill doesn’t start to churn. You know what people will say — that you supplied the detcord that nearly killed two of our children. Once the news is out there, your name and credibility will be mud. No one is going to listen to or care about any fraternizing charges you may trump up against me.”

“Just how dumb do you think I am, Flynn? If you had any hard evidence against me, any actual proof that I supplied the saboteurs with detcord, I would already be in shackles.”

“Do you deny it?”

“Of course, I deny it. Charge me or set me free.”

“I have no present intention of doing either. Lou is still investigating. Until I say different, be warned — you remain our principal suspect. But, as you say, we lack incontrovertible evidence against you. So, for the time being, you remain a free man, at least until after LeClerq’s memorial service. But threaten again to have me brought up on charges and you will find yourself in shackles so fast it will make your head spin. In the meantime, I suggest you move out.”

“Move out?”

“Yes. Vacate the premises. Move out of the married quarters. Find yourself another bed to sleep in for the next few days, or at least until this thing is over.”

“And if I refuse?”

“Then you will be charged as a saboteur in front of a tribunal, slapped in irons, and dispatched to the brig for further processing.”

Doyle was about to take issue with that last statement, when the buzzer on Chief Flynn’s comm came alive.

“Chief, it’s high time you got down here,” Administrator Winston Hanrahan said. “The memorial service for Antoine is about to begin and I need you here in the chapel, standing behind the podium, ready to deliver the eulogy.”

“Me? No way. I’m too close to this thing.”

"I'm not asking," Hanrahan said.

"Christ. I can't stand in front of people, not today. Besides, I'm not prepared to deliver a eulogy. I still need to interview Nora and Mitch and that young teacher lady, Sarena What's-Her-Name."

"This isn't a democracy, Flynn. Your interviews can wait. Better still, I can conduct the interviews myself. Her name is Lopez, by the way. Sarena Lopez. Now get your hairy ass down here and make the eulogy sound like you wrote it and practiced it and that you care. People are waiting. Every pew is full."

"Okay. I am on my way. Flynn out."

CHAPTER SIX

Day Two, 1000 hours

"Last night's thrashing by Hanrahan was mounds of fun," Chief Flynn said unamused.

"I understand he tore you a new one," Lou Santini said. The two men were suiting up to enter the tunnel system for their first sweep since yesterday afternoon's detonation. Antoine LeClerq's memorial service was behind them. Flynn had done a passable job, despite not being much of a public speaker, and delivered a brief yet touching eulogy. LeClerq had been a popular and well-liked member of the staff and the memorial service had been well attended. In a community as small as this one, where everyone lived close to the edge each hour of every day, the loss of even a single individual was felt deeply by one and all.

Now, though, time was at hand for Flynn and Santini to get down to serious business assessing the base's security risks.

"The bastard tried to ream my ass because my signature was on that field trip form. Only, I wasn't having any," Flynn said, his face still red with anger. "His Lordship Hanrahan sees himself as a first-class administrator. But what he is, is a first-class asshole. Combine that glaring character defect with a major-league case of pathological stubbornness and you have the makings of a full-blown disaster. I recognize that Hanrahan did a stint at the Station, so, perhaps, he has the proper credentials. But the man is either too stupid or too arrogant to fully grasp the central principle of what it takes to live and work inside a pressurized tin can; much less keep order inside one."

"Ah, more pearls of wisdom from Professor Know-It-All Flynn. So tell me, Professor. What is the central principle when it comes to living inside a tin can?" Santini asked, sprinkling talc on his skin before zipping the suit closed. The talc cut down on skin rashes and irritation.

"Professor Know-It-All Flynn nothing. The central principle for surviving in a place like this is to accept that anyone with enough determination, anyone who has made up his mind to fatally cripple this place we live in, can do so rather easily. Humans are fragile creatures. We can only live a short while without clean water and fresh air. If some demented, evil son-of-a-bitch decides to poison our water supply or foul our breathing air, they would make short work of us. Decimating the habitat is a relatively simple matter to orchestrate. Hanrahan is a fool. He thinks that if he issues the right order or installs the proper protocol that afterward we will all be safe. Bots in the corridors, my ass. I told him it was hogwash."

"I heard you used somewhat stronger language."

"You heard? From whom did you hear? That goofy secretary of his? Edith something or other?"

"No matter."

"You agree with me, right?" Flynn demanded to know. "It is no great shakes to introduce a biotoxin into our water supply. Nor does it require any brilliant feat of engineering to poison our air supply or cut off our electrical power. Every last one of us survives on this hunk of rock thanks in great part to the goodwill of everyone else. Military rank and honor is what keeps us alive, and not much else. Rank, honor, and goodwill."

"Even men in a submarine get the occasional shore leave," Santini said, reaching for his helmet.

"What exactly is your point?"

"The psychological eco-system of confinement onboard a submarine is the closest known parallel to life inside the moonbase. The only thing that keeps submariners from killing one another during a long-term deployment is military rank and honor, just like you said, Chief. That, plus a patrol sock and regular shore leave. This place has no such escape valve. The new park helps, but only a little. If nothing else, a few hookers would help keep the peace around here."

"Hookers, eh? Would Hanrahan then be their pimp? You want I should put that suggestion in my official report?"

"Do as you please. But my recommendation stands. This level of confinement doesn't suit every psyche, not even those who have trained for it. Why do you think I am so opposed to children being here?"

"I can see both sides of that argument. Allowing children here keeps parents from worrying."

"And makes other parents worry even more," Santini interjected.

"Their playfulness keeps others calm. And what are the risks really? Fewer than five generations ago, when the pioneers left the tidewater region and pushed inland into uncharted and dangerous wilderness, they took their children and families with them, had babies along the way. The risks were incalculable — Indians, wild animals, other settlers, deprivation, you name it — and yet the continent was settled."

"Sorry, mate, but I don't buy it. Those people could breathe fresh air, chop wood, swim in open bodies of water, hunt live game, live off the land. They didn't live in a bottle; we do. Hookers and patrol socks is what I say."

"And what is a patrol sock anyway?" Chief Flynn wanted to know.

"Men masturbate when there are no women around. Hell, men masturbate even when there are women around. A *patrol sock* is what navy men use when they're lonely, especially submariners."

"And you know this how?"

"Well, I suppose it's better than a WUBA."

"Dare I ask?"

"Woman Used By All," Santini replied. "An onboard hooker."

"Okay, Lou. Let me get this straight. You think this act of sabotage is the work of a distraught employee? Someone with cabin fever? A horny sailor? I hardly think so. More likely a stowaway, someone we don't even know exists. Or maybe someone with a grudge, a longstanding grudge, perhaps an agenda."

"Chief, is it even possible for us to have an undocumented worker on-station, a stowaway? More to the point: Have you considered what seems to me more likely, an unauthorized robot, perhaps one small enough to avoid detection, yet sophisticated enough to set and place an explosive device?"

By now the two men were suited up and moving towards the first set of pressure doors. Each tunnel, connecting node, and building could be compartmentalized to keep the occupants safe in case of a decompression event elsewhere in the hab. Keycards and voice ID matches were required to enter most areas.

"Even an undocumented worker must eat," Flynn said, as they moved clumsily along, compensating for the low gravity with exaggerated body movements. "An undocumented person must also breathe and take the occasional piss. He has to consume consumables and exhale carbon-dioxide. He must poop and wipe his ass and flush a toilet. There would be ample evidence of a stowaway's presence on-station. The habitat is pretty much a closed system. Our stowaway would leave behind a chemical signature. As for an unauthorized robot — even a small one — it is pretty much the same situation. A bot requires electricity to run and to recharge. Power consumption is a closely monitored utility throughout the hab. The service computers would notice the anomalous change in power usage almost instantly."

"Okay, no stowaways, no undocumented bots. Where does that leave us?" Santini said. "The saboteur must be one of us."

"Yes, has to be," Flynn agreed. "Someone we know and work alongside every day has it within them to wreak havoc and destruction, perhaps kill us all. That's why we need a security detail, to start sorting out the risks."

"Boss, you know as well as anyone that space can kill a man a thousand different ways. How can a security detail of just a handful of people possibly safeguard every square centimeter of this place?"

"Obviously, they can't," Flynn replied. "We must sort the greater risks from the lesser risks."

"And how exactly do you propose we do that? Decisions of this sort are purely subjective and arbitrary."

"These bad-guy terrorists want headlines, the messier the better," Flynn said. "They want to destroy buildings and obliterate symbols. They want to do something reprehensible, something that will have a lasting impact — either economically or psychologically. — And they want to do it with a splash of showmanship. It has to look good on camera. So, these bad-guy terrorists are not going to simply set fire to a couch in a public lounge and leave it at that. A burnt couch doesn't set people's hearts to fear. No, the terrorists want to do something big and noisy, something that will generate lots of blood, inflict injuries, cause countless deaths, and generate photographs of body bags. More than anything else, they want to do something that interferes with commerce, that has an economic impact."

"So we begin by identifying the biggest economic targets and protect those first."

"That shouldn't be difficult," Chief Flynn said. "Paddington Sinclair's about-to-be-built lunar space elevator has to be high on the list. The railgun paddock. The lunar accelerator. The water treatment plant. The electrical power storage system. Those are among our most valuable assets here on this desolate piece of rock."

"Okay, then we ought to take a team and inspect each one of those for signs of foul play or sabotage. The inspection team can mark and identify likely spots where a bomb or explosive might be rigged. Then they can tag those areas for additional surveillance, both cams and roving guards."

"Lou, you know as well as I do that there have often been threats against the railgun. It's the second-oldest installation on the moon and the least well protected. After we're finished here in the tunnels, what say we make our next stop the railgun paddock?"

"But who can we trust to be on the security team? Until we made Doyle out to be a possible suspect, I would have counted him among the good guys. He's one of the Clay Pots, after all; a member of our little seven-piece combo. And you can't ignore Doyle's background and training. The man ought to be on any inspection team we assemble. Unless, of course, you still consider him to be a Bad Guy."

By now they had reached the main tunnel entrance outside the Admin Building, completed their voice ID clearance and were about to insert their keycards into the reader. They would pass first through Node C on the way to the Water Processing Center this side of the Ice Quarry. The entire length was part of the original lava tube network where the first residents lived.

"All the evidence points to him," Flynn said. "And that is precisely what bothers me. Too many breadcrumbs. Besides, I have known the man a good long time. Doyle Baldwin never impressed me as being smart enough to have masterminded something as clever as this. But I would wager that the actual perpetrator is someone close to him, maybe in his department. Put Doyle on the inspection team. At least by having him on the roster, we can track his movements better."

Santini nodded. "Even a physical examination of these facilities can reveal only so much. What we really need to do is place a network of passive devices, sniffers for instance. They can detect miniscule traces of compounds like trinitrotoluene that accompany most modern explosives. That's TNT in case you have forgotten."

"I haven't forgotten, Lou. A sniffer may work well indoors, within an enclosed space, but I hardly think one will do us much good detecting an externally placed device. The moon has no air. Nothing to sniff."

"Fair point. On the other hand, bot technology has become quite advanced. We can place fixed sentinel units, as well as roving guards that will detect suspicious movements. And never underestimate the value of a spider swarm to check on anomalous features. They are cheap, cost practically nothing to operate, and are very sophisticated nowadays."

Flynn seemed unconvinced. "Everything you say is true, Lou."

"I smell a 'but' coming."

"But . . . it seems to me that we need to be smarter than all that," Flynn said. "If the perpetrator is indeed an insider as we suspect, he knows our security protocols. He will be able to guess ahead of time what steps we will take to observe his movements and to catch him. So he will take steps to thwart and defeat any known defenses we have."

"Ah, game theory. My field of study before I transferred into mechanical engineering. Rather than Tit for Tat, you are playing Tit *before* Tat."

"Yes, something like that. The bad guys will likely have anticipated our security moves before we make them. They will do something we don't expect them to do, something off-book."

"What are you thinking?"

"Maybe the bad guys mean no harm to the railgun itself. Maybe they mean to use it in a harmful way instead."

"You mean arm it with a dangerous payload?" Santini said.

"It is a possibility we have to consider. What is the most lethal payload you can imagine?"

"Usually, the payloads are large ingots of mined lunar ore," Santini said. "Aluminum, titanium, stuff like that, metals that have been extracted here, then flung outward toward factories and mills in Earth orbit."

"Yes, usually," Flynn said. "But what about the nuclear wastes stored on the farside? Governments of every stripe have been dumping this crap on the moon's farside for decades. You must know that the stuff is still hot and quite lethal when it is dumped here. What would it take to stitch together some sort of dirty bomb with that garbage?"

"It would be dangerous to handle, even for a bad guy," Santini replied. "Besides, you couldn't actually make an atomic bomb out of that gunk, if that's what you mean. Too many impurities."

"If not a bomb, then what? An ordinary projectile? It wouldn't have to actually explode in order to be lethal."

"Quite right, Chief. It's a bit like soldiers in the Middle Ages trying to take a well-defended castle. They would sometimes catapult a diseased horse carcass over the castle walls hoping to infect everyone inside and force them to surrender."

Flynn nodded. "The bastards could use the railgun to hurl a cauldron of hot nuclear wastes into Earth's atmosphere. It would be like drinking poisonous soup. Even an unarmed nuke would burn up in the atmosphere. Plutonium would be spewed across the landscape and into the oceans. The planet would be poisoned for a thousand years."

"Not a thousand. But I do get your point. How easy would it be, do you think, for an amateur to operate the railgun and launch a payload?"

"In my estimation, not difficult at all," Chief Flynn said. "I can show you the guts of the machine when we get up there, but you know how it works. The lunar railgun system is passive, which makes it easy to operate. The gun employs neither a superconducting magnet nor an energized electromagnet, but rather what amount to a series of ordinary bar magnets."

"Only much more powerful, for those of you not playing the home game."

"Oh yes, much more powerful," Flynn said. "The launch vehicle has roughly the same shape and size of a large sled. On the underside of the sled is a rectangular array of magnetic bars arranged in a special pattern. The magnetic orientation of each bar is placed at a right angle to the orientation of the bar in front of it. In this configuration, the magnetic field lines overlap to produce a very strong magnetic field beneath the array. Above the array, the field lines cancel one another out.

"The Trak beneath the sled is inclined along its entire length, and at a steadily increasing angle of attack. Embedded in the Trak are closely packed coils of insulated wire. They form a closed circuit in the shape of a rectangle. Taken together, the coils produce a levitating force. It is a well-known phenomenon. When an ordinary dipole magnet is moved laterally near a loop of wire, it will induce an electric current to flow in that wire."

"The Faraday effect, yes?" Santini noted.

"Yes. Michael Faraday. Englishman. Dates to the mid-1800s. To reach the minimum speed at which levitation occurs, the sled cars come equipped with auxiliary wheels and a conventional drive train. When the sled first begins to move forward along the Trak, it does so under conventional power. Magnets in the array induce powerful currents in the Trak's coils. These currents generate an electromagnetic field which in turn repels the arrays. The arrays levitate the car a few centimeters above the Trak's surface.

"As the sled begins to move forward, the levitating forces rise quickly. The magnetic field behaves much like a compressed spring, with the levitating force increasing exponentially as the separation between the Trak and the sled decreases. This property makes the Trak inherently stable, which allows it to easily adjust to an increasing load or to acceleration forces. That is why even an untrained amateur can probably operate it successfully and without difficulty."

"Okay, I am beginning to grasp the truth now." Santini stopped to catch his breath. Even under one-sixth-earth-normal gravity, walking and working inside a spacesuit was exhausting.

Flynn continued. "Drive coils interspersed among the track's levitating circuits generate a series of electromagnetic pulses. By pulsing the drive coils in synchronization with the car's forward motion, they can achieve a steady and strong acceleration at or near the 10-g level. The payload — which on an ordinary day is nothing more than an ingot of solid ore — could just as easily be a rocket or a nuclear warhead in the hands of an anarchist."

"And therein, I guess, lies the mortal threat to the safety of Earth," Lou Santini added. The man knew enough physics to grasp the essentials. "The bad guys don't need a functioning nuke to create an extreme hazard. They don't even need an end-loader full of spent nuclear rods. An ordinary hunk of granite rock, accelerated to a high enough velocity can pack a remarkable amount of kinetic energy."

"Yes, it can. But the scary part is that our Earth-based antiballistic shield isn't much of a defense. Those missile and laser systems were designed to protect cities and infrastructure. That big rock you're talking about could strike the atmosphere practically anywhere and wreak havoc and destruction like mankind has never seen."

Lou Santini frowned as they made their way out of Node D and into Tunnel Twelve. It had been a long day already and was about to get longer. The day began at the Water Processing Center beside the Ice Quarry. Then into Regolith Processing and Nodes C and D. Now into Tunnel Twelve which terminated at the Railgun Paddock hundreds of meters away. Santini had assembled a surveillance package consisting of three sensors — thermal, sonar, and motion — along with a radiological sensor. Once their initial sweep was complete, the follow-on team would begin installing surveil packages on the walls of each node and at regular intervals inside each Tunnel. No one was going to enter or leave any part of the facility without being seen or heard.

"In this next section of tunnel, we would ordinarily face a special problem," Santini said.

"The railgun's magnetic field?" Flynn offered. "That has been a longstanding issue. The field has been known to affect the Comm Center, which is two hundred meters away. The solution has been to run super-cooled air around the rim of the railgun which reduces the reach of the magnetic field."

"This is an impossible task," Santini said. "We have three dozen newcomers arriving here tomorrow, next day at the latest. Sinclair's entire Moon Beam team. How can we possibly keep track of all these new arrivals? They are already on their way."

"A security nightmare, to be sure," Flynn agreed. "But no less than the entirety of this facility. It was not built at a single point in time according to some master plan. There are probably side tunnels we know nothing about, chambers and the like that were drilled years ago, then abandoned, perhaps sealed and left behind. Consider the colonists' original lava tube. Back in the day it was mapped, the ceiling reinforced and the walls made airtight. That section is still central to our tunnel system, parts of it anyway. But there are also unmarked sections, some up to 500 meters wide and half a klom long. To this day, there are caverns that have never been explored. Our security net is as full of holes as a wheel of Swiss cheese."

CHAPTER SEVEN

Day Two, 1200 hours

"Here, help me with this pressure door," Chief Flynn said. He was laboring to turn the manual wheel that controlled access to the airlock at the end of Tunnel Twelve. "Damn thing won't budge."

"Stand aside, old man," Santini said, pushing forward. "You must be getting weak in your old age."

"Lactic acid, you fool. Anyway, you're ten years older than I am. So please do act your age."

"What's that you say? That you're lactating? What an old mother hen you are. And it's only eight years that I am older than you, not ten."

"Lactic acid. Muscle fatigue."

"Quit griping. I got it already," Santini said as he cranked the wheel and pushed open the pressure door.

The two men moved through the airlock and into a ready room where they could safely remove their suits. Their air supply was running low, and they were both hungry and dehydrated. Working inside a spacesuit was brutal and exhausting work. The knee and elbow joints were stiff and the gloves cumbersome.

"Time to eat," Santini said as he removed his visor and helmet. The inner lining of the pressure suit smelled earthy, like a boys' locker room.

"I'll call the mess and see what they got to eat around these parts."

"I have energy bars in my backpack," Santini said. "Plus there is plenty of distilled water in the suit recovery system, if we need a quick something to wet our whistles."

"You want me to drink your recycled sweat? Not in this lifetime."

"Don't be a fool, Chief. Everything we drink on this rock, I mean every last drop we drink, is someone else's recycled sweat or urine or dishwater. When did you start getting picky?"

Chief Flynn scowled. What Santini said was not strictly true; they did distill a certain volume of consumables from mining the ice quarry in the neighboring crater. But that stuff was valuable, and most of it was used to irrigate crops at the Farm.

In fact, clean drinking water was the most valuable asset in the solar system, bar none. Space travelers required water, as well as the oxygen that could be derived from it. Water was a source of fuel as well. Once the oxygen was broken free of its hydrogen bonds, the hydrogen could be burned as fuel to power everything from lunar rovers to spacecraft to HVAC units.

While the two men ate and drank, they talked. "So tell me what you know about the history of this place, the habitat," Santini said. "You were saying something earlier about the hab not having been built according to some master plan."

Flynn nodded. "Architecturally speaking, the moon is a mess. Nothing matches, nothing meshes properly. The place is like a bunch of square pegs that have been forced by pneumatic hammer into little round holes."

"Those little round holes being the pesky junctions between the moon's natural formations and our manmade tunnel sections?" Santini asked. "No matter what kind of sealant we apply, we are constantly springing leaks along those seams."

"Incompatible technologies applied without forethought or plan," Flynn grumbled. "At times, the base has been under international control; other times not. The lunar settlement strategy has been much the same as it has been on Mars: make use of local terrain, burrow underground for safety."

"You're referring to our labyrinth of lava tubes, yes?"

"Yep. Our underground squirrel holes are the safest place on this rock to live and work."

"On Mars, the choices were obvious. The western slopes of the basaltic shield volcanoes, *Elysium* and *Olympus* Mons. We saw the entrances to those lava tubes on some of the first satellite images ever captured more than a century ago."

"The first robot mission confirmed it," Flynn said. "Those ancient volcanoes were found to be honeycombed with klom after cubic klom of lava tubes, all filled with valuable minerals and frozen volatiles, including vast ice deposits. Face it: we lucked out on Mars. Those natural caverns have roofs that are tens of meters thick, thick enough to shield people from most of the surface risks Mars has to offer — solar radiation, extreme temperature fluctuation, wind, dust storms, not to mention those nasty micrometeoroids which can put a quick end to any man's day."

Santini seemed to agree. "The risks are no less awesome here on the moon, minus the wind and dust storms, of course. On the plus side, lunar regolith is an excellent insulator. Forty meters below the surface, with a thick layer of solid basalt lying above your head, the subterranean temperature is stable and borderline balmy, minus 20 degrees or so centigrade."

"Most people say Celsius nowadays, not centigrade."

"Is that so?"

"I'm not trying to be a smart ass, Lou, but yes. In the mid-twentieth century, the centigrade scale was renamed to honor Swedish astronomer Anders Celsius, who was the first to derive it."

Santini glared at his friend, but did not comment.

"Living on the lunar surface was never a realistic plan for settlement," Flynn continued. "Oh, those Quonset hut-style surface dwellings connected by pressurized passageways made for wonderful book covers and maybe even a few grade-school science fair projects. — But the reality of living on the surface is much less forgiving. No wonder people opted to live underground. It was the logical alternative, learn to make a home of the extensive network of caverns and lava tubes."

"No argument there," Santini said. "The tubes and caverns are the backbone of our present node and tunnel system. Annex B was formed from one of those large underground caverns. A little plastic explosive, some reinforced concrete, and voilà, Annex B."

"Part of the reason for our architecture being so bizarre is because people and governments have never been able to properly agree what the Moon is good for."

"Go on."

"At one time, the Moon was seen to be valuable as a research station; then later as a waste dumping ground; then later still as a source of valuable minerals — titanium, Helium-3, other exotics."

"That is still true today. The regolith separators run night and day on the far side of the *Mare*."

Flynn seemed to agree. "The lunar accelerator was the first mega-project ever built on the moon. And we both already know about the DUMP, which was one of the earliest of lunar enterprises. There was a time when it was a thriving business. Mammoth shuttles used to arrive every fortnight or so, their cargo bays laden with red-hot nuclear wastes. The shuttles would engage a trajectory that conveyed them towards the farside, where they would soon dump their load. Their cargo was — and still is — the most noxious poison known to man. Radioactive sludge. In years past, the crap poured forth in an unending stream from Earth's many hundreds of fission reactors."

"Geez, Chief, I didn't take you for one of those save-the-planet nutball types. You a Greenie?"

"Far from it. But stupid is still stupid. Fission reactors? Transporting nuclear wastes through Earth's atmosphere so we can dump the stuff where no one else will see? Stupid. And dangerous."

"Yeah, Chief, I got that. But what were they supposed to do with the stuff? There were no longer any satisfactory places left on Earth for safe storage of those spent fuel rods. So why not the Moon? It was uninhabited."

"The operative word being *was*. It *was* uninhabited," Chief Flynn said. "Now, a hundred years later, we are still contending with the deadly muck. Modern-day terrorists can scoop up that shit any ole time they please and use it to bomb Earth. I don't think that is what those people had in mind when they negotiated the Moon Treaty."

"A subject I never learned much about in school."

"And why would you?" Chief Flynn sighed. "Only the most important, dumbest piece of paper ever signed."

"Dumb? In what way?"

"Can a man of your advanced age sit still long enough for a short history lesson? Or do you have to go to the potty?"

"This is going to be boring, isn't it?"

"To you, perhaps." Chief Flynn smiled. "What bores one man to tears, fascinates another. Drawing lines, fighting over territory, making treaties. These are all part of the human experience. Ever since the first primitive nation drew its first line in the soil of that first populated savanna, countries have been steadily extending their boundaries, always jockeying lines for maximum benefit."

Chief Flynn continued as he chewed on the energy bar. "The property lines began simply enough. A circle of stones around the campfire. Then a wider zone that reached from the edge of the campfire circle out to the nearest mountain range. Then to the coast. Then beyond the coast to a three-mile limit in the ocean. Then, after the dawn of the space age, the three miles changed to two hundred, and the direction began to shift from out to up. That's when people started drawing lines in outer space. First, key orbital zones around Earth. Then, the asteroids. Finally, the Moon."

Lou Santini shook his head. "Yeah, but allowing us to draw lines in space is a little bit like a fish arguing with his neighbor about who owns the coral reef they dart in and out of. No one can actually own outer space."

"Possession is nine-tenths of the law, Lou. Those folks back then negotiated a treaty *before* the fighting began. That is probably a first in human history."

"Go on."

"The first treaty, the treaty on which all subsequent treaties have been based, was supposed to ensure that there would be no lines. It was supposed to guarantee that outer space would remain forever de-militarized, that no country would declare any Earth orbital zone as their own, and that land claims would never be made on the Moon, the planet Mars, or any other place that humanity's rockets might one day reach."

"Hah!" Santini chortled.

"Hah, indeed. Just thinking about it makes me laugh. Such naiveté! *No lines in space?* What a laugh! *Forever demilitarized?* Whoever thought that one up must have been smoking some off-brand weed."

"So what are you saying, Chief?"

"The harsh realities are quite different, aren't they? As soon as someone figured out how to turn a decent profit in space, they started drawing lines everywhere. First on the agenda? — Geosync orbit. Then later, ice-laden craters on the moon. More recently? — The asteroid belt. Still to come? — The lunar elevator. — After that? — Who knows?"

"Turning a profit is still a decent motive for doing things, as far as I'm concerned," Santini said. "Or are you a Socialist along with being a Greenie?"

"Neither. I am not passing judgment, mind you — just explaining the crazy patchwork history of this place. Profits drove its development. Valuable ore was discovered, ilmenite, aluminum, other things. Mine workers and machinery arrived. Strip-mining operations got underway. Living conditions were cramped and spartan. But the money was good. Before long, a burgeoning moontown had burrowed itself into the protective rock of a nearby crater wall. Luna City, as it was then called, boasted more than a hundred residents — miners, engineers, cooks, crooks, medics, and bimbookers."

"Yes, I remember the stories my father used to tell me when I was a boy. Dad was one of those miners. Six months on, six months off. It all sounded so exciting to me at the time. Those early comers called themselves Lunatics, didn't they?"

"That's right. Some still do. But unlike the frontier towns of early Earth, life for the citizens of Luna was highly-regimented. Luxuries were few and always at a premium, same as today. If the sheriff of this frontier town sent a miscreant packing, it was a death sentence. Beyond the tunnels and walls of the tiny city there wasn't so much as one ounce of liquid water or a single millibar of fresh air. Lethal radiation and sub-zero temperatures awaited anyone who, even for an instant, ventured outside the cocoon of the colony without wearing a double-density spacesuit."

"I think I get the picture," Santini said. "It must have been just like my father said. Fear kept the Lunatics in line, not the law."

"Nicely put. The strip-mining operations of those early days were reminiscent of similar big industrial enterprises back on Earth. Giant quarry machines with huge buckets and Caterpillar-style tractor treads. The regolith in the highlands is rich in aluminum and silica; the regolith in the *maria* are basaltic rocks rich in iron and magnesium. On the nearside are areas containing high concentrations of the titanium-based mineral ilmenite."

"Valuable stuff," Santini observed.

Flynn quietly nodded and continued. "The machines mashed the moon rocks into rubble, along with the occasional miner. Then they cooked the gravel in these enormous kettles until the pure ore oozed out and bubbled to the top. Some of the ore was destined for lunar-based manufacturing — foamed aluminum production and the like. But most of the molten metal was poured off into bullet-shaped molds before being cooled and shot back to Earth by railgun. Not the railgun we use nowadays, but something similar, an earlier model. The ore-bullets were snagged in orbit and then passed onto surface factories for further processing."

"We couldn't exist up here on a long-term basis without foamed metals," Santini said. "Our lunar economy depends on them, metallic foams mainly, but also ceramic. Internally, these metals have a cellular structure. The cells consist of solid metal or ceramic material infused with a large percentage of the volume consumed by gas-filled pores. Makes these metals ultralight and with very high porosity. As much as ninety percent of the volume consists of void spaces."

"I am familiar with foamed metals. We used the stuff on the wings and airframe of the jumpships I tinkered with in my salad days."

"Salad days?" Santini harrumphed.

"What would you call them, if not salad days? Anyway, the strength of a foamed metal derives from a power law relationship to its density. A twenty percent dense material is more than twice as strong as a ten percent dense material."

"Perfect stuff for our heat exchangers," Santini observed. "Increased heat transfer at the cost of reduced pressure. That's why we export only a portion of what the diggers extract from the ground. The rest remains here, like you said."

"Not just heat exchangers; radiation shielding as well. Composite metal foams are in heavy demand. Hollow beads of one metal are formed within a solid matrix of another metal, usually steel within aluminum. A less than one-inch-thick plate of the stuff has enough resistance to turn a standard issue M2 armor piercing round to dust. A plate not much thicker is a brilliant shield against gamma rays and neutron radiation, with twice the resistance to fire and heat as plain metals."

"Manufacturing the stuff is just one of our many budding industries. Other industrialists followed in the footsteps of the ore-handlers," Santini said.

"The waste handlers, foremost among them. Thanks to the Moon's inert surface and its distance from Earth, the Moon soon emerged as the preferred dumping ground for every manner of toxic human waste, from spent radioactive fuel to an unimaginable array of medical refuse.

"But life on Luna was hard," Santini said. "I often heard my father complain between six-month tours."

"Certainly no migratory haven, not like some envisioned at the outset of the space age," Flynn added. "Certainly no new frontier to conquer, at least not in the sense of the American West or the Brazilian Outback. The Moon proved to be a miserable place to live. It soon conquered the people who came to settle here in much the same way that North America conquered the hardy Vikings a thousand years earlier."

"Yes, and by the turn of the century, virtually all mining operations had been automated and permanent habitation of the moon had essentially ceased," Santini said. "All that remained of man's once robust presence on the Moon were periodic visits to recalibrate the lunar railguns and occasionally repair the robot-driven milling equipment. That is, until we arrived with a new mandate and a new mission."

Flynn washed down the last of his energy bar with a sip of recycled water. But he nearly gagged. The water they drank every day was flat and bad-tasting. It had to be flavored to be palatable.

"Okay," Flynn said. "Story time is over. Time for us to suit up and get back home. We have a lot of work to do beginning tomorrow."

Lou Santini grudgingly agreed. "I hate this thing, you know?"

"You hate your suit? Everyone hates their suit."

"No, I mean I think I have had this suit too long. It is beginning to smell." Santini sniffed the inside of his helmet and jerked back his head at the stench.

"They have been known to do that," Flynn said. "Body funk gets into the lining and there is no good way for getting it out."

"Body funk?"

"Yeah. Sweat. Urine. Farts. BO. Body funk."

"Well, when you say it like that, it all makes perfect sense," Santini said. "But I need to apply some sort of super strength suit liner deodorant if I'm to get this stench smelling sweeter."

"Good luck with that," Flynn said, snugging his helmet into place.

A modern spacesuit was a compound garment. It had multiple layers, an inner pressure suit surrounded by a protective outer shell, the so-called Mag 10 suit. For a man to be able to work productively both inside and outside a spacecraft or hab, a suit had to perform multiple functions. Maintain stable internal pressure. Provide for a reliable supply of breathable oxygen and a method for eliminating excess carbon dioxide. Collect wastes. Provide a radiation shield. Repel lunar dust. Regulate internal temperature.

"Suit tech is complicated fare," Santini said as they began to move. "The funk accumulates in the LCVG. That layer is highly absorbent, like a form-fitting set of long johns."

"Now who's being a know-it-all?" Flynn asked.

"Yes, the Liquid Cooling and Ventilation Garment, or, as the monkey wrenches call it, the sanitary napkin. What we slip on before we slip on the hard shell. In zero-g, there is no convection. Heat will not rise; cold will not sink. Excess body heat must be absorbed directly into the napkin's web of thin plastic, water-cooled tubes, then dumped into space via an umbilical with the PLSS, the portable life support system."

There was suddenly, now, an audible crackle over the comm.

"Put a sock in it," Flynn said, interrupting Santini's explanation. "Incoming transmission."

"That be a patrol sock?" Santini quipped.

Chief Flynn glared back at him and said into the headpiece. "Say again?"

The line had a great deal of interference on it. The comm system operated through a specialized cap worn over the head, a so-called Snoopy cap. It was a name given the head gear by early spacemen. The name stuck because the color of early caps matched the coloration of a then-popular comic strip character named Snoopy.

"I need you two back at base right away. Stat."

It was the voice of Director Hanrahan.

"Damn it, Hanrahan. We're in the middle of something important here," Flynn replied angrily. He was tired and hungry and fighting a splitting headache after so many hours in the suit.

"I need you two back at base," Hanrahan insisted. "Sinclair is already on the ground and the rest of the Moon Beamers are expected to land at any time. The explosion and your rescue operation has put us behind schedule. I have only two Z-bots to spare on corridor duty. The three of us — you, me, and Santini — have security details to work out. We have to process all these inbound visitors, get their particulars into the database, work them into the feeding schedule, run them past Doc Runyon for their physicals, issue them keycards, locker room space, and who knows what else. Big job. Plus, Doyle is becoming a giant pain in the ass. Return to base right away. That is an order. Hanrahan out."

Flynn shook his head in disgust when the line went dead.

"You go ahead," Santini said. "I'll finish up here, then grab a junior tech and go do my quarterly track check with him instead of with you."

"Are you sure you can handle that without me?"

"Heh, this is me you're talking to, remember?"

"I don't want to go see Hanrahan alone," Flynn muttered.

"Oh, don't be such a cry baby."

"Bugger off."

"Okay, already," Santini relented. "I'll come back in with you. But only for a short while. I'll clean up, slip on a new sanitary napkin, and then after the meeting, head back out with one of the newer techs, like I said. Those track welds need to be checked and this is as good a time as any. Might be a good way to get Junior Mate Gunderson up to speed on such things, a teaching moment for me, a learning moment for him."

CHAPTER EIGHT

Day Two, 1400 hours

"It's a job I have to do every three months or so anyway," Lou Santini said through his mic. Chief Flynn was at the other end of the line. Flynn had removed his flightsuit and was getting ready to go topside to see what was up with Doyle and Hanrahan.

"It's part of my job description," Santini continued. "You know the drill. Safety first. Four times a year I have to walk the track to check for loose bolts or broken welds. So what if it's a few days early? You were the one who ordered a moonbase-wide security check."

"Yeah, I know what I ordered," Flynn grumbled. "It's just that I would feel a whole lot better if I was there walking the tracks with you."

"I'll be fine, Chief. Gunderson is here with me. Catch up to us when you can."

"Gunderson?"

"Junior Mate Gunderson. Tech in Training. Santini out."

He clicked off the comm and knelt down beside the electrical panel in the dimly-lit tunnel. There were nine of these panels inside the tunnel complex, one every 500 meters or so. For the moment the only sound Santini heard within the confines of his space helmet was the rhythmic sound of his own breathing. In, out. In, out. A raspy sound. His throat was dry from the compressed air inside the tanks.

Then the silence was broken by the sound of the younger man's voice.

"Is every day a lesson with you?" Gunderson asked.

"Don't grasp your meaning, son," Santini replied, loosening the cover of the electrical box and peering inside. Behind the dustcover, the inside panel was part printed circuits and part solid-state digital breakers. "You're my TIT, and don't you ever forget it."

"Oh, how could I? You remind me of that fact twice a day. What you seem to forget is that I'm a Tech In Training, not your indentured servant," the young trainee said. Gunderson had bushy blond hair, a strong build, and quick wits.

"I got that, newb. Now bend down here and take a look at this electrical panel with me. My contract is up in a few months. Then I'm going home, perhaps for good. If you ever hope to replace me as Supervisor, you'll need to buckle down and learn. Understanding how this place is wired is a must. Consider it Priority One. Digital circuit breakers, surge protectors, diode couplings, chain wiring."

Gunderson shook his head. "So many things can go wrong around here. How can one man possibly learn all the hab's systems?"

"Time and experience, boy. Time and experience. They are your only teachers. Pay attention, put in the hours, and you will learn."

"But this place, the moon. Every day something new breaks down up here. Something spills, something leaks, something shorts out, something needs fixing or replacing. You and I, we're not engineers; we're high-priced plumbers and electricians. One day toilets, the next day turbines, the day after that cooling systems."

"And Junior Mate Gunderson, that is precisely what our job is here today, checking rivets in the track for microfractures and replacing brushes in the turbines, if they need replacing."

"Yeah, I got that, Mr. Santini. But why turbines in a tunnel? That is what I don't get. And why here of all places?"

Santini shook his head in irritation. "Do you not understand how we Lunatics store electrical power up here? Don't they teach you newbs anything in engineering school anymore?"

"There's no need to be mean about it, Mr. Santini. I have the general outlines. But it would be nice if someone filled in some of the blanks for me."

Santini slid the dustcover back into place, snapped shut the electrical panel, and got to his feet. There would be eight more panels to check before the day was through. "Every day is a lesson, like you said."

"And today's lesson is?"

"Hours of sunshine," Santini replied without further explanation.

"Come again?" Gunderson said.

"Hours of sunshine. Full Moon to New Moon to Full Moon again. Twenty-eight-day cycle, or thereabouts."

"Honestly, Santini. This is not news. Humanity has known about the 28-day lunar cycle since at least the time of the Sumerians, probably longer."

"That is how it appears to an observer on Earth. What counts up here is how it looks to us. The number of hours of sunlight that strike the lunar surface changes over the course of the lunar month."

"Go on."

By now the two men in spacesuits were moving slowly up the tracks, stopping to check rivets at each tie. Lou Santini held a scoping device that scanned the metal for metal fatigue, a constant problem because even the most exotic of metals became brittle in the sub-zero temperatures of lunar night. Beryllium copper was the most resistant. Non-sparking, yet physically tough and nonmagnetic. The stuff could be heat-treated for increased strength, durability, and electrical conductivity.

Santini spoke. "One face of the Moon always faces the Earth."

"Your point is?"

"My point is that the length of a moon day changes over the course of an earth-month. At the start of the lunar month, a given location on the moon is bathed continuously in sunlight. Fourteen days later that same location is completely dark. Days of various lengths both precede and follow the New Moon."

"I think I get it," Gunderson said. "The number of hours of sunlight interferes with a consistent level of electricity production throughout the month, yes?"

Santini nodded. "At full-on darkness, power usage surges. People turn on more lights for more hours each day. Evolution has set our body-clock to a twenty-four-hour day regardless of where we lay our heads down to sleep. There are psychological challenges to coping with continuous darkness. But this is something different. What I am talking about here is not psychological at all. Solar power generation falls to zero just as power usage soars."

"You're talking about load-balancing, yes?"

"Indeed, I am. And how does one balance load, junior engineer man?"

"With a battery. Shift excess power generation from long solar days to short solar days by storing it up in the present so it can be drawn down and used later on."

"Ain't no chemical battery big enough for our needs up here," Santini retorted. He looked closely at the rivet scan on his monitor, made a note on his handheld of one that might need replacing.

"If not a battery, then what?"

"You have to think outside the box on this one," Santini said. "One of the lowest tech ways to squirrel away a large quantity of electricity in times of plenty so that it can be used later on when power is in short supply is not to store it in a battery, but rather to pump it uphill in the form of water and place the water in a storage facility. Pumped storage has been widely employed where local geography and surface water conditions permit. The Brits use this method to great success on their little island, as does the State of India."

"This, I have never heard of."

"Local topography rarely cooperates fully," Santini noted. "A system of this sort requires two, sometimes three water reservoir basins stationed at different elevations, along with enough water to fill them all. To make the reservoir system function properly, one of the basins will often have to be manmade."

"What are you saying? Two lakes? One above the other in just the right spot?"

"Two reservoirs at two different elevations. The reservoirs are linked by tunnels and pumps in order to create a head of water whose pressure, when released, can drive the pumps backward to act as a power generating turbine."

"This is for real?"

"Oh yes, quite real. The connecting tunnel or giant water pipe must be large enough to allow water to flow freely between the reservoirs without escaping. And the tunnel pipe needs to have a large enough diameter inside to house multiple turbines. The turbines are designed to do double duty, first as motors to turn the turbine blades when they are lifting water from the lower reservoir to the upper one, and secondly, as generators when the blades are spun in the opposite direction by a down rush of water after the upper sluices are opened."

"So, your genius battery consists of moving water up and down a blinking hill?"

"In essence, yes," Santini said. "And it is genius, sheer inspired genius. Gravity is a form of stored energy. That gravitational potential can be released by running downhill."

"But of what good is pumped hydropower as a storage system in places where there is no water, like the desert?"

"Or the Moon?" Santini offered.

"That is, after all, today's lesson, is it not?"

"I am not the genius, Paddington Sinclair is. He adapted an earlier idea for an alternative to pumped water storage and crafted it to a moon-specific application."

"That's the lunar elevator guy, right? The guy who is scheduled to arrive here any time now and oversee its construction?"

"One and the same. In fact, I'm told he has already landed," Santini said.

"So, if this Paddington fellow stole someone else's idea, why claim that he is a genius?"

"Paddington Sinclair's breakthrough idea was an alternative to pumped storage, one that could be used on the moon. Instead of moving water up and down a hill, why not move something else that is heavy up and down a hill? He settled on a chain of large, concrete-filled boxes moved up and down by railcar. A bit like Sisyphus."

"Don't know the guy. Is he that gay guy in merchandising?"

"Ancient story. Greek mythology. Sisyphus, the first king of Ephyra. He was condemned by the gods to push a rock to the top of a mountain, only to have it roll back down again. He had to repeat the punishment over and over again for all eternity."

"Mr. Santini, if you have a point to make, I wish you would just hurry up and make it."

"No point; just a metaphor."

"I do think you mean allegory."

"Piss off," Santini snapped. "In Paddington Sinclair's modern take on that ancient story, concrete boxes stand in for the weight of the water in a pumped water storage system. Instead of turbines lodged inside a giant water pipe, his system — the system he installed here on the moon — employs empty boxcars running up and down on a track inside a tunnel, this tunnel."

"So, this railroad track is like the water pipe in your story? It is the connector between reservoirs."

"Yep. Concrete boxes loaded onto flatcars. Like the electrical kit of a pumped water storage system, the motors that drive the train act as a turbine when the loaded train cars run uphill. Then they act as a generator when — pulled along by gravity — the train cars run in reverse and roll backward downhill to the bottom."

"But why does the rail line have to be built inside a tunnel? I can understand water in a pipe, but tracks inside a tunnel?"

"Dust," Santini replied curtly.

Gunderson nodded as if he understood. "Yeah, the crap is everywhere, isn't it? Outside, we are knee-deep in that shit every moment of every day. Once the microscopic particles stick to your suit, they are damn near impossible to wash off."

"That's why the track had to be built inside a tunnel rather than laid out on the surface, and that's why there are dustcovers inside all our electrical panels."

"So why the crater?"

"To gain maximum change in elevation. That is the other part of the equation," Santini replied. "You need height to gain kinetic energy. But the moon is actually quite flat in most places. To gain maximum advantage of the moon's relatively minor changes in elevation, Sinclair's team chose to build the tunnel we're standing in as a series of concentric rings stacked one atop the other running counterclockwise around the inside of a large crater — this crater — from its upper lip to its rounded bottom. Folks around here have a name for this crater — the GAPS Crater."

"What is that short for?"

"Gravity Assist Power Station Crater."

"So, explain to me the mechanics of this concrete block battery gizmo. How does the damn thing work?"

The two men were walking along the catwalk that ran directly alongside the railroad track, stopping every once in a while to check the connectors and flash the rivets for the presence of microfractures. The second electrical panel was just ahead.

Lou Santini stopped to explain. "When solar production is high, the turbines drive the loaded railcars up the track. Once the cars reach the top of the track, the concrete boxes are lifted off the railcar by jacks built into the beds of the railcars. Once the blocks have been lifted off the railcar, they are then rotated and placed on sturdy racks located beside the track at the top. Then, freed of their load, the empty train cars roll back downhill to fetch another load. They continue to run uphill and down until the upper storage facility is completely filled. When it later becomes time to generate power . . . "

"You mean when the days become shorter and solar cell output falls to zero."

"Precisely. When solar output falls to zero, the concrete boxes are put back on the railcars and the stored kinetic energy becomes a source of generated power as gravity drags the heavy cars downhill and spins the turbine blades in the opposite direction."

"Clever."

"Yes, it is. And you are about to meet the man behind that cleverness."

"Paddington Sinclair?"

"Yes. The genius who conceived of the storage system and oversaw its construction."

"And his next project?"

"Man's first space elevator — the Moon Beam."

CHAPTER NINE

Day Two, 1450 hours

Chief Flynn looked Doyle Baldwin squarely in the eye when he spoke. "Didn't I tell you that I would have you detained if you didn't move out of the apartment and into bachelor quarters?"

An hour earlier, Flynn and Santini had rushed back to base on Hanrahan's orders, showered, and quickly eaten. After a quick bathroom stop, Flynn had come straight up to the comm center. Santini had gone back out with Junior Mate Gunderson to check the rails.

"Why the hell should I be forced to move out of my own place?" Doyle barked. "Just so you can shag my wife whenever you please?"

"Watch your mouth, Doyle. This isn't about me shagging your wife. This is about you and what you have been up to since last we spoke."

The communications center of the moon habitat was one of the most secure locations in the facility, double-thick pressure doors, encrypted comm units, fire-walled computers. No one would be able to observe or overhear this interrogation.

"Chief, I'm telling you that I am innocent," Doyle said, pushing against the leather restraints that bound him. "You have got the wrong guy."

"Every guilty man says the same. Can you prove it?" Flynn asked. He was sipping hot cocoa from a narrow-mouthed porcelain growler. Easy to heat in the microwave; tough to accidentally knock over. A flagon of hot cocoa was his favorite mid-afternoon beverage.

"Innocent men don't think about alibis when they are out NOT committing crimes. Only guilty men think about alibis," Doyle said.

"Everything we have points to you, Doyle. Access to explosives. Means. Opportunity. All we lack is motive."

"We? Who the hell is we?"

"Lou and myself."

"The two of you don't even have the authority. How dare you? Sending those two knuckle-draggers down to my flat to arrest me? Placing me in restraints? I have rights, you know."

"Not as many as you think. Besides, I am acting within my authority, I assure you. As Chief of the boat, I can keep you in restraints for up to two days without a hearing. I can have you confined to quarters for up to three. So, put aside your trumped up anger and indignation and answer my effing questions. To this moment right now, everything we points to you and only you."

"Everything points to me? How can that possibly be? What exactly do you and Santini have on me?" Doyle asked. "It can't be much. Plus, I would guess that whatever you do have is entirely circumstantial."

"You had access. Not many people do." Flynn moved to the other side of the interview table, undid Doyle's restraints, gave him something to drink.

"Access? That's a laugh," Doyle retorted, shaking his hands to restart the circulation. "Access isn't hard to get, even in a relatively secure place like this. What does a man really need? A keycard? Easy to steal or copy. A password? Any small bot placed in the right spot can observe someone entering a password on a computer. A fingerprint? All you need is a drinking glass from my kitchen or the mess hall or the pub. A voice match? Child's play to a determined saboteur."

Flynn turned thoughtful. "Fair points all. But if not you, Doyle, then who? Point me in another direction."

"Chief, you are one of the smartest men I know. And you have an amazing singing voice, no matter how much the other Clay Pots make fun of you. But use your clicking head. Start with the people closest to me and work outward." Doyle placed his hands flat on the table between them.

"Ouida?"

"Why not?"

"That doesn't seem possible," Flynn said. "She hardly seems the type."

"Just shows how little you actually know about her," Doyle replied.

"You would use your wife as a scapegoat to hide your own treachery?"

"You don't see it, Chief. You don't see it because you spend all your free time between her legs."

"You disgust me," Flynn said.

"I disgust you? You disgust me. You are having sex with my wife and hiding your malfeasance behind your rank."

"And you know this about me how?"

"She flat-out told me," Doyle said. "But don't worry, old friend. You haven't been the first and you certainly won't be the last. The woman hasn't been right in the head since the accident."

"What accident?"

"Her first husband, Jaxson Cooke. She nearly got the man killed. I have never met him, mind you, but I understand that the fellow is permanently disabled. After the accident she apparently parked him in a hospital bed somewhere. The woman is certifiable."

"If you knew that Ouida wasn't right in the head, then why the hell did you marry her?" Flynn was doing his best to suppress his surprise upon learning that the woman he'd been sleeping with had a husband before Doyle. *How had Flynn not known this about her?*

"A question I ask myself every day. A weak moment, I guess." Doyle fell quiet, then said. "Flynn, all I'm asking you to do here is to consider the possibility. Ouida had the means and perhaps the motive. By bedding you, she may have hoped you would first look elsewhere before looking at her. Before you judge me guilty, consider my lovely wife as a suspect."

"What motive? You said she may have had a motive."

"Ouida has absolutely convinced herself that her husband's accident was the fault of the mining company."

"And was it?" Chief Flynn asked.

"Not at all. The two of them, Jaxson and Ouida, were wildcatting on company time with salvage equipment destined for the storage heap. The drill shaft splintered and kicked back into the man's face. The impact broke his neck, which left him permanently crippled, a quadriplegic."

"The medicos couldn't fashion a neural bridge to repair the break?"

"The accident occurred too far from a med facility to do either of them any good. It took weeks instead of days to get him help. By then it was too late. The nerve endings had died. She blames everyone but herself."

"And why should she blame herself?"

"Because Ouida lied about the equipment, told him it was good stuff, when it was actually rubbish. I've read the official accident report from the insurance carrier. They denied her claim to cover her husband's medical bills."

"That would make me angry too," Flynn said, although he found a certain logic to what Doyle was saying. "You're telling me

she lied about the equipment? Not very sporting of the girl.
When did this dreadful accident take place? I'm trying to
establish a timeline in my head."

"Ten years ago, give or take," Doyle answered. "She
caught you on the rebound, right after that terrible jumpship
accident. You two first met at the Station, yes?"

"It was little more than a fling, a one-night stand, two
nights actually."

"Long enough to get her pregnant, if you believe my wife's
story. I took up with her right after that, though I didn't know
about you and her until much later."

"Adam cannot possibly be my son; I already told you that.
She and I only had sex while we were in zero-g. But you've made
your point, Doyle. Lou and I need to dig deeper."

"So, you'll let me go?"

"Can't do that," Flynn said. "Not yet anyway."

"You can't keep me locked up like this, Flynn. I'm your
man on drums, remember? Percussion. You need my skills to
make the Clay Pots complete."

"No lie there. But the band will have to wait. And you,
Doyle, will have to be patient and remain under house arrest
while Lou and I continue our investigation. If Ouida is actually
the one behind all this, I don't want to tip my hand to her by
setting you free."

"Confinement is what I fear most. Please don't leave me
rotting in this hole."

"Two days tops. I promise. Two days."

•

•

"May I come in?"

Chief Flynn stood at the intercom outside the door to
Doyle and Ouida Baldwin's flat. He had come here directly after
interrogating Doyle.

Her voice was angry and husky when she answered the
intercom. "You detain my husband then prance over here to fill
the void in my bed? How dare you?"

"It's not like that, Ouida."

"What's it like then, you bastard?" She still hadn't opened
the door or allowed him access to the premises.

"You may not be so angry with me once I tell you why I am
here."

"Okay, why are you here?" she shouted through the locked door.

"May I please come in?" Flynn asked again.

"Can I stop you?" she retorted haughtily, then keyed him in. The electronically controlled door rolled smoothly open.

Flynn was intimately familiar with the place. He had been here in this flat countless times before, usually as a guest of them both, sometimes alone with just her. He crossed the room to his favorite chair and made himself comfortable. She brought him his usual soft drink.

"How are you, Ouida?"

"I think when my parents chose a name for me, they expected me to go through life with an agreeable attitude."

"How so?"

"My name. Translated, it means — Yes, Yes."

"Is that Welsh?"

"No, silly. *Oui* is 'yes' in French. *Da* means 'yes' in any number of Slavic languages. My father was Russian; my mother French Canadian."

"So, you have a reputation for being easy? Is that what you are saying?"

"This is funny to you?"

"Not hah, hah funny. But yes, a bit amusing."

"So, tell me, Chief Flynn. Why are you really here, if not to bed me?"

"So now it's Chief Flynn, is it? Not Flynn? Not Chief? Not Clay?"

"Why are you here, Chief Flynn?" she persisted.

"Doyle says you are the saboteur who blew up the tunnel, not him."

"And you believe him?"

"I didn't say that."

"What then?"

"He seemed pretty convincing."

"Maybe my husband is a good liar."

"He says you have a motive."

"What motive?"

"Something to do with a first husband you never told me about."

"Oh, that."

"Yes, that. And there is only one way to clear all this up. I would like your permission to search the premises."

"And if I refuse?"

"Then you force me to go see Hanrahan about an administrative order."

"What is it that you hope to find if you execute a search warrant for our flat?"

"I hope to find nothing."

"But you think there may be something hidden in this apartment that might incriminate either Doyle or me?"

"It's my job, Ouida. You get that, right? I have no choice. I have to sort this thing out for the good of the colony. The evidence points to Doyle, and now he has pointed his finger at you."

"You're an ass, you know that, right?"

"Are we going to do this the easy way? Or are you going to make me do this the hard way? Either way, it gets done."

"Make you? I am not making you do anything, Flynn. Go see Hanrahan. Get your plucking administrative order and then get the hell out of my life and don't you ever come back!"

CHAPTER TEN

Day Two, 1520 hours

"If not Doyle, then who?" Santini asked. He had just returned from the spot-check of track welds with Junior Mate Gunderson. They identified six bolts that required immediate attention, and twice that number for the repair-as-soon-as-we-can list.

"His wife," Flynn replied with a long face.

"Seriously? Now you suspect Ouida?"

"The simple truth is that I'm less sure of anything now than I was six hours ago. Otherwise, why else would I be on my way to see Hanrahan to have him issue me a warrant to search their place?" Flynn said. He had come out of Ouida Baldwin's flat and run almost immediately into Lou Santini in the corridor. "For all I know, the two of them are in this together."

"You do this and she will never sleep with you again."

"Who says she is sleeping with me now?"

"Come on, Chief. Look who you're talking to. You may think you're fooling the rest of these lugnuts up here on this blinking rock. But you're sure as hell not fooling me."

"I can't be with a woman who I suspect of treachery," Chief Flynn said as the two of them worked their way slowly up the narrow passageway in the general direction of Winston Hanrahan's office. Their route would take them past the newly built green space, indoor park, and manmade stream.

Chief Flynn continued. "The only way for me to know for certain whether or not Ouida is in the clear is to conduct a thorough search of their premises. If I lose her, then I lose her. There are more than a few lives at stake here, not to mention a huge capital investment."

Santini put his hand on his friend's shoulder. "Well, before you breach the topic of a search warrant with Hanrahan, what say you and me first talk this thing through together and see if we can't come up with another way. Since we don't even know who it is we are dealing with, maybe we can make an educated guess where he or she or they will strike next."

"Who you kidding? There's no possible way for anyone to make a guess like that. This is a big place. Lots of people. Lots of places for a bad guy to hide."

"Standard game theory," Santini said.

"Now who is our resident Professor Know-It-All?"

"Guilty as charged."

Chief Flynn shook his head. "Is it even possible to outthink a bad guy using game theory? Seems rather farfetched."

"Lassoing an asteroid was once considered science fiction. Now we do it regularly, once or twice a year. Building a lunar elevator was once just a bunch of unsolved equations on a yellow legal pad. Now construction is about to get underway. Outthinking a bad guy? Within the realm of possibility. You have heard, perhaps, of the Prisoner's Dilemma? We are playing a version of this game with our unknown saboteur."

"If you say so," Flynn replied unconvinced. They had proceeded up the corridor to where a small wooden bridge crossed the manmade streambed and exited on the small, green space beyond.

"It is economics or, rather, mathematics. Nash Equilibria."

"Now you have really gone and lost me."

The manmade indoor stream ran roughly parallel to the corridor, past the aptly named pub, Perdition's Cup, past the cafeteria and the rec center. There was a tall waterfall at the headwaters of the stream, two footbridges, one on either side of the park, and a small lake at the lower end where the recirculating pumps were hidden behind a set of faux boulders. The park was in a clearing about midway down from the waterfall, live trees, tall grasses, several park benches, a wind machine, and plenty of simulated sunshine overhead. A perfect place for a quiet chat or lovers' embrace.

"I've gone and lost you, have I?" Santini quipped. "Nash Equilibria. John Nash. American mathematician. Twentieth century."

"You know about such things, Lou? I thought you were just a tech."

"I studied economics for two semesters before I switched to mechanical engineering and then later to space materials. The game is called the Prisoner's Dilemma. Two mobsters. They have been arrested in connection with a brutal murder. They are being held in separate cells and cannot talk to one another. They have been left in separate cells to sweat out the same deal offered to each of them by the district attorney."

Flynn inquired, as he sat down on one of the four park benches. "Just to be clear. Each prisoner knows that the other has been offered the exact same deal?"

"Yes. And this is the deal they have each been offered. If they both confess to the bloody murder, they will each face ten years in prison. If one stays quiet while the other snitches on his partner, then the snitch will get a cash reward and be put in witness protection, while the one who holds his water will face a life sentence with no chance for parole. If they both hold their water and neither confesses, then they will each face a minor charge and serve only one year in the clink."

Chief Flynn thought a moment, stared blindly into the babbling brook, watching the air bubbles form, melt, and form again. "I'm no mathematician, Lou. Neither are you. But given those parameters, my guess is that they will both confess."

"And you say this why?"

"It would seem the best strategy. My guess is that each mobster will reason it out the same way. Since the other might spill the beans, snitching avoids a lifetime in jail."

"Unless, of course, they have some means of communicating, in which case they will both keep mum," Santini argued.

"But I thought you said they were not permitted to talk to one another?"

"Not during," Santini replied. "But perhaps prior."

"Lost me again."

"What if the two mobsters talked beforehand — before the murder — and came to an agreement?"

"What sort of agreement?"

"What if they made a pinky swear that if either one snitched — if either one dared open his mouth — that spilling the beans would carry with it lethal consequences?"

"Pinky swear?"

"You know what I'm saying, Chief — a pact. Mobsters have codes, codes that are often enforced with force. Snitching may carry with it a death sentence."

"Which is why the district attorney offered the snitch a chance for witness protection. But I get where you are going with this, Lou. We have to outthink our opponent."

"Indeed," Santini said.

"The thing is, I see two weaknesses to the confession game you have just described."

"Go on."

"Theory aside, in real-life games the players aren't likely to know one another as well as our hypothetical mobsters do.

Actual people may be unsure what their opponent truly wants. So, they will be at a loss as to what their next move ought to be."

"Go on."

Flynn warmed to the subject. "Imagine two lovebirds. Their first date was an alcohol-fueled frenzy, with no thought given to consequences. Now they are trying to select a mutually acceptable location for a second date. But the two would-be lovebirds face a serious problem. They are trying to make the choice of an acceptable location for their second date with no idea what the other person prefers, movie or dinner, pizza or steak. Each is afraid to make the first move, in case their choice will ruin any further chance to be with the other."

"An interesting version of the game, Chief. The wrong move can lead to what game theorists call a death spiral. He says steak, but it turns out to be a critical error. She is a strict vegetarian, a fact unknown to him, and the second date is called off."

Chief Flynn nodded.

"You said there were two weaknesses."

"Ah, yes. This thing you call a Nash Equilibrium. It requires that both players exhibit rational behavior. That presents two further problems, as I see it."

"Yes?"

"Some people are rational. But because of poor information — or perhaps due to a lack of information — their decisions are no better than seat-of-the-pants guesses. Other people are truly irrational — as in nuts — and they will do stupid or unexpected things even when endowed with all the information required to make an informed decision."

"What's your point?" Santini asked, as they got up from the bench and strolled along the canal.

"My point is that we don't know enough yet about our opponent to correctly judge his behavior. Does our saboteur have an agenda? Or is he just nuts? I don't think your theory of games is going to help us figure out what or who this person is going to target next. We should follow our leads wherever they take us, and my best lead so far is getting a search warrant for the Baldwin's flat. Are you with me?"

"With you, Chief. Always with you."

"I do love being by the water," Flynn said wistfully.

"It is peaceful here. No place finer this side of low Earth orbit."

"When they built this stream and park, I thought it would be a big waste of time and money, not to mention living space," Flynn remarked.

"And now?"

"I was wrong, flat out wrong."

"Never thought I'd ever hear those words come spilling out of your mouth. You okay, Chief?"

Flynn looked hard at the other man.

Santini grinned. "Remember our discussion about patrol socks?"

"Your solution was to import hookers, if I recall."

"Yes, that would definitely help. But studies have shown what people missed most when they traveled off-planet was the sound of rushing water."

"More of your submarine psychology?"

"Rain. Babbling brooks. Waves crashing on the beach. Waterfalls. Lakefronts. Water lapping against a pier. That is what people missed. The sound of rushing water. That's why we built it."

"Makes sense," Flynn mused. "The civilizations of man evolved on the water. Mesopotamia. Indus Valley. Phoenicia. Egypt. Greece. Rome. What did they all have in common?"

"Navigable rivers. Seafaring trade. Harbors. Lakes. Watercraft of all sorts. Canoes. Rowboats. Keel boats. Rudders."

"Geez, let's get the hell out of here before somebody breaks out in a rousing chorus of *Kumbaya*."

CHAPTER ELEVEN

TWELVE YEARS AGO

"We hit pay dirt and you and I are going to be richer than you can possibly imagine," Jaxson said with a glimmer in his eye.

The two, Jaxson Cooke and his wife Ouida, were in the cab of the tread-mounted electric cart bumping along the mottled surface of the asteroid toward the wildcat zone. They were following the computer-generated grid lines laid down two months earlier by the swarm of survey bots.

"You mean *if* we hit pay dirt, don't you, honey-love?"

"You dare doubt me?" he answered with feigned anger. "*When* we hit pay dirt, girl — not if. Have faith."

"Oh, I do love it when you dream like that," she cooed, turning up the heater inside the small rover. The windshield was fogging up. Outside, on the surface of the asteroid, it was bone-splitting cold.

Law and custom dictated that after a new asteroid was lassoed that freelance ore-hunters were permitted to wildcat any tracts the big mining companies did not bid on. Wildcatters were permitted to search for valuable ore on their own time and at their own risk and expense. Fortunes had been made this way. Lives had been lost this way as well, more lives than anyone cared to keep count of.

"It's only another half klom or so," Jaxson said, fiddling with the knobs on the directional finder and banging once or twice on the insulating panel. Asteroids were not at all like ordinary, rocky planets. Their spins were irregular, and their surfaces treacherously uneven and jagged.

Wildcatters rarely ventured out this far from base without at least one mech to assist. In the asteroid mining trade, robots of one form or another did most of the heavy lifting and essentially all the dangerous work. These robots came in several classes, from the simple automatons that were little more than mechanized tools; to the slaves, smart bots that took orders from superiors but were not self-aware and could not reason problems out for themselves; to the master bots, smart and entirely self-aware machines that could think for themselves, yet still obeyed human command. The humaniform Z-bots were at the top of the hierarchy — smart self-aware, self-actuated bots capable of making their own decisions independent of human thought or input.

Normally, when a new asteroid was captured, the first order of business was to dispatch a swarm of survey bots across the surface of the big rock to identify prime locations to drill. The bots mapped out the richest veins of ore, as well as any dangerous fault lines the drillers ought to steer clear of. As the swarm of bots spread across the rocky mass, they blanketed the asteroid's surface with geo-markers that acted as fixed reference points on a static grid-map before the bidding began. The markers also helped keep the peace in the event of a claim-jumper.

After the assay samples were retrieved and analyzed, mining companies would then bid on large tracts they wished to drill on and later extract ore and other valuable minerals from. Inevitably, large tracts of land were left un-bid. Enter the wildcatters.

Wildcatting an asteroid was the most human of pursuits; bots need not apply. This was a job for men in spacesuits, armed with little more than their wits and a pneumatic drill, perhaps a Geiger counter and the odd portable laser to cut out and extract rock samples, plus a rover or electric cart to haul themselves and their booty home.

Ore-hunters often worked in teams, sometimes husband and wife, more often close friends or drinking buddies. The 'catters, as they were called, often worked full-time for an ore company during the day and wildcatted on their own time, at night or on weekends, scavenging equipment from their employer. The employer usually looked the other way, as the scavenged equipment was often second-rate and on the verge of breakdown anyway.

"When do we have to have this equipment back?" Jaxson asked, craning his neck for a better view of the terrain ahead. There were no roads, of course, but plenty of false shadows and dangerous terrain. Even a skilled driver could roll an electric cart in such conditions. Hazards were many — geysers of oddly shaped particles, loose chunks of rock, ice crystals, steep inclines, uncertain surface features.

"Not ever," she answered, gripping the roll bar with the glove of her spacesuit. Ouida was thrilled by the danger. It made her heart race. So did the prospect of one day striking it rich. Jaxson Cooke was her ticket to Easy Street.

"What do you mean not ever? Don't tell me you nicked all this drilling equipment on the sly?" Jaxson had never thought of his wife as a thief, although every day brought new revelations. Most women were risk-averse; not Ouida.

"The pneumatic drills were parked in the front of the salvage yard. The company was about to get rid of them. The handheld lasers too."

"Jesus God, honey-love. Please don't tell me this stuff was on the garbage heap, tagged as unsafe."

"Not at all," she lied. "The stuff was blue-tagged. It had already passed inspection and was being prepped for resale. The company will be auctioning off these used drills and diamond bits soon enough. All the stuff I spirited away can go to the auctioneer after you and I are done using it. Besides, I only had a hundred quid in my pocket. After I bought food and supplies, how much do you think was left over for equipment rentals?"

"We are here," Jaxson said, slowing the cart to a crawl at the assigned grid coordinates. "The Z-bot said to drill here."

"Now you are taking advice from a Z-bot?" Ouida said as she lumbered out of the cart. Her arm was still sore from the session with the tattoo artist. Skin art was part and parcel of the 'catter lifestyle. It often told a story, a sad one at that; skin-poetry for those who could understand the verse.

"Taking advice from a Z-bot is no worse than stealing equipment from the company. Or did you trade the equipment for sexual favors?"

"You know I don't do that anymore. Knees are getting too old for that kind of deep squat work."

"Not too old, I hope. Once we strike it rich, I may be needing some of that on-your-knees therapy. Anyway, what the hell is wrong with taking advice from a bot? Bots are okay. Three Laws and all that."

"You actually believe that shit?" Ouida questioned.

"And you don't?"

"Bots are as corrupt as anyone else," she said as she worked her way around to the back of the electric cart where the drilling equipment was lashed down.

"How can a bot possibly be corrupt? First Law. A robot may not injure a human being or, through inaction, allow a human being to come to harm."

"So much odious crap," Ouida said. "People acquire their moral codes from their upbringing, from their genetics, from their religion, from the people with whom they associate."

"Yes, and robots get theirs from their programming, from a sequence of behavioral laws hardwired into their positronic brains."

"Unless, of course, they do not," she retorted.

"Huh?"

"Robots don't get their moral code from their programming; they get their moral code from their programmer."

"What is the difference?"

"Evil people can write evil computer code. Or did this not occur to you, love? Robots can just as easily be programmed to be immoral as they can be to obey that famous sequence of behavioral laws. Whatever limits those three laws are supposed to place on robot decision-making can just as easily be neutered or done away with by someone smarter or meaner. With a few keystrokes, any savvy programmer can render the Three Laws moot."

Now, with Ouida's help, Jaxson unloaded the reciprocating drill from the back of the rover, inserted the diamond drill bit, tightened the chuck and slowly wheeled the drill assembly the few meters over to the marked point.

"Can a robot deceive itself into believing it is actually a genuine flesh and blood human being?" she asked, lending a hand.

"I suppose that is possible," he replied, positioning the tripod support.

"In that event, the Three Laws are history. Any bot that has deceived itself into believing it is actually a human being will no longer feel bound by the Three Laws. He can willfully violate any or all of the Laws and not give the violation a second thought."

"I get your point," Jaxson said, nearly stumbling to the ground on a pile of loose rock. "Any robot that believes it is a human being will find it has no obligation to obey the Laws of Robotics. Thus, in contravention of those laws, it could indeed harm another human being, no questions asked, and do so with a clear conscience."

"Exactly."

"Therefore, to remedy this inherent loophole in their programming, we need to devise a fourth behavioral law, don't we? One law that overrides the other three."

"It would seem so. Have you a solution to offer?"

"Yes, I believe that I do," Jaxson Cooke said, standing the drill upright and fumbling with the starter motor to drill their first core sample. The drill was big and unwieldy. "We shall call it the Fourth Law of Robotics. *A robot must at all times know that it is actually a robot.*"

"Yes, hubby, I suppose that might work. But I still don't see how making a robot self-aware will stop people from writing malicious code that allows a humaniform Z-bot to misbehave. But you just keep right on doing the thinking, honey. That's what you're best at — thinking."

"Time to stop thinking and jawing and start drilling. Get ready, honey-love. You are about to become the richest woman this side of Deimos."

"Come again?"

"Deimos. One of the two Martian moons. Phobos and Deimos."

"Oh, that does have a nice ring to it," she murmured, lost in thought.

"Which part?" he asked.

"The rich woman part."

The machine sputtered to life and began to spit bits of rock and regolith to the side at it penetrated the surface.

"This stuff is pretty soft," he muttered into the comm unit. "Nothing of value here near the surface."

Minutes passed and the bit dug deeper. Jaxson stopped a moment, attached the first extender bar and continued to dig. He was now down about one-third of a meter. Suddenly, the hammer began to shake violently in his hands.

"Did you check the seals on this drill before you walked out of the salvage yard with it?" he asked, his voice cracking with doubt. "This infernal shaking makes me think the seals are ready to blow."

Ouida nodded yes, but said absolutely nothing. It was hard to make herself heard over the racket of the reciprocating hammer.

"It was blue-tagged as safe for resale, safe to use, yes?" he asked her with worry in his voice. Jaxson Cooke had nearly five hundred hours of experience with drills of every sort. He knew trouble when he felt it tremble in his hands.

The lateral movement worsened. If a drill operator lost control of his drill, any number of bad things could result, the worse being that it could fly apart and kill its operator.

She nodded. "All the unsafe equipment is stored at the back of the yard. The newer stuff is kept out front. That is where I got it from, out front." Ouida didn't take the time to say that this particular drill assembly had no tag whatsoever on it. She just assumed it was okay and took it.

The core sampling hammer shook violently. It tried to shake free of Jaxson's grip. Clearly the bit was dull from use and was perhaps now shaking loose of its bushings. Catastrophic failure was but seconds away.

"Was it tagged safe to use or not?" he asked breathlessly.

"It was tagged," Ouida lied, yelling at the top of her voice. "Do you really think I would risk losing my best guy to an accident just to cut corners and save a little scratch? Do you trust me or not?"

As Ouida shouted her reply, the bit struck something extremely hard: solid iron slag from an ancient tectonic event, most likely volcanic. The jack hammer kicked back like a mule.

"Shut it down!" she shouted. "Shut the bloody thing down."

Her instructions were at least ten seconds too late. The handle kicked back and struck Jaxson high in the chest, just below the chin.

Jaxson's head snapped backward with a hard crunch. If not for the protective suit, the impact would have punched the handle straight through his throat and taken his head clean off. Instead, it snapped his neck, fractured his spinal cord just above the shoulder at C4.

Jaxson collapsed in a lifeless lump. The spacesuit had not ruptured, so it was still pumping in oxygen and recycling carbon-dioxide exhaled. All modern suits were programmed to perform auto-compressions whenever it sensed a cessation of breathing, a form of emergency CPR designed to keep a suit's occupant alive until help could arrive or the victim could be transported to safety.

Accidents in space rarely ended in a scraped knee or bruised elbow. Most accidents in space ended in death. Radiation burns. Massive trauma. Penetrating blows. A torque hammer, a pneumatic drill, a piton gun. If something went wrong or misfired in space, it rarely resulted in just a disjointed finger or a broken toe. More likely, an entire appendage would be torn off.

The clock began to run the moment the accident occurred. *Could she get Jaxson to competent medical help before it was too late?*

The technology existed. Severed spinal cords could be repaired. Neuron bridges could be built. But for such repairs to have a good chance at success, the optimum time to get under the knife was within 120 hours of the injury, five days. He was five weeks from the nearest outpost, too long for even the simplest repair, let alone something this severe.

If Jaxson lived, his paralysis would be for life, and Ouida was to blame.

CHAPTER TWELVE

Day Two, 1610 hours

"No way am I going to hand someone as pigheaded as you a search warrant," Winston Hanrahan said, sternly. "Not now, not ever. If the Baldwins' premises need to be searched, it will be me doing the searching, Flynn — not you."

Chief Clay Flynn bristled with anger. Hanrahan had cut short his and Santini's security sweep of the tunnels and was now being an obstructionist, interfering with his investigation.

"Listen, you toad. I can only hold Doyle for forty-eight hours. Heading up an investigation of this sort is part of my job description. Look it up in the Manual. My area of responsibility." Flynn turned to Lou Santini for moral support, but Santini remained mum. "You want to toss the Manual, then toss me as well."

Hanrahan said nothing, which angered Flynn further.

"Damn it, man, make up your mind. Am I in charge of this investigation or not? Use me or shitcan me. But whatever you do, do it now."

Administrator Hanrahan shook his head. "Chief, your judgement is flawed. People will see your search as a personal vendetta. Any evidence you unearth in the Baldwin flat will be tainted and highly suspect."

"How so?"

"You are sleeping with the man's wife, for God's sake, and in his own bed."

"And you know this how?"

Hanrahan harrumphed. "While you and Santini were out playing tunnel rat together, I interviewed them both, Ouida and Doyle. I have a good mind to bring you up on charges."

"So, go ahead," Flynn dared the other man. "But you won't. And do you want to know why? Because you know full well that Lou and I are on the right track with these two. One of the two — either Doyle or Ouida — is responsible for all that has befallen us in the past twenty-four hours. Within a day or two, either or both of them together will try to pull off something even more spectacular and damaging than what they have already done. And, unless you want a bloody nose for your trouble, don't ever call either one of us a tunnel rat again. Capiche?"

"Yeah, I capiche," Hanrahan said. "But she's a cold one, that woman, Ouida Baldwin. You know that, right?"

"What makes you say that?" Flynn asked, though he privately agreed with the other man's assessment.

"Two things. Earlier, when Adam's fate was still uncertain, the woman never shed so much as a wet tear for her boy's safety. I sat with her for a time while you and the others were out risking your lives trying to rescue her kid and that girl. Ouida just kept staring at her chron like she was expecting a call or a visitor."

"People handle stress differently," Santini remarked. "You said two things bothered you."

"I interviewed her earlier this afternoon, like I said. The two of you were in the tunnels. Her, Doyle, Nora, Mitch, the two children. I talked to them all. Even that Mexican girl, Lopez, the counselor on the field trip who cocked up this thing to begin with."

"You're a bigot, you know that?" Santini cursed.

Winston Hanrahan answered him with a blank stare.

"Sarena Lopez. That's her name," Santini said. "She's as American as you or I. Dutch Lopez is her father, Captain Dutch Lopez, United States Marine Corps."

"Boy, you are touchy today," Hanrahan snapped. "Do you want to find out what I learned from them or not?"

"Yes, and what did you learn?" Santini asked sarcastically.

"The little girl — the daughter, Kyra — used her father's security code to gain access to that side tunnel, just like you and Flynn supposed. Turns out that counselor — model citizen that she is — was busy giving her boyfriend a hummer in the bathroom when the two kids wandered off unobserved. Some boy named Phelps from the Equipment Department. Carson Phelps. That's her boyfriend."

"Wonderful," Flynn chided. "Just clicking wonderful."

"Yes, wonderful," Hanrahan said. "Aside from a terrorist attack, I have about two dozen infractions of the rules I must deal with — Mitch taking his daughter with him on rounds, giving her a security code; two of my senior officers committing adultery; a counselor on her knees when she ought to have been on her toes watching out for the safety of our little ones."

"Forget the rule infractions already," Santini said. "Focus on the main event, the big picture."

"But rules must be obeyed. They were codified and written down for a reason."

"Don't be an ass," Santini said. "We need all hands on deck, not on report. Once the Beamers step off their ship, we don't need to be distracted by having good people bilged."

"Bilged?"

"Naval term. Flushed. Thrown out like garbage."

"Quite right," Hanrahan said. "Not to change the subject, but Chandler Tattersall just texted me. The arrogant twit has time to see you and Santini now. But he says, you'll need to hurry. Chandler's a busy guy, or so he says."

"Tattersall's an arrogant twit? Kettle calling the pot black, wouldn't you agree?"

"Are we done here?"

"Not quite. You still need to authorize a warrant?" Flynn tried one last time.

"Ain't happening. Give me something more than circumstantial evidence. A print, a frame shot on a surveillance tape, a witness, something, anything."

CHAPTER THIRTEEN

Day Two, 1700 hours

"Our biggest import in days past was food and medicine," Professor Tattersall said in his absentminded way. Before him sat his friends Chief Clay Flynn and Senior Tech Lou Santini. They were listening but antsy and eager to get on with what was left of their day.

Professor Chandler Tattersall continued. "But now, with the Farm operating smoothly, food is no longer a pressing need. We are nearly self-sufficient in most of the staples — corn, wheat, rice, potatoes. Of course, we still import much of our animal protein from Earth — as well as nearly all our pharmaceuticals. Also, a laundry list of specialty items — food, sure, like lobster tail and chocolate, but other things too, like strings for our guitars and reeds for our woods. But protein is the big thing. Raising cattle or sheep has proven problematic. No fields of grass on which to graze them. Chickens harbor too much disease. Fish farming eats up too much clean water. Goats do okay, though."

"Goats, eh? Never knew that," Santini remarked. "I suppose that's why lamb chops are never on the menu."

Tattersall chattered on. "Which is also why, aside from flash memory chits and pharmaceuticals, much of what arrives here each month onboard the rapid descent vehicle is animal protein in one form or another. Lunar soil is largely devoid of nutrients. It has been a learning process coaxing crops to grow. You boys would be amazed by the varieties of fertilizer that can be harvested from human wastes, especially when it is mixed in with fish krill raised in our aquatic tanks."

"Stay on point, will you?" Chief Flynn said in an irksome tone. Lou Santini seconded Flynn's frustration. It was time to eat supper and this intellectual detour seemed a bother.

"What was your question again?" the old guy from the laboratory asked. Professor Chandler Tattersall knew more about everything than most people knew about anything. He was well-liked and orderly and was possessed of a first-rate mind. But, the man was easily distracted. The only time he seemed truly focused was when he was on keyboards playing his heart out for their little string and brass band.

"Professor, my question had to do with the lunar elevator that Paddington Sinclair and the Moon Beamers are about to build here at EML-1. Let's say they get the thing up and running. Let's say that after the thing is operational and we have come to depend on it, what then? If it were ever to be knocked out of service, what would be our most pressing need? What would fall into shortage first? Because that is where we must bulk up."

"This is a game, right? Some sort of test dreamed up by that megalomaniac Hanrahan? A complex what-if scenario, yes?"

"Yes," Santini said. "Let's approach it that way for now. A hypothetical test run."

"Yes, quite right," Tattersall said. "What would fall into shortage first, you ask? Aside from medicine? — Machine parts. Computer keyboards. Flash memory. Together, those three probably account for 70 percent of our imports nowadays. Electronics are in chronic short supply. Dust, solar flares, magnetic disturbances from the railgun, overuse, extreme cold. We constantly burn out electronic components. Flash memory chits. They are the worst. We go through those buggers like there is no tomorrow."

"And why is that, exactly?" Lou Santini wanted to know.

"Sometimes the sun burps, bad as you do after band practice," Tattersall answered laughing. "Only instead of burping up bad breath, the sun flings off mighty arcs of hot plasma. What we call coronal mass ejections."

"Like a plasma storm, then?" Flynn observed.

"Indeed. Space weather. That's what the ground techs at Los Alamos call it. Space weather. But we don't need a full-blown solar hurricane to stir up trouble for us here on the Moon. Space drizzle is trouble enough."

"Of all things," Santini exclaimed. "Space drizzle? I've worked up here two days short of forever and never once heard mention of space drizzle. What the hell is that?"

"The Earth and Moon are bombarded by a steady stream of high-energy subatomic particles. Some of these particles come from the sun. Others are cosmic rays, which originate outside the solar system. Space drizzle; that's what they call it. Galactic shrapnel, more like. The stuff is dangerous to man and machine alike. If one of those high-energy particles should happen to strike a computer chit, it can inject an unwanted electrical charge into the circuit. Goodbye memory. Goodbye software. The tinier and more densely packed the chit, the larger the problem. A modern computer might incur a hundred space-drizzle-induced errors per billion transistors per billion hours of operation."

"That doesn't sound like much," Santini reckoned, lost in the math.

Professor Tattersall nodded as if he understood. "Modern chits have thousands of millions of transistors, and modern data centers have billions of chits. Operate a data center containing a billion chits, each with a hundred million transistors, and in one hour you have already racked up a hundred million billion hours of operation. The numbers add up quickly."

"So, paddling backwards to our original question," Flynn interrupted. "If the elevator is built and later there is an interruption in the elevator service — a hypothetical interruption, of course — there would soon be bottlenecks in comm and in electronic controls? Is that what you're saying?"

"For purposes of this what-if test, without a doubt. Environmental stabilization would be one of our biggest concerns. To maintain a near constant air pressure across all parts of the facility at all times is an electronics nightmare. Think of it — tens of thousands of tiny sensors, complex feedback loops, servos, pumps, hydrostatic air cleaners, motors, valves, radiological detectors — all controlled by easily damaged electronics. People notice the tiniest smells. They panic, think it's a fire, call Control. A slight dip in air pressure and alarms sound everywhere, inside and out. The calls start coming in fast and furious. So, yes. Electronics. That is our Achilles heel. That is where they will cut us, in the heel. Stop those essential deliveries and inside of ten days, two weeks at the outside, and we are done."

"But how long could we go without fresh meds?" Santini asked.

"That's anyone's guess," Tattersall replied. "Not long. Maybe a week, maybe two. To survive up here on a long-term basis, we require a constant supply of new and better meds. The biological dangers are constantly changing. To stay one step ahead, we constantly need new pharma formulations, new chemical structures, improved antibiotics, even re-jiggered antivirals."

"Yes, and again why is that?" Flynn asked.

"It's a problem we frail humans have been facing since the dawn of the space age."

"So, you're up to speed on this as well?"

"Oh, yes. Micro-gravity screws with our body's immune system. It makes us less able to ward off infection. But the danger from low-g is magnified by another threat. Bacteria grow much more quickly in low-g. The little buggers also mutate more readily. Taken together, these risks make bacteria more infectious. It also makes them more resistant to antibiotics. What we have learned from the past hundred years or so of space travel is that relatively harmless pathogens can change and become more lethal in unpredictable ways. Entire crews have been lost on account of debilitating disease."

"I got that," Flynn said. "But have we learned why? Do we know what mechanism is responsible for turning ordinary bacteria lethal?"

Tattersall nodded. "We have a partial answer, thanks to years of careful measurement and observation. We have established that cells grow more quickly in outer space. Not only that, but changes take place down at the sub-cellular level, in the double strands of DNA and its messenger chemicals. It turns out that unexpressed genes become active when the pull of gravity is low or zero; also that *more* genes become more active, which makes the outcome nearly impossible to predict in advance."

"What if I told you this wasn't a test after all, that this wasn't a game of what-if?" Santini asked. "What if I told you this was an actual scenario being played out right now by actual people?"

"Not a Hanrahan bogey-man chase? The actual real thing?"

"Flynn and I believe the elevator may become a target, even before it is built. Aside from the Moon Beamers themselves, you, Tattersall, probably know more about the space elevator than anyone on this rock. How easy will it be to damage or destroy the thing? What part will be most vulnerable? What part is second-most vulnerable? How do we protect those parts from damage or sabotage?"

Professor Tattersall scratched his chin in the usual manner. "You have come to the right place, you have."

"We know that," Santini said at the end of his patience. "Now we need you to focus, Professor. Focus on the question being asked of you. What part is most vulnerable? How do we protect it?"

"Either one of you boys know any science?"

"A little, I guess," Santini answered grumbling. Tattersall knew full well that his visitors had advanced degrees in science and engineering and were well versed in such matters.

"Well, no matter," Tattersall said. "Maybe I can teach one or the other of you gents a bit of history, maybe some science as well. Now sit down, both of you, and pay attention."

Flynn looked at Santini, and Santini looked back. They each found a chair and tried to get comfortable.

Tattersall cleared his throat to speak. "The lunar elevator may be easier to bring down than you think."

"Do tell," Santini harrumphed.

"An amazing marvel of human engineering, to be sure. Like the pyramids of Egypt or the Panama Canal, monuments to our ability to marshal massive resources to achieve an important end. This elevator thing is one part brilliant engineering, three parts Newtonian physics. But, unlike the Pyramids or the Panama Canal, the elevator is little more than a fancy kite with a very long and quite tenuous string. Gravity is a heartless bitch, and she would like nothing better than to crash your kite. The structure remains aloft only because it finds a place of equilibrium in a balanced and carefully orchestrated dance with the very same forces that hold the solar system together."

"Believe it or not, I do understand the basics," Santini said. "One very long, very strong cable with a counterweight attached at the far end."

Tattersall nodded. "The cable is woven from some of the strongest materials known to man, Zylon or Dynemma or Magellan M8 fiber. The elevator boys call this cable a tether. The thing that moves up and down on the cable is called a tether climber — specifically, a Pearson Tether Climber — what ordinary folks might call an elevator. The elevator will carry both people and cargo up and down the tether, though in separate compartments, one above the other. The lower part of the cable hangs down from a depot parked at L1, and the depot is attached by a further length of cable to a counterweight. The longer the cable, the lighter the counterweight can be. The entire assembly is suspended above the moon's surface at L1, one of the five lunar libration points. You know what a libration point is, yes?"

Both heads nodded. Santini said, "Back in the dim ages, before the birth of Christ, when I first got an education, we used to call them Lagrange points."

"Ah yes, the mathematician Joseph-Louis Lagrange . . . Everything looks so simple with a piece of chalk in hand and a blackboard. Lagrange did geometry; we do reality."

"There is a difference?" Flynn asked.

"Yes, and a mighty big one. Once we depart the realm of chalk and chalkboard and enter the realm of reality, we find that the so-called Lagrange points are actually not points at all, but rather oddly shaped regions. The geometrically defined points are actually at the centers of two regions on opposite sides of the moon. Objects anchored in these regions will tend to drift around the centers of these points in erratic orbits. They will appear to orbit the geometrically defined points in a noncircular and nonelliptical fashion without ever leaving the region and without requiring much station-keeping propellant to remain anchored in the region."

"I did not know that," Flynn said.

"Nor I," Santini admitted, though he did. "It seems that we have come to the right man."

"It is a common mistake," Professor Tattersall said. "Mathematicians make geometry appear altogether too simple. But reality is rather more messy. The L4 and L5 points are located in Earth orbit sixty degrees in front of and sixty degrees behind the path of the Moon around the Earth. When the Moon accelerates or decelerates an object at L4 or L5, it changes the object's centrifugal force relative to Earth and hence its orbit around Earth. This, in turn, causes the object to climb away from or fall towards Earth, in which case its orbital speed decreases or increases as it climbs away or falls towards Earth. As a result, it falls behind or passes up the L4 or L5 point and the cycle repeats."

"Professor, you couldn't be more obtuse if you tried," Santini chided. "I am smarter than most. I even know some mathematics. — And yet, I failed to understand a single word you just said."

Professor Tattersall harrumphed. "Let me water it down some, so the engineers among us can understand. An object placed at a lunar libration point does not orbit the Moon; it orbits the center of mass of the Earth-Moon system and it does so once each month. To further complicate matters, the Sun's gravity likewise perturbs any object anchored at an EML node."

"EML?"

"Earth-Moon Lagrange. The mathematics are daunting, and the picture becomes murky awfully fast. But the name of the game is preservation of angular momentum."

Chief Flynn interrupted. "Excuse me, Professor. But the last I heard, the three-body problem has never been properly solved. How can it possibly be the foundational principle that makes the elevator work?"

"No one has adequately explained dark matter either, and yet the universe exists," Professor Tattersall replied. "The analysis of an anchored lunar satellite is an application of the restricted three-body problem, one of a veritable handful of versions of the problem that have indeed been solved. But, as you say, other versions of the problem remain intractable. No formula or equation or analytical shortcut exists that can provide a solution in those cases."

"None?" Santini asked.

"None," Tattersall answered flatly. "To determine the future positions of three bodies orbiting one another, a predictive model has to be run in real time at ordinary speeds. A simulation, even a sophisticated one run on your best computer will differ noticeably from the true positions of the three bodies before they have even completed their first revolution. Our reality here on the Moon is perhaps even more complicated."

"Is that even possible?"

"For an anchored lunar satellite, the effective gravitational field is defined by the vector sum of five contributing forces."

"Only just five?"

"Do I detect a note of sarcasm? Five vectors; count them. The gravity of the Earth. The gravity of the Moon. The centrifugal acceleration. The Coriolis acceleration. And the linear non-inertial acceleration. The primary bodies are, of course, the Earth and the Moon, and each is assumed to revolve in circular orbits about their barycenter."

"Barycenter," Santini interrupted. "Something I actually do know about. Barycenter. The mass-adjusted center of gravity."

"Yes. Quite right," Tattersall said.

"The equilibrium points discovered by Lagrange. Points L4 and L5 are stable positions for third bodies; the collinear points L1, L2, and L3 are unstable equilibrium points. The dynamics of a body released from a tall lunar tower are extremely complex, because the gravity effects of both the Earth and Moon must be taken into account. The motion must be analyzed as a restricted three-body problem, which has received extensive analytical treatment. But, as you said, it is still not properly solved."

"And yet this Paddington Sinclair fellow knows how to build the thing?"

"Oh, indeed. In fact, Sinclair is already here, on the ground. He arrived early this morning during all the excitement. Barfing his guts out ever since he landed, or so I gather. Something about the lightcraft experience, or so I am told. Doc Runyon's got him up in sickbay for the moment."

Flynn couldn't help but smile. *The lightcraft experience.* Flynn knew everything there was to know about the physics and aerodynamics of a lightcraft. He had helped engineer the previous generation of lightcraft early in his career, the jumpship series. In fact, that was how he first met Ouida, during one of those tests.

Flynn thought back now to those days, crew and designers working together to perfect a dangerous and unproven technology. Hard, dangerous, rewarding work.

A ride onboard a rapid ascender pod was bound to be frightening no matter who sat at the flight controls, frightening even to an experienced space traveler like Paddington Sinclair.

The experimental launch vehicles went by several names — pod, rapid ascender, lightcraft, jumpship. Regardless of what people called them, these were no ordinary spaceships. In fact, they were enormously sophisticated craft, with hulls of high-tensile-strength metals. Quick and easy to launch. Difficult to slow down once in motion. Equipped with g-chairs for five passengers. Full complement of emergency gear. Med kit. Pressure suits. Portable life support systems. Umbilicals.

The launch of a lightcraft was unlike any other. A full pulse from a ground-based laser. The sudden slam skyward. Six minutes straight up into the atmosphere. High-g acceleration. Sudden weightlessness.

Had a jumpship been a solid-fuel rocket like one of those used at the dawn of the space age, there would have been a bright orange flame, followed by a volcano of blinding smoke and a tremendous thundering roar as the big fuel tanks ignited and the towering rocket lumbered slowly skyward picking up speed as it broke its earthly bonds.

But with a lightcraft everything was different. No orange flames. No blinding smoke. No big fuel tanks filled with volatile chemicals. Just raw acceleration, blinding heat, and ground-rattling vibration. The roar grew exponentially as the lightcraft's acceleration rapidly compressed the air in front of the ship into an increasingly thick wall. Inside, the passengers would be compressed into their seats like flattened pancakes.

Then would come the air spike. Just thinking about it made Flynn's pulse quicken. From the moment of launch, physics ruled the ship's destiny. The wall of air that piled up in front of the vehicle would become superheated by the annular mirror. An instant later, the dense wall of air would collapse in a brilliant flash of white energy. This was fluid dynamics hard at work. The violent noise would abate and the jumpship would fairly leap into space. Only four minutes to low-earth-orbit; two more to docking orbit.

The solution to achieving cheap access to space lay in the nature of a lightcraft itself. It rode a beam of high-intensity laser light that was pulsed up to the space vehicle from a transmitter down on the ground. It was a complicated arrangement, one which took decades of tinkering and experimentation to perfect. After years of trial and error, including two horrible accidents, the aerospace engineers working on the project — including one Clay Flynn — finally came up with an arrangement that worked, one that did not malfunction midflight.

A fully functional lightcraft had three parts. A forward aeroshell. An annular, ring-shaped cowl. And an aft part consisting of an optic and expansion nozzle.

During atmospheric flight, the forward section compressed the air in front of the craft and directed it to the engine inlet. The annular cowl took the brunt of the exiting thrust. The aft section served as a parabolic collection mirror.

The mirror concentrated the incoming infrared beam into an annular focus. This ingenious design offered the added benefit of automatic steering should the craft begin to stray outside the diameter of the beam. The thrust would incline and nudge the spacecraft back into line. The advent of lightcraft meant that pilots no longer lived in a stick-and-rudder world.

Once the craft reached an altitude of about fifty kloms, where air became scarce, the ship had to switch from riding the laser beam to burning onboard liquid hydrogen propellant.

Chief Clay Flynn leaned back, now, clasped his fingers behind his head, and consciously tuned out the other two men. Those were his salad days — Experimentation. Achievement. Hands-on engineering. Flynn took great personal satisfaction from reliving these fond memories, all of them good, with one big exception, the last one.

Ten years ago, during high-altitude testing, there had been a terrible accident, a crew-killing fire in low-earth orbit. Horrible. He was still haunted by the events of that day.

CHAPTER FOURTEEN

TEN YEARS AGO

The test run had begun in the ordinary way. Five crew members strapped in, the cabin pressurized, the bullet-shaped ship lowered onto the launch pad by a retracting crane. Now it rested on a railcar-sized tripod which left the ship's curved bottom suspended over the business end of the light tube.

Thirty meters below the surface, at the bottom of the light tube, sat an enhanced chemical laser. While chemical lasers were not cutting-edge technology, incremental improvements in legacy technology allowed them to be put to use in novel ways. A carefully calibrated chemical reaction permitted a stupendous amount of energy to be released in a matter of nanoseconds. It was mated to a standard free-electron laser to achieve amazing energies, enough to power a small spaceship to orbit.

The theory behind the revolutionary propulsion system was simplicity itself. Light had momentum; concentrated light had even more. The energy of that momentum could be focused by reflective, mirror-like surfaces at the base of the lightcraft into a ring beneath the craft. The focused beam of energy heated the air to temperatures nearly five times hotter than the surface of the sun. The superheated air expanded explosively, providing thrust.

Shielding the occupants of the passenger compartment from the kinetic energy of that superheated air proved to be one of the most daunting engineering obstacles designers had to overcome to make the ship fly. Cargo had been lifted to Earth orbit by lightcraft for years, but never human beings. Flynn's team believed they had finally solved the shielding problem once and for all.

The day of the disaster was the fifth test run of this model, but only the second test with actual humans onboard. Flynn remembered that day with pained agony.

Half the engineering team was aloft at the orbiting space station, their job to observe the launch from above. The other half of the team remained feet firmly planted on *terra firma* to observe the launch from below. Other observers from the university and the military circled the launch site in aircraft pre-positioned at various altitudes.

Clay Flynn, newly minted Ph.D., was one of the observers aboard the space station at the time of the launch. He had been accompanied to the station by his robot assistant, Claybotta. By virtue of Flynn's training and connection to the project, he and his robot were ordered to join the investigative team that descended by shuttle down to the burnt-out hulk from the space station after the accident.

The initial launch of the jumpship had been picture perfect. The ship was beyond the boost stage and gliding at zero acceleration into orbital position when it happened, a single devastating explosion. What looked at first to be a successful test-launch destined for the record books ended in tragedy.

The terrible thing about a fire onboard a spaceship is that it may burn virtually unnoticed for a long time. In space, in the absence of gravity, heat does not rise in the ordinary way. Convection currents are absent. Fires often burn without flame. A ceiling-mounted heat sensor, while useful when the craft is parked in its lorry down on Earth, becomes a useless party decoration aloft. Thus, a treacherous fire may be quite hot and dangerous, yet remain completely undetected for an extended period of time.

This particular fire started beneath the floor of the crew compartment in the locker where the liquid hydrogen propellant was stored for the final jump to orbit. Once the craft reached an altitude of about fifty kloms, where air became exceedingly scarce, the ship had to switch from riding the laser beam to burning onboard liquid hydrogen propellant, highly volatile stuff.

The investigation proved that what actually caught fire first was a grease-soaked hand towel left behind by the ready team when they were performing their final prelaunch check. *Human error, of all things!* The towels smoldered in the propellant compartment for many minutes before igniting. The ship was already in orbit by then, and the launch termed a success. But when the temperature in the propellant chamber rose high enough, the ventilation fans spooled up and fed oxygen to the smoldering flames. Flash fire followed within seconds.

Within minutes of the accident, the observation teams, both on Earth and in space, realized there had been a serious malfunction. Then followed a quick series of conference calls between team leaders, the university, and the military. Space Command quickly dispatched a military shuttle to the Station, picked up the lightcraft team and transported them all to the wrecked ship. Their job was grim: recover bodies and prepare a preliminary report describing what had gone wrong.

The crew of the jumpship was undoubtedly dead; that was a near certainty. This was not going to be a rescue mission; it was going to be an investigative and body recovery mission.

In those days, space crews normally included a robot as part of every team. Not that bots were indestructible, for they surely were not. A sophisticated Z-bot was just as mortal as any human being, especially when exposed to high radiation or extreme pressure or temperature.

But the value of sophisticated bots when undertaking a dangerous mission was measured by a different metric. Bots did not panic, not like a human being. They had no adrenal glands and were devoid of any programming that mimicked its effects. Bots could be counted on to remain calm and dispassionate, even under extreme stress.

It was not that robots were fearless, for they surely were not. Intelligent, self-aware Z-class robots had no more interest in dying in a horrible accident than a human being did — but their behavior was governed by the Laws of Robotics. It made them seem part of the family. Humans gave them pet names. This particular Z-bot went by Claybotta, a nickname earned in no small part because she was Clay Flynn's favorite.

As the recovery team descended in the shuttle down from the Space Station to the deteriorating orbit of the mortally wounded jumpship, Flynn could only imagine the terrible sequence of events. The flash of fire. An instant of bright yellow. A moment of horrifying screams. A flash of red. Then pitch blackness dotted only by pockets of glowing ambers. Finally, silence. Utter, terrifying silence.

The test crew onboard the devastated jumpship would have gone aloft wearing insulated pressure suits. The suits might have kept them alive for thirty seconds or so after the fire broke through the floorboards and before the explosion. But then the intense heat would have cracked the hull of the ship and it would have been game over. Thank God sound waves could not propagate in an airless vacuum. The screams, had there been any, would have been unbearably horrible.

A trained stickman from the Academy was at the helm of the military shuttle as it descended from orbit. Despite his experience, it took the man the better part of thirty minutes to maneuver the craft to within tether distance of the burnt-out hulk. A sergeant fired a grappling hook from a small chain gun and the two orbiting bodies did a slow spiral dance closer and closer to one another. Flynn could barely contain himself. *Friends of his were dead.*

Once the pilot had maneuvered the shuttle to within a few meters of the dead jumpship, the military shuttlecraft had to be held steady and in a fixed position long enough to allow the four adult humans and their robot assistant to make their way from shuttle to pod and back again with the evidence.

Now, as the shuttlecraft came to rest beside the charred hull of the jumpship, the four men and their robot companion from the Station scrambled out of their seats and onto an umbilical that had been stretched between the two space vehicles. The umbilical had handholds spaced every meter or so along its entire length, so a man could drag himself rapidly along. It functioned as a temporary bridge linking one spacecraft to the other.

"Steady the pod," Claybotta ordered the military pilot who was keeping it hovering alongside. "Hold it steady and extend the grabber." A robot was sanctioned to give humans orders when the danger was extreme.

Claybotta was the first to cross the bridge to the other craft. Pieces of the jumpship had come loose — and continued to come loose. The jagged, floating pieces were a hazard to both ship and man.

Claybotta broke the seal on the jumpship's airlock, cranked it open. That is when the harsh reality of their situation hit home hard. Two corpses floated lifeless in the chamber. More dead bodies lay in the short passageway beyond. They had all died trying to get out of the ship alive before it was incinerated.

When Flynn saw the first of the dead bodies, revulsion welled up inside him. *Only yesterday he had had lunch with this man.*

Flynn thought he would be ill. He brought his hand up to his mouth to catch the bile. The hand motion was instinctive.

But the visor on Flynn's helmet blocked his hand. Then he remembered. If he threw up inside his suit, he would likely choke to death on his own vomit. Barfing was something he simply had to avoid doing at all cost.

Flynn turned his head, swallowed what he was about to gag on, tried to change the focus of his mind.

"Pull it together," Claybotta ordered. "No time for delay."

Flynn nodded, tried to slow his breathing. The fire danger had passed. The vacuum of space had zeroed out the remaining fumes, extinguished the flames, and flushed away the heat.

Flynn steeled himself for what had to be done. He grabbed one dead body from where it sat, then another. Ned Lognasto, another team member, did the same. Jinnaro would not touch the dead.

"Help us, you jink," Flynn said.

"Screw off, friend. I am here to save the living, not dispose of the dead."

"They are all dead, you jink. No one survived that blast."

"I don't care, I'm not touching them," Jinnaro said. "Bad *juju.*"

Flynn was in no mood to argue. There was something exceedingly strange about the corpses, something he had not expected.

The fire had not charred their skin — not even a little.

Claybotta answered his question before Flynn could ask. Mechs were smart that way. They self-adapted. If a man worked with one long enough, the robot knew what the man was thinking before he could even think it himself.

"The fire swept through the ship so rapidly, it consumed every molecule of available oxygen almost instantaneously. The flames burnt themselves out before they had time to do more than singe the hair on these people's arms."

Flynn accepted that answer. It had a certain commonsensical ring of truth to it. Still, it unnerved him when Claybotta outthought him that way.

The singed hair came off, now, like fine dust, as Flynn slid the first two inert bodies out through the airlock and into the vast emptiness of space. It had the consistency of talc, a cloud of fine white powder.

The two bodies spun away from the ship and disappeared past the pod into the darkness.

But then something happened which changed the urgency of their mission. The lightcraft lurched to one side. *It was falling out of orbit.*

"What the hell?" Jinnaro yelped, grabbing hold of the bulkhead.

"Steady the pod!" Claybotta yelled at the pilot through the comm link. "Tighten the gripper! If the cable breaks we are all dead, every last one of us!"

The car shuddered for a second time, then seemed to stabilize. "We have to hurry," Claybotta said. "We need to find the blackbox, recover the last of the bodies, and get out of here."

"The box isn't black," one of the military people said, the voice soft and feminine. "It is bright orange and should be to the left of the main panel. Magnets or Velcro or both hold it in place."

For the first time, Flynn realized that one of the military persons onboard the shuttle was a woman. The team had left the Station in such a hurry there had been no time for introductions. All the military personnel were already strapped in their seats and bundled in their Mag 10 flightsuits, a garment hardly known to compliment the female form.

"We are running out of time. The orbit is deteriorating."

It was the same pretty girl speaking now. At least she looked pretty through the fogged visor of his spacesuit. Two things were for certain. She had glowing red hair and her spacesuit had two well-meaning bulges in exactly the right places on her chest. She wore two medical stripes on her left shoulder.

"Hurry now," Claybotta said. "Only two minutes remain before the umbilical bridge shatters under the stress. I do not know how much longer our pilot can hold the shuttle still. He's only human."

Claybotta grabbed Jinnaro and shoved him bodily through the open airlock of the lightcraft. "Quickly. Find a seat." Claybotta manhandled Flynn the same way.

"Do you have the blackbox?"

"Yes," Claybotta said, flinging the orange crate through the airlock. "We are down to seconds now. Strap in and get ready to cut the umbilical loose. Hurry, damn it!"

Robots were not known to swear except under extreme conditions. It was part of their programming. "Sit down. Strap in. Shut up. Only twenty-five seconds."

"Retract gripper!" Claybotta yelled at the pilot. "Detach from cable!"

"Everyone! Cinch your straps tight as you can!" the military woman yelled. "Ten seconds!"

The shuttle shuddered as the gripper was retracted. For an instant, it felt like they were in freefall.

The woman turned her head and screamed an order at Claybotta. "Seal the hatch! Now, now, now!"

"On my mark . . . Five . . . Four . . . Three . . . Two . . . One . . . Mark!"

▲

Ouida sat now, right forefinger poised on the trigger of her gun. She flexed her muscles, admired the bold tattoo of a Phoenix burned into the supple flesh of her upper arm and shoulder. Its hawk-like eyes stared wantonly at her breasts, the raptor's fire-red plumage the color of her hair.

Ouida took the gun from her temple, laid it in her lap. She had been here before, on the verge of ending her life, and had always changed her mind at the last possible moment.

Was there another way? She wondered. *Perhaps a better way?*

Ouida pulled the bone-handled hunting knife from its sheath at her waist and touched the hardened steel blade to the bare skin of her leg. Blood oozed from the shallow cut as she dragged the razor-sharp knife edge across the skin of her thigh. Then the evil thought popped into her head.

She could plunge the knife deeply into the flesh of her thigh, slice her femoral artery, bleed out in a few minutes, a gentle slide from pain to drowsiness to eternal sleep.

And why not? It might be a good way to go. End her pain in a single explosion of blood and tears.

She debated which was worse, the accident that had crippled her Jaxson or the way he had sent her away the last time they were together? Jaxson had dismissed her as if she were nothing, a pebble on the beach, a cockroach on the floor — Nothing! *But why?* Why had he ordered her to leave as if she were no better than one of his dimwitted tool jockeys?

Or was it the guilt she felt because she hadn't put up a fight, hadn't even argued with the man? He had told her what to do, and, like an obedient puppy, she had obeyed his commands.

But why had she obeyed? Wasn't that the deeper question? *What the hell was she made of inside, after all?* Is that what her anger was truly about, about her having given up without a fight?

Ouida played it back in her head now. Their final meeting. Their final conversation, three months ago, on her last trip home.

"I apologize for not coming to visit you more often."

That is what she said to him when she first entered his hospital room in San Diego twelve weeks ago.

"I wish you wouldn't come back here at all," he answered woodenly from his bed. His head was propped up on a pillow but held in place with stainless steel rods. Jaxson was paralyzed from the neck down and unable to control his movements or his bowels.

"Never would I abandon you," she said. It wasn't a hospital room, not in the truest sense of the word, more of a ward, a ward for the permanently disabled, those with no future but this one.

"The company abandoned me; not you. It was their negligence, their carelessness that left me in this state; not yours," he said.

Jaxson knew he faced a bleak future. Bio-repair had come a long way in the past few decades. But a severed spinal cord was still severed. Neuron bridges could be built, but not always, and only at great cost. Weeks had elapsed between the date of the accident in deep space more than a decade ago and the first attempt at a neural graft in a hospital equipped to deal with such injuries. For such repairs to have a good chance at success, the optimum elapsed time was under five days. He was five weeks from the nearest outpost when it happened; too long for such a delicate repair. This was one accident he would never recover from.

"If only we could have gotten you home sooner," she cried, "this might never have happened."

"If only, if only, if only. All that anger, Ouida. No one can live that way, not you and certainly not me. I cannot bear it any longer. I cannot bear for you to see me this way. Find a new man and get on with your life."

Ouida turned away. She had always hidden the truth from him. She had already found a new man and a new bed to sleep in. It didn't take her long after the accident; only a matter of weeks. Ouida had remarried, but had never told him. That made her a bigamist, even under modern law, as she and Jaxson had never been divorced.

"I mean it," he said. "Go away and don't you ever come back here again. That's an order. Leave me alone to die in peace, and get on with your life."

"What are you saying, love?"

"You heard me right, Ouida. I don't want you to ever come back here to this hospital again. It breaks my heart for you to see me this way, and I'll have no more of it."

"But . . . "

"Leave!" he shouted. "Leave, and don't you ever set foot in this room again. I never want to see your ugly face at my bedside again."

"I will make them pay," Ouida muttered as she slowly lifted herself out of the hospital room chair and turned for the door. "You'll see. I will make the bastards pay."

CHAPTER FIFTEEN

Day Two, 1930 hours

Paddington Sinclair was an arrogant SOB. Selfish, self-centered, insufferable. Exceptionally smart. An all-round general pain in the ass.

The man knew just about everything there was to know about the complex systems required to keep the lunar habitat up and running. What he didn't know was how to keep from tossing his lunch every time he rode in an automobile or train, boat or spaceship. His arrival at the hab eighteen hours ago had begun inauspiciously with bile in his mouth.

Paddington Sinclair was here to get the Moon Beam space elevator project launched and running smoothly, a mammoth undertaking. But Sinclair was no stranger to challenges of this magnitude. His last mega-project, begun five years ago, was to oversee construction of the electrical power storage system, a feat of engineering in its own right. Everyone agreed that Sinclair's power storage system was considered a prime target should the tunnel saboteur strike again.

Paddington Sinclair had been an early proponent of taking steps to make the Moon a self-sustaining colony. *But how, exactly, does one go about doing that?*

People need to eat food and consume liquids. They need to breathe air with sufficient levels of oxygen. They need to urinate and they need to poop. How can these needs be met in a place where you can't breathe the air or go outside unprotected?

As it turns out, these needs could be met easily enough, but only so long as electrical power was available in sufficient quantity and with absolute reliability.

Obtaining such a happy result on the Moon was easier said than done. Producing copious amounts of steady and reliable electricity was an engineering problem of the highest order. No weather meant no wind; no wind meant no wind farms. Nuclear power was difficult to build and harder still to manage and maintain. Oil and gas were not part of the geology. Hydro seemed equally out of the question. Although water in the form of ice had been discovered on the moon long ago, it was still considered an extremely precious resource and not subject to wide-scale mining.

By process of elimination, solar seemed the only logical choice. But even solar power had its drawbacks. Dust, for starters. The quantities of dust encountered on earlier missions had proven immense. And, given its proven tendency to "clump," solar panels had to be constantly swept clean. They degraded rapidly under the relentless bombardment of highly-charged gamma rays.

All of these thoughts and more went through Paddington Sinclair's mind as he sat on the edge of the narrow bed and began to unpack his few things.

How he wished he'd brought along some mouthwash to flush out the foul taste of his latest tosser.

But, it was a wish that would go unfulfilled. Even with today's advanced rocketry methods, weight limitations for space travelers were extremely tight, twenty klogs maximum, not much for a man of his stature. Clothing wasn't the problem; it could be manufactured onsite in a matter of hours by a 3-D printer and milling machine. No, it was everything else that made space life bearable: electronics, toiletries, writing tools.

Sinclair had been much too sick from travel to unpack earlier. Now he had to hurry. His first briefing was in an hour.

The room was not much to look at. A metal frame bed. A desk and a rolling desk chair. A dresser with four drawers. A closet barely wide enough to accommodate eight hangers.

Paddington Sinclair had great difficulty adjusting to the room's overhead lighting. It was his eyes. Natural lighting, filtered through Earth's wonderful atmosphere, was nonexistent here, although modern diodes could produce a reasonable facsimile thereof. Indeed, the pattern of light and darkness that came with living on the moon was a challenge for nearly everyone to cope with. It was a question of evolution. Humans were accustomed to a twenty-four-hour day.

Sinclair had a reputation to protect. He had been credited with solving the moon's long-term power generation and storage problems with his railroad cars and neat stacks of concrete-filled boxes.

But solar power generation was confounded by the everpresent dust. He thought he had devised a solution to that problem as well, but hadn't yet discussed it openly with anyone else.

A knock came to his door.

"May I come in?" Chief Flynn asked through the intercom from the corridor. He had just come from his and Santini's long meeting with Professor Tattersall.

Sinclair pressed the contact and the door opened. He looked at the man standing in the doorway and said, "Flynn, right?"

"Yes. Chief Clay Flynn, or just Chief. May I come in?"

Sinclair nodded. "I recognize you from the briefing dossier I was given earlier during that hellacious ride up here."

"And how was the ride, smooth as always?" Flynn asked, knowing the answer.

"Is that what passes for humor up here among the Lunatics these days?"

"Forgive me. I will get straight to the point. It is a busy time for us all," Flynn said.

"The saboteur, yes?" Paddington asked.

"Yes. As of this moment, still unidentified."

"Shame. It is a distraction, I should imagine."

"That's not why I'm here," Flynn said.

"Then what the hell are you here for?" Sinclair snapped, his eyes red and his head pounding.

"I have it on good authority that you may have devised a solution for our dust problem," Flynn remarked.

"Solved is a strong word. What I have is more like a working theory, the basis on which to maybe build a prototype."

"It also looks like you have a bad headache. Rule number one of space travel — drink plenty of fluids, then drink some more. The headaches will soon go away."

"Thank you. I should have remembered from last time. That's what they always tell you. Drink plenty of fluids. Which brings me to my first question. Where is the nearest watering hole?"

Flynn pointed across the room to what looked like a metallic chest of drawers, but with a vertical handle on one side. "May I introduce you to a recent invention, the refrigerator?"

"Smart ass. You're just like everyone else around this toilet," Sinclair chided.

"Whatever you do, avoid alcohol, at least until your stomach has settled."

Sinclair grumbled.

"I know you're the smartest man in the room, Sinclair. But have you solved the dust problem or not?"

"First, I drink. Then we chat, yes?"

Chief Flynn nodded as the other man went to the tiny fridge and took out something cold to drink. "The dust is bad here," Flynn said, "and getting worse every day. But if you want to do something fun, try getting used to tacking back and forth across the solar system by solar sail."

"Sorry. Never had the pleasure. Truth be known, space travel is not my thing at all. But do it I must, if I am to reach the destinations where my manifest skills can best be applied."

"Manifest skills?"

"Building things, of course — big things. But I'm happy to bide my time listening to your little old space story. Tell me, Clay: What was the solar sail experience like?"

"Noisy, for one. Frightening, for another," Flynn said. "And don't call me, Clay. Chief or Chief Flynn or just Flynn, even Asshole. But not Clay."

"Okay, Asshole. But could anything be more frightening than what I just did? — Traveling to the Moon on top of a chemical rocket or lifting off from Earth on a lightcraft?"

"There is really no comparing the two. Riding the solar wind is not unlike being aboard a three-masted sailing ship on Earth prior to the steam engine. Tacking into the wind, riding the Trades, pushing for exotic lands, the currents of air at your back."

"And seasick meds in your hand . . . "

"They said you were a bit weak-chinned."

"Is that a reference to my homosexuality?" Paddington Sinclair declared in an accusatory fashion.

"Not at all. Until you just told me, I had no idea and, honestly, could not have cared less. I was referring to your reputation for throwing up at the drop of a hat. If your sexual preferences are such a sensitive subject, I suggest you keep them to yourself. Rules of fraternization are the same regardless."

Sinclair's tone softened. "The world is not as accepting of men with men as one might wish."

Flynn shook his head. "My degree is not in philosophy, and I would be lying if I said I understood your ways. I like women; you like men. So long as you don't try to crawl in bed with me, I could not care less what you do in your spare time. Can we leave it at that?"

"Yes. Do go on with your story. Solar sails. So, why are they so noisy?"

"Static electricity," Flynn said. "The same reason why the lunar elevator cable has to be grounded. Static electricity. Or, as you physicists say, triboelectricity."

"So you flew on the S.S. *Ticonderoga* to Mars and back?"

"*Ticonderoga*, yes. Mars, no. Did a short stint on the X52 asteroid mining project for ASARCO. Came home on the *Alexander Hamilton.* But the solar sails are something else again.

"Use your imagination, Sinclair. Imagine you are sitting there. The ship has already broken anchor from the space station and is in motion. Then you hear a sound and feel a bit of buffeting. The S.S. *Ticonderoga* is unfurling its giant, titanium-ribbed sails and turning them into the sun. Your two-week voyage is about to get underway."

"Two weeks, eh? I would be sick from the get."

Flynn laughed. "It can be a bit unnerving. Unfurling the sails is neither a quick nor quiet thing. The two halves of the immense sail are stored in a pair of footlocker-like compartments, one on either side of the big ship. The compartment doors, made from the highest grade of beryllium copper, ride on a series of huge hydraulic pistons. The pistons draw out the guide wires on which the sail's titanium ribs are suspended.

"Now you settle back into your acceleration couch, take your pills or your meds or slap on your patch, whatever will keep your stomach quiet. You look out the windows, small and oval-shaped like a porthole on an ocean liner. You can see the solar sail being slowly unfurled. It is a mammoth thing, half a klom long in every direction, from center to edge, a circumference of more than three-and-a-half kloms with the giant ship at its center."

"I had no idea it was so large. Three-and-a-half kloms? Really?"

"Oh, yes. When the sail is completely unfurled and set at the proper angle to the sun, the thin filaments that line the body of the sail catch the solar wind and fill, just like a canvas sail does on a lake back home when stretching tight against the wind. Think of a large-masted sailing ship before the age of steam or coal or diesel. Once it is fully extended, the solar sail is slightly egg-shaped, a giant ellipse more than one full klom from tip to tail, with the *Ticonderoga* at its focal point."

"But what makes it so noisy?"

"I'm coming to that. The tech is rudimentary. Untold megavolts of static electricity build up on the sail's surface each minute as it billows. A sudden flash of light, an explosion of noise. Under the pressure of all that kinetic energy, the ship begins to lurch forward. Velocity is slow at first. But acceleration is nearly constant.

"Noise is an unfortunate side effect of the massive energy build-up on the sail and subsequent discharge. A nearly constant crackling, practically a roar, as the charge on the surface of the solar sail is bled off every few seconds with a loud pop and a flash of white light. — But the big ship itself keeps right on accelerating."

"But surely a big ship like the *Ticonderoga* must be heavily insulated."

"Even so, the noise makes talking difficult at first. Plus, the jarring flashes of bright light take a bit of getting used to. Sometimes the sail looks like it is on fire. The annoyances lessen after a few days' time, once the accelerating ship reaches a velocity of about one percent of light speed."

Flynn paused thoughtfully. "The truth of the matter is that I had a tough time adjusting to being away. I could not wait to get back home. The *Ticonderoga* is a big ship, twelve decks in all. On Level Eight, at the rear, is a large aft lounge — the so-called Entertainment Deck. There are windows back there, fairly large ones, where a person might look safely outside at space without risking damage to his corneas.

"But no amount of tinting can blot out the glimmering visage of a trans-comet hurtling through space. It begins its long journey in the outer reaches of the solar system on the way to its eventual rendezvous with Venus. Just like we do here on the Moon today — Man fiddling with his environment. That is the crux of the problem, isn't it? Maybe even the reason for the sabotage. For every man who wants to change the environment to better suit his needs, there is another who thinks it wiser to leave it alone, even if leaving it alone means that others would suffer a lower standard of living or shortened lifespan as a result."

Paddington Sinclair interrupted. "You talk as if the Garden of Eden were an actual place and every bite of the apple since that idyllic time has somehow distanced us from a world of plenty, a world of grace where we all lived in perfect harmony with nature. Hah! What a load of crap!"

Chief Flynn smiled but said nothing. Then he changed his mind and spoke. "I want to hear more about your working theory."

"What working theory?"

"Didn't you say something earlier about having solved our dust problem? That you had a working theory of how to do it?"

Sinclair took a sip of his drink, cleared his throat and began to speak. "Lunar dust consists of rock pulverized to the consistency of talcum powder. This is thanks to millions of years of unrelenting micrometeoroid impacts."

"I am no geologist," Flynn said. "But this is not news."

"The fragments are sharp. And because the moon has no weather, no wind, no erosion due to water, those fragments remain sharp more or less forever. Then comes the influence of that solar wind you seem so fond of. When it bombards the dust particles, it imparts to them a static charge, same as what would make an ungrounded lunar cable so dangerous, same as what causes all the fireworks and noise on the *Ticonderoga*'s solar sail. The static charge is what makes the tiny dust particles cling to everything they come in contact with."

Flynn nodded. "You have described the problem adequately enough. Those jagged dust fragments blacken our spacesuits. The dark color causes our pressure suits to absorb too much heat. The sharp-edged buggers tear tiny leaks in joint seals, which cause pressure leaks and eventual suit failure. They scratch visors, hinder visibility, and cake batteries until they overheat and fail. The damage costs us big money. And it's even worse when the dust gets inside the hab. It gums up our air filters and endangers the health of our residents."

"Well, I may have a solution," Paddington Sinclair declared.

"So you said."

"What I propose is a new sort of spacesuit material, a polymer-based coating that could be applied directly onto the fabric of the suit."

Flynn shook his head. "I don't think so, Sinclair. Space engineers have already tested hundreds of mixes, dozens of coatings. Why should we expect yours to work when none of the others have?"

"Ah, my own special brew. Quite novel, really."

"Novel in what way?"

"Bit of a trade secret until the patent is approved. But this much I can tell you. The coating is impregnated with tiny dust-like particles of its own, a sort of slippery paste. This goop makes it harder for the moon dust particles to stick to the material."

"Hardly seems enough of a difference to change the outcome," Chief Flynn said, somewhat disparagingly.

"It isn't enough, not taken by itself. You are right about that. But I have added one further twist. Also embedded in the material is a yarn made of conducting nanotube fibers. Connect those fibers to a power source and the fabric generates an electric field strong enough to repel the charged dust particles. The particles can then be brushed off the fabric with nothing stronger than an ordinary hairbrush."

"This is on the level?"

Sinclair nodded.

"My God. If that conducting fiber stuff works, you will be richer than the lords of avarice."

"Who is to say that I'm not already richer than you can imagine?"

"Are you?"

Sinclair smiled. "They don't call me a genius for nothing."

"No one calls you a genius."

"No?"

"Arrogant and conceited; that is what people call you. Arrogant and conceited."

CHAPTER SIXTEEN

Day Three, 1915 hours

"Antoine LeClerq is going to be one tough pick-and-string man to replace in time for this weekend's dance," Doyle Baldwin said without emotion. The six remaining members of the brass combo had gathered in a nearly soundproof room at the farthest end of the rec level to practice their music.

"Not much of a eulogy," Lou Santini said unpacking his slide trombone from the large, felt-lined case. He oiled the slide and cleaned the mouthpiece with a small piece of soft white cotton cloth. "The man is barely cold and in the ground and already you want to replace him on our crew? Just be happy Flynn sprang you from holding long enough to come jam with us."

"Sorry, Lou. That came out sounding colder than it was meant to be," Doyle replied. "I'm grateful for having my restrictions lifted, no doubt about it. And yes, we're all going to miss that bum. All I was trying to say is LeClerq was one hell of a bass guitarist. No man alive can anchor a beat like he did. What are the Clay Pots going to do without a man of his talents?"

"I hate that name, you know," Flynn said as he instinctively pumped the trio of piston valves on his trumpet in rhythm with his favorite tune.

"Yeah, you wanted the Clay Pigeons," Santini laughed. "Why does the band have to be called the Clay Anything at all? Just because you pretend to be the lead singer? Hell, Flynn, you can barely carry a tune. Why can't it be the Moon Dusters? Or, why not the Regoliths? — we have been known to play hard rock on occasion. Or the Crater Heads? Anything but the Clay Pots."

Tattersall chuckled. "Why not call our little band the Lunatics? Every last one of us is certifiable."

"You want we should name the band after you, Chandler?" Nora Goldman teased. When she wasn't playing footsies with Doyle Baldwin after hours, she played lead electric guitar for the band. "Clay and the Chandlers? Clay and the Tattered Sails? Maybe just the Tattered Sails." Nora paused to let that last one sink in. "Truth is: I miss LeClerq badly. He and I were mellow together, his bass, my metal strings. The man was quite the plucker."

"You do mean plucker, right?" Santini quipped. "Not that other word."

"Yes, I do mean plucker," Nora replied. "Just to watch that man on his electric bass — his fingers, thumbs, plucking, slapping, popping, strumming, tapping, thumping, or picking with that big ugly red pick of his. And what about LeClerq's solos? Pure magic." She sighed.

"Not to change the subject," Doyle said as he changed the subject. "Maybe one of Sinclair's Moon Beam kids plays. Nobody will be using LeClerq's bass now that he's gone. There it sits."

Doyle pointed to the guitar stand in the far corner of the room. A bass guitar was similar in appearance and construction to an electric guitar, but with a longer neck and scale length. LeClerq's bass was a genuine antique, an early twentieth century Fender jazz bass made from real maple and alder woods. It was easily worth more than a month's salary to a Lunatic, and it cost him much more than that to get it shipped up-orbit from Earth. For the moment, no one was thinking much about it, but LeClerq's family was certain to want the Fender back.

Chief Flynn pursed his lips and played a few notes on his brass trumpet.

But the instrument was out of tune, its pitch all wrong. Moon-normal gravity at one-sixth-g played havoc with the sound of a brass instrument.

Flynn placed the mouthpiece in his pocket to warm it, emptied the spit reservoir, and made a slight adjustment to the tubing. A trumpet had a slide mechanism for the first and third valves. He could compensate by throwing (extending) or retracting one or both slides, using the left thumb and ring finger for the first and third valve slides respectively. For some tunes he would pull out his piccolo trumpet, which had four valves and half the tubing length of a standard trumpet. In his able hands, he could use the piccolo to perform thrilling trills. But not today.

"We need seven people," Flynn said. "Just like in Herb Alpert's group — *four lasagnas, two bagels, and an American cheese.* That's how he described his group, the Tijuana Brass. Four lasagnas, two bagels, and an American cheese."

"What do you suppose he meant by that?" Tattersall asked, adjusting the stops on his keyboard.

"I am supposing it was deep metaphor," Flynn replied. "Four lasagnas; four Italians. Two bagels; two New York Jews. One American cheese; a smartass Yank from the West Coast. He was a Jew, you know, not some Mexican from south of the border like everyone supposed."

"Who was a Jew? Herb Alpert, the trumpet player? He was a Hebrew?" Santini seemed genuinely surprised.

"You got a problem with Jews?" Nora Goldman asked.

"Not at all," Santini answered defensively. "I didn't mean it that way. I've seen pictures. The guy looked Hispanic to me, that's all. South of the border and all that. You know how the man dressed."

"He was born in the United States," Chief Flynn said. "But his family were recent imports from The Ukraine. I read somewhere that his first name was actually Tito or something along those lines."

"Our Mister Know-It-All makes his second appearance of the day," Santini jabbed.

"Are we going to jam or are we going to jaw?" Doyle asked, sitting down in front of his drums and tightening the catch on his cymbals. He had a pair of hi-hats operated by a foot pedal, as well as a suspended cymbal that could be played with a variety of oddball mallets, some made of yarn, some of sponge, some of cord, each one wrapped to achieve a specific sound.

"Plugging in, tuning up," Chandler Tattersall said from behind his multi-level electronic keyboard and digital synthesizer. It could reproduce virtually any sound known to man.

"Same," Nora Goldman chimed, adjusting the volume on her electric guitar and strumming a few chords to verify that it was in tune with a reasonable volume setting.

Now, suddenly and quite unexpectedly, the hallway door opened and in strolled two young people, a man and a woman, both in their mid-twenties and casually dressed. They seemed to be a couple.

Doyle Baldwin looked up. "Sorry, this room is taken. If you two lovebirds want to be alone, you'll need to find somewhere else to be."

"No, it's not like that," the young man said, embarrassed. He was good-looking, with a dark complexion and a ready smile.

"What then?" Doyle asked. "Do you mind telling us who you are? I know everyone on staff."

The young man reached out his hand to introduce himself. "I'm Guillermo. My friends call me Guy. This is Neena. We came to listen, maybe join in, if you'll have us."

"Moon Beamers?" Tattersall said with some disdain.

"We don't mean to be a bother," Guy answered. "But yes, we are with the Moon Beam contingent. It's been said around the hab that you folks have a good sound, a good old-fashioned sound. I'd love to hear you play."

"Can you handle a bass guitar?" Flynn asked. "We're one man down."

Guy smiled widely. "I play."

"Are you any good?" Tattersall asked, tapping out the opening keys of their signature song.

"Some say that I am."

"Then get up here, boy, and show us," Lou Santini said, ignoring the pretty girl standing beside him. "I'll do the introductions. This is Nora Goldman on electric guitar. Chandler Tattersall on keyboard and synth. Doyle Baldwin on drums. Tonni Kalash on trumpet. You got to watch out for Tonni, he farts whenever he plays. Me — I'm Lou Santini — on slide trombone. And our founder, after whom the Clay Pots are named, is Chief Clay Flynn, lead trumpet and occasional vocalist."

"Clay Pots, eh?" Guy said as he shook hands all around.

"You read music?" Flynn asked.

"I play electric and bass guitar in a blues band back home. We're throwbacks, actually. Still doing it the old-fashioned way, on paper sheet-music most days."

"No paper here," Santini said. "Bars and lyrics on an e-pad set into the frame of your music stand."

Guy nodded, went to the corner of the room and picked up Antoine LeClerq's bass. It was a beautiful instrument, made from the finest woods, and he immediately recognized it as such.

He came back to the others with the instrument cradled lovingly in his hands and plugged into the amp.

"Got my own pick."

Guy reached into his pocket, pulled out a small, bright blue piece of plastic and, in the key of A major, played the opening baseline riff to Bobby Troup's classic *Route 66*. Then he stopped to tighten the metal strings, followed by a rapid-fire slap and pop on the strings, followed by a palm mute. The others were impressed.

Palm-muting was an advanced technique, hard to master, yet often tried by bass players with varying degrees of success. Outer edge of the hand on the bridge, palm pressed against the strings, which muted them, shortening the sustain time.

Cruz clearly knew his stuff and didn't mind showing off a bit. He looked up from his instrument and said, "Ready." The girl, Neena, smiled from the sidelines. Santini continued to ignore her, as if she wasn't in the room.

"Okay, Clay Pots," Flynn said, trumpet in hand. "Tune in, or tune out. Let's first try *This Guy's in Love with You.* It's trademark Herb Alpert."

"Oh, God, he's going to sing," Santini said, feigning distress.

"Music's on LeClerq's e-pad," Nora said, directing Cruz to his music stand.

"You told us you could sight read," Flynn said. "Db major, about 90 beats per, just like it says at the top of the sheet."

Doyle Baldwin set the beat by striking the butt end of his wooden drum sticks three times against the metal frame of his snare drum.

"And a one, and a two, and a three . . . " Then Flynn began to sing,

"You see this guy, this guy's in love with you
Yes, I'm in love. Who looks at you the way I do?
When you smile, I can tell it know each other very well . . .

My hands are shakin' don't let my heart keep breaking
'cause
I need your love, I want your love
Say you're in love and you'll be my girl, if not I'll just die"

CHAPTER SEVENTEEN

Day Four, 0600 hours

"Gentlemen and ladies, in a little under three hours we begin dropping cable for the lunar space elevator. This is the big moment we've all been waiting for, though none more than me. Once our triangulation is complete and I give the signal, mechs stationed on the temporary platform at EML-1 will begin to unreel line. These are exciting times we live in, if I don't say so myself."

Paddington Sinclair positioned himself behind the large, wooden podium in front of the audience of forty or so engineers, scientists and cable jockeys. Some of them were meeting for the first time. Sinclair enjoyed the trappings of power, when all eyes were upon him. This was his stage, and he was the star of the show.

"Four years of planning and twenty years of dreaming are finally coming to fruition," he said.

"Twenty years? Try two hundred," the young engineer in the first row rebutted. This young man, Carl Rosen, had a serious unresolved crush on the older man. But Sinclair had thoroughly, and quite recently, snubbed the younger man. The rejection had left a sour taste in Rosen's mouth and he was looking for payback.

Paddington Sinclair got up on his high horse. "The concept of a tower that extends all the way into orbit originated in a science-fiction story. The year was 1895. The author was Russian rocket pioneer Konstantin Tsiolkovsky. He realized that a tower tall enough to reach geostationary orbit would experience a net gravitational force of zero at the top. But at the time Konstantin wrote his story, he did not see how such a tower could be built."

Sinclair continued. "The problem of building a tower of this sort was first solved, in a theoretical sense at least, seventy-five years later by another Russian, Leningrad engineer Yuri Artsutanov. Artsutanov was the first to recognize that the tower must itself be a satellite in geostationary orbit. This satellite could then be greatly elongated both upward and downward, using the gravity gradient for stabilization, until the lower end of the balanced tower reached the surface at the equator. Artsutanov envisioned a structure large enough to support passenger capsules shuttling back and forth between Earth and orbit. He called it a heavenly funicular."

"Yes," Rosen interrupted for a second time. "But Artsutanov's claim to have been the first to think of it cannot be substantiated. The man never published so much as a technical paper on the subject. Pearson is the one we should be talking about. Jerome Pearson. He is the one who did the first practical work on the concept."

"It's true," Sinclair conceded. "We owe the entire field to JP. That's what his friends called him in those days. JP. Jerome Pearson. He is the reason we call those elevator cars Pearson Tether Climbers. But you are wrong. Artsutanov did publish. One article that I know of. Around the time of the Bay of Pigs, maybe a little before. An article in a Russian periodical. It was later translated into English."

"So, we done with our nostalgic trip down memory lane?" Rosen snapped, his unrelenting sarcasm on full display. Rosen was a master at reading micro-expressions. He could always sniff out a bluff in a poker game.

Sinclair was angered by the continuing disruptions. Self-important men of exceptional stature could not tolerate interruption mid-lecture. "The point I was trying to make is that it is ironic."

"In what way?" Rosen asked. The other scientists and engineers in the room were becoming uneasy at the test of wills between the two men. Some of them had seen it unfold before, most recently in their prep meetings weeks ago. It always ended badly for the lesser man.

"The original concept of a space elevator was to make lifting mass up from the Earth's surface cheaper and safer," Sinclair lectured. "The irony is that the first test case of a lifting elevator is to be built here on the Moon, not back on Earth, where it was first envisioned. Any payload released from the far end of the lunar cable will reach Earth in under half a day with zero expenditure of fuel. The underwriters of this Moon Beam project consider what we are doing here today on the nearside to be essential techdem."

"Techdem?"

"Technology demonstrator. Phase 2 — if we ever get a chance to build it — will be a farside elevator to support the existing radio telescope. But before any sort of elevator system can ever hope to be deployed on Earth, it first has to pass muster here at L1 on the nearside. That is our present challenge — to prove that the concept can be properly engineered and made to work."

"If indeed it is a test case," Rosen said, still prickly.

"Whatever do you mean?" Sinclair was becoming impatient with his arrogant underling. The boy had made a pass at him three weeks ago, back on Earth, a pass which Sinclair had rebuffed. Now Paddington found Carl Rosen to be an unwelcome distraction.

"As an essential techdem, this effort is second-rate," Rosen said, his voice brimming with arrogance. "Not only are you building the thing on the wrong side of the Moon first, almost nothing we learn from building an elevator at EML-1 will be applicable to later building a similar one on Earth."

"Wrong side of the Moon first?" Sinclair retorted angrily. "The decision to build the prototype on the nearside at 0° East 0° North was made long ago — and by people much smarter than you or I. Their reasons were sound back then, and they remain sound now. — Less cable, for one. 278,500 kloms versus 297,300 kloms if it is built on the farside. Less cable means burning through less capital. Easier comm connections. Easier observation of the cable and the Pearson Tether Climbers from Earth-based satellites. The three comm nodes — counterweight, Supply Depot at EML-1, and Landing Platform — will each be instrumented to monitor the elevator's performance."

"Yes," Rosen admitted. "But a farside elevator at 180° East 0° North could support a radio telescope with good result. The farside is totally shielded from terrestrial radio transmissions. That makes it arguably the best place in the solar system to site kit for a radio astronomy telescope. During the lunar night, when radio interference from the Sun is blocked, radio astronomy can be conducted. The EML-2 landing site is near Lipskiy Crater and just north of Daedalus in very rugged and heavily cratered terrain in the lunar highlands. The orbiting platform at EML-2 would provide a comm mast visible from any location on the farside and could thus serve as a relay for communications with Earth."

"Well put, young Rosen . . . " Sinclair tried to regain control of the classroom.

"Excuse me, but I am not done speaking," Rosen said, his voice tightening. "As I was saying: as an essential technology demonstrator, this effort is second-rate. The moon has no wind. The gravity well is one-sixth that of Earth. Solar tides are minimal. There is no ionosphere to contend with. No magnetic field. No ocean to test-float the marine node. No aircraft cruising at altitude to get in the way. Except for counterweight thrusting on a monthly basis to counteract cyclical movement of the libration point, I would say that as proof of concept, the lunar elevator is one big waste of time and money. — Okay, now I'm done."

"Carl, impertinence is not a virtue. If you don't believe in what we are doing, then why the hell did you volunteer to join the team and go through all the training and testing?" Sinclair exclaimed.

"The experience will look good on my resume."

Sinclair's face reddened. "All the same, that is what we are here to do today. Make up your mind, Rosen. Either you are in. Or you are out. Which is it?"

"I am in, of course."

"Good. Now let's get on with it, shall we? The satellite node has already been launched. It is stable and in lunar-sync orbit. We have a cargo ship anchored overhead beside the construction platform at the EML-1 libration point. Onboard the ship are tens of thousands of kloms of coiled cable and equipment, about 80,000 klogs worth. Unless there is a ghost in the machine, before the day is out we will have begun reeling out two cables from the libration point simultaneously, one descending down toward the lunar surface and a second cable ascending three times as quickly in the exact opposite direction and pointed directly at Earth. The ascending cable will be anchored to a counterweight. The object is to avoid disturbing the satellite's orbit as the two cables are reeled out. You people sitting in this room: — you are the ones who have to make this thing come off without a hitch. You need to watch the weight balance; you need to scan for static electricity build-up; and you need to constantly be on the lookout for trouble of any kind. The counterweight will wheel into and out of Earth's magnetosphere twice each lunar month. That means no less than one pass through the magnetosphere during the unreeling. We cock up this thing and we all go home in disgrace; that is, if we get to go home at all. So, let's wrap our minds around the enormity of the undertaking, shall we?"

Now a new voice made itself heard. "But, sir," Guy Cruz said, stealing a sideways glance at his girlfriend Neena. In public forums like this, they did their best not to be too familiar. "Didn't I recently read in a journal somewhere that until the cable is fully extended and anchored to the ground, that even coming into contact with the cable is exceedingly dangerous?"

Cruz was clearly of Hispanic descent, with an easy smile and a mop of curly dark hair. Women of every size and shape were attracted to him. For the moment he was spoken for, however.

"Where did you read such malarkey, son?" Sinclair wanted to know.

"Last summer's edition of <u>Lunar Physics</u>, I believe."

"<u>Lunar Physics</u>?" Sinclair said in a dismissive tone. "A second-rate journal, if ever one was published. The people who write for <u>LP</u> are charlatans."

"Even so, can you really afford to ignore them? The authors say that static electricity can build up to dangerous levels on the line as it is being unreeled," Guy Cruz said. "The solar wind is electrically charged. According to the prospectus, this cable unreeling process is going to take some time. If I understand my physics correctly, until the cable is completely unreeled and lowered all the way to the moon's surface, where it can be grounded, the electrical charge build-up will accumulate and cannot be easily sloughed off."

All heads turned now in the direction of the podium. If Cruz's assertion was correct, this science project had just become a whole lot riskier than advertised.

"We have taken all contingencies into account," Sinclair replied curtly.

"Have you? It's a question of timing. How long do you reckon this cable unreeling process will take?" Cruz pressed his attack. "Electrical charges can build up rather quickly."

"I'm glad you asked me that question," Sinclair said. He appreciated the opportunity to once again be the scholar. Chin jutting, Sinclair came out from behind the podium and moved over to a large screen. A complex set of schematics were displayed on the screen. He pointed to one and said:

"Fifty-five thousand kloms of cable will be descending from the libration point down to the moon's surface. Three times that amount will be ascending skyward out from the libration point in the direction of Earth. Down-reel-rate of fifty meters per second, nearly 180 kloms per hour, in excess of 4,000 kloms each day. Two weeks, folks. Two weeks of pure living hell. If all goes well, that is how long it will take us — just under twelve and three-quarters days to out-reel 55,000 kloms of very expensive, very twitchy cable. That assumes no cock-ups, no malfunctions, no ghosts in the machinery."

"And what about the tether climbers?" Rosen asked. "They need to be assembled, tested, and attached to that cable."

"It's a brilliant system, really," Sinclair said. "The kinetic energy gained by a descending load is stored in the counterweight. Later, that same kinetic energy can be transferred to an ascending payload. It is an amazingly modern and efficient system using simple block-and-tackle methods the Greeks devised nearly three thousand years ago. Whatever energy is lost to friction in the raising and lowering of loads is reacquired by solar cells, both orbiting and ground-based. No further need for fossil fuels here, or for volatile chemical brews," he concluded with a flourish. Sinclair seemed awfully proud of himself, as if he personally had invented the Pearson Tether Climber that made it all possible.

Carl Rosen shook his head. "Once again, you have avoided the question. The Pearsons have to be assembled, tested, and attached to what I now understand to be a potentially hot and dangerous cable."

"I am coming to that, Carl. We will divide up into eight, four-man teams and stagger the start time of each team. Each day each team will begin their rotation by first working three hours on the out-reel detail. Then that team will have three hours off to eat and relax. Then that same team will work three hours on the tether climber detail. Then they will have fifteen hours off the clock. We stick to a 24-hour day up here, regardless of the solar day. During those fifteen hours off the clock, you and your teammates are expected to sleep, get physical exercise, and complete all your written reports. Then, the next day, you will repeat the same cycle all over again."

"Sounds more like a military drill than a scientific pursuit," Rosen said, continuing to badger Sinclair. "You don't need top-flight scientists for this project; you need trained monkeys plus a few Z-bots. And you still haven't answered Guy Cruz's question."

Sinclair became red-faced. "I do not need whiners on my crew. Either get with the drill or hit the bricks and book yourself a seat on the next shuttle home. Capiche?"

"Yes, sir. Sorry."

"Son, in case you have forgotten, we work for a private consortium. They have stockholders. The Board of Directors is expected to turn a profit for the stockholders. Experience is a good teacher. If we are to stay on budget and within time and cost constraints, we must adhere to a strict schedule. If it sounds regimented, that is because it is regimented."

"What I was trying to say is that regimentation is something better suited to mechs, not human beings. We are not robotic drones, after all," Rosen said.

"What you are, son, is fired," Sinclair ordered. "Pick up your things, pack your bags, and get the hell out of my face this very instant. You are off the team."

"Up yours, Sinclair. Fuck all of you," Rosen said as he got to his feet, an indignant look on his face.

When the younger man had left the room, Sinclair's body language relaxed. Suddenly more at ease, he smiled and said:

"That man annoys the crap out of me. But he does have a point. There is a difference between a robot drone and a human being kept on a tight leash. The laws of robotics seem almost romantic in their simplicity, maybe even quaint. Laws written down before the first robots had even been assembled. Laws conjured up by a brilliant mind, the mind of Isaac Asimov. Anyone here know what I'm talking about?"

A hand in the third row shot up.

"Yes?" He pointed to a cute brunette sitting roughly in the center of the room in the second row. Though Sinclair did not bat for that team, he did like being surrounded by pretty women. "Introduce yourself to the others please."

"Neena Petronas."

"Okay, Neena Petronas, have at it."

She nodded. "A robot may not injure a human being or through inaction allow a human being to come to harm. That is First Law. Second Law states that a robot must obey any order given to it by a human being, except where such an order would conflict with First Law. Then there is Third Law. A robot must protect its own existence so long as such protection does not conflict with First or Second Law."

"But that is science fiction, Petronas. Ancient science fiction at that. You and I have to make actual decisions within the real world. The Three Laws only apply to higher-level robots capable of thought, the so-called Z-bot."

"I am aware," Neena replied.

"Well, then you must also know that the Laws are a bottleneck in terms of brain sophistication for lesser machines. For years, engineers have used simpler constructs to control the behavior of simpler bots."

"Would you mind elaborating, please?" Neena asked respectfully.

Sinclair liked it when someone said *please*. "Under specific conditions, the Three Laws can be modified or tossed out altogether. It all depends on a robot's actual design and its intended use. Robots of low enough value can have Third Law deleted. Those sorts of bots don't need to protect themselves from harm; thus, their brain size can be greatly reduced. Other robots, those that are designed to operate autonomously and without specific human command, may safely have Second Law deleted as well. So long as these sorts of bots do not require Third Law as part of their programming, they can be built with smaller brains still. Finally, robots that are both disposable and designed to operate autonomously, without ever receiving orders from human beings, do not even require First Law, not so long as they operate in places where no human being can come to actual harm, like a deep mine. For an extremely simple bot, the sophistication of positronic circuitry can render a brain so small, it can fit comfortably within the skull of an insect."

Neena pressed her case. "In principle, I find no argument with what you are saying, Dr. Sinclair. But that still does not preclude a Z-bot from operating within the confines of the Three Laws. Your friend was right. Repetitive tasks are best done by simple machines, not humans, not Z-bots, not even advanced slave bots."

Sinclair countered. "Just because our life for the next two weeks will be regimented doesn't mean that what we do can be better done by robots. You are among the most gifted, most intelligent, most qualified young people available in this price range."

Everyone laughed. The tension in the room lessened.

"Seriously," Sinclair said. "You folks are among the most talented people available and I mean to exercise and stretch your mind and your skills to the breaking point. What we humans do cannot be done by mechs."

Neena Petronas wasn't done with him. "The truth is that I don't trust these newer bots. We ask these machines to make complex decisions. We ask them to decide whether or not an action they take will allow a human being to come to harm. How does a robot decide? An older bot, with more hours of experience, will make better decisions than a newly built one fresh off the production line. In my opinion, First Law is bogus."

Paddington Sinclair harrumphed. "A strong statement, Petronas. Do you have any evidence to back up your theory?"

"Forget evidence; it's common sense. Adults make better decisions than teenagers. The same must be true of synthetic life. When a robot starts to make judgment calls on the basis of algorithms and nothing more, I think we will find ourselves up shit creek without that proverbial paddle."

"It sounds to me like you have your thesis statement for your dissertation," Sinclair said in a condescending tone.

"Must you belittle everyone, Dr. Sinclair? Predictability is the cornerstone of expected robotic behavior. Without it, robots lose their reliability, which is their entire purpose for being."

Sinclair snapped back. "One of the foundational principles of science, one that goes back to the days of the first proto-human watching that first nut falling out of that first tree, is that the same experiment will always yield the same result, no matter who performs the experiment. This is the key to understanding robotic behavior. Predictability."

Neena replied, "A robot is a tool, Sinclair. Does a hammer argue about who is gripping the handle when there is a nail to be pounded? I think not."

"Okay, enough about robots already; enough about rules. We are now one man down. That man will shortly be on his way home. Okay, go grab some chow. Then report back here in one hour. You will get your team assignments after breakfast and the first team will begin its first three-hour shift right away. Every three hours we will set a new team on its daily routine. Except for Petronas, you all may leave now. Good day."

As the others filed out of the room, Paddington Sinclair turned to the young woman and said in a threatening tone, "Are you and I going to have a problem, Petronas?"

CHAPTER EIGHTEEN

Day Four, 0630 hours

"So you're keeping me after school to punish me for speaking up in class? Is that what this is about?" Neena asked, her stomach growling. It was early and she was hungry for a big breakfast. "I happen to agree with you, you know."

"Didn't sound like it in there," Paddington Sinclair declared. "It sounded more like you were fighting me at every turn."

"No, not at all. At one level, I agree with you. An elevator running to L1 will be an essential techdem, just like you said, an important project in its own right. Still, at the end of the day you have to admit that the two elevator projects — Earth versus the Moon — can hardly compare. Rosen was right about that. A lunar elevator is orders of magnitude more stable than an Earth elevator, just by virtue of its location and design."

"Okay, I'll give you that one," Sinclair said. "But more stable or not, there will still be ongoing disturbances to the lunar cable and counterweight that we must train ourselves to reckon with. We can learn much from dealing with those movements, things we cannot learn in any other way. Solar tides. Lunar libration. Extreme cold. As the Earth-Moon distance varies throughout the lunar orbit, so too does the effective gravity force at the elevator's counterweight."

"Don't take that holier-than-thou tone with me," Neena chided. "I've seen the sims; I know my physics. We will have to model and test suitable countermeasures for each motion. Counterweight thrusting is one possibility. Tether reeling and unreeling on a monthly cycle. Load variance. That sort of thing. Active countermeasures."

"Yes, that about sums it up."

"Tell me why you are really doing this."

"You are direct, aren't you?"

"Always."

"If you must know, I'm in it for the money," Sinclair declared, thinking back over his life's work. "The consulting fees are delicious. Plus, I like the media attention. But no government or mega-corporation is going to finance the building of an Earth elevator or any similar lifting device, unless I can first prove by demonstration here on the Moon that the risk of catastrophic failure is negligible."

"And how exactly do you propose to do that?"

"By emphasizing the differences. With an Earth elevator, we have no choice but to address the dangers from impact with orbiting material. Earth's orbital paths are strewn with objects big and small. Not so much the Moon."

"But even that is changing, isn't it?" Neena said.

"How so?"

"Enough with the questions already," Neena said, losing her composure. "I'm hungry. Starving, actually. Can we please go up to the mess, so I can grab some breakfast before your next frigging meeting at 0700? We can talk as we walk."

"Fair enough," Sinclair answered, as he grabbed his notes and followed her out the door. "You were saying . . . "

"The volume of debris accumulating in key lunar orbital paths is growing rapidly," Neena said. "Surely you must realize that ore pellets go awry all the time. Not a month goes by that one or two pellets don't miss being captured by the orbiting mass catcher. It is cheap to mine and extract certain materials here. The moon is, after all, one of the most accessible sources of minerals and metals in the inner solar system. Thousands of tons of lunar surface material go aloft every year."

Paddington Sinclair nodded his agreement. They exited the meeting room and started up the narrow corridor towards the mess. "And, much like the space elevator we are about to build, the ore pellet launch system was first conceived of and written about in early science-fiction novels. Arthur C. Clarke described the passive railgun, what some call an electromagnetic launch system."

"I prefer the term linear motor myself," Neena said. "But no need to quibble over terminology. We all mean the same thing. Big ugly contraption placed here, near the Moon's equator. Magnetic field arrays suspend the outbound freight above an inclined track and accelerate it to very high speeds. The freight normally consists of bins of lunar ore pellets drawn from the nearby processing plant, mostly aluminum and titanium ore. The launch trajectory of the freight car tosses them towards Earth. An orbiting mass catcher retrieves the pellets as they pass by and dispatches them along a sort of conveyor belt to a waiting space freighter. But, like I said, sometimes the railgun misfires. Sometimes the mass catcher fails to make the grab. Sometimes one or two of the pellets bounce off the conveyer belt. It's like billiard balls on a pool table after the opening break, only without gravity or friction. The balls go everywhere. So we end up with a huge mess, an orbiting debris field, like the rings of Saturn, only smaller."

Sinclair admired Neena's understanding of physics, yet he wouldn't yield any of the high ground. He continued to argue:

"The elevator we are about to build is going to change all that. No more need for a railgun. No more misfires. No more debris field. Everything raised effortlessly up to an anchored satellite by tethered climber. Henceforth we will be able to launch payloads using nothing more than the energy of the Moon's own rotation."

Neena chuckled outloud, then, hungry or not, stopped in the corridor to make her point. "An economist, you are not. For a man who says that he's in it for the money, you know nothing at all about it."

"How dare you!" Sinclair exclaimed.

"Hear me out, Oh Great One. An entire industry has built up around the railgun. Huge sums of money have been sunk into the building and upkeep of the mass catcher. Same goes for the freighters, the conveyors, the architecture of space mining, the training of employees. The owners of these giant businesses are not going to simply stand idly back while you swoop into their backyard and upset their apple cart. They are not going to shutter their profitable monopoly and grant you and your backers a new monopoly without first putting up a fight and, I might add, a nasty one. As on Earth, canals compete with railroads which compete with overland truckers that compete with airliners that compete with volume vacuum tubes. Space isn't about physics; it is about dollars. Profit drives space exploration, not noble intentions. That's what my father always says."

"Your father?" By now the two had begun moving again along the corridor toward the mechanical lift that would take them up to the mess level.

"Lou Santini."

The clanging of dishes, silverware, and plates could be heard just ahead, the smell of bacon and waffles riding the air currents in the elevator shaft.

"Lou Santini is your father? As in the hab's chief tech?" Sinclair seemed genuinely surprised by this news.

"Yep. One and the same."

"Did not know that."

They exited the lift and entered the mess. It was busy with people, Moon Beamers and regular staff. The two went straight to the hot food line.

"See? Now I have gone and taught the great man something he did not know, something new. Aren't you glad, now, that I stayed behind after class so willingly?"

"Smart ass woman."

"Which bothers you more, Sinclair? The smart ass part? Or the woman part?"

"Next?" It was the voice of the food bot behind the counter. To make the bot look presentable to human patrons, it wore an Aunt Jemima-style apron and paper cap. "What'll you have, young lady?"

"Two eggs over easy," Neena replied. "A cup of yogurt with fruit at the bottom. One piece dry toast. A glass of orange juice."

"What kind of fruit at the bottom of your cup of yogurt?" the bot kindly inquired. "We have sim berries."

"Yes, that will be fine."

"Okay. Please proceed to the food pickup window. Wait for your order number. It is forty-eight. Next?"

Sinclair ordered his breakfast, then followed Neena to the pickup window. While they waited for their food, he picked up the conversation from where they left off.

"Construction of the Moon Beam will need to begin from above, like I explained in the meeting. It begins in space, from the building platform we placed at the libration point months ago. Both the line being dropped to the surface and the longer one being extended into space will need to be extruded more or less simultaneously. It's a balancing act. As the line reaching down towards the surface becomes heavier with the increasing gravitational pull of the moon, the system can be kept in balance by the weight of the line reaching out into space."

"I understand all that," Neena said as their food order number was called. They found an empty table and sat down. She ate her eggs hungrily then spooned down the sim berry yogurt.

"My good friend Guy Cruz says you have understated the risk," Neena murmured as she washed down the last of her food with the small glass of orange juice.

"That Cruz boy is still wet behind the ears. Why in the world would a smart girl like you listen to advice from a grad student with mediocre grades and a half-baked thesis topic for his Ph.D.? I certainly have no intention of doing so."

"Mediocre grades or not, Guy knows his stuff as well as anyone in the room. Guy says that L4 and L5 are stable equilibrium positions for third bodies, whereas the other three — L1, L2, and L3 — are not. Unlike an Earth-anchored satellite with a stable GEO orbit, should the Moon tether ever be severed near the base, the upper part will fly off into space while the rest will crash down to the Moon's surface. He says that will happen even if the counterweight is released. Care to comment on that?"

"What is it with you and Cruz?" Sinclair asked.

"You're avoiding the question," she pressed.

"Just the same. What is it with you two?"

"If you must know, he and I are bedroom buddies."

"Is that what they call it now?"

"They do. But I don't see how with whom I sleep is any of your business."

"It isn't. But I do love to gossip."

"As much as you love to avoid answering hard questions?"

"You want to know the truth?" he asked.

"That would be nice for a change."

"Okay, here's the truth. To prevent Guy's scenario from unfolding, an emergency stabilization method will be required, probably a powered module near the balance point, a module capable of lengthening or shortening the cable on a moment's notice."

"Funny," Neena said. "I didn't see one of those powered modules in the budget or on the manifest."

"Truth is — I didn't ask the backers for all the money we actually need to build the thing."

"You lied to them?" Neena was taken aback.

"Is that a statement or a question?"

"I just want to be on the right side of this fiasco when the truth comes bubbling out and the whole thing blows up in our collective faces. No one has properly solved the three-body problem. But you are acting as if it has been solved," Neena said.

Sinclair finished his breakfast and got up to leave. "No, you're right, Petronas. No one has ever properly solved the three-body problem, not I, nor anyone else. But the motion of our anchored satellite can be analyzed as a restricted three-body problem and that has received extensive analytical treatment. Honestly, the unknown in this equation is none of the above. It is the strength of the materials we are planning to use. Do they have enough give? We tested them all. Boron-nitride nanotubes. Carbyne. Diamond nanothreads. Graphene. Carbon nanotubes.

We finally settled on something much more ordinary, a core of Zylon cord wrapped in a mesh of Magellan M8 fiber."

"I guess we will soon find out whether or not you made the right choice of materials, won't we?"

"Perhaps sooner than you think. Later on this morning, you and Guy will be the first team on the surface. Your initial assignment will be to position the three telemetry laser pods."

"You're sending out just the two of us? I thought we were being broken up into four-man teams, not teams half that size?"

"The other two members of your four-man team will be in the hab with me, monitoring your progress from inside."

"And you thought it would be smart to pair me with my boyfriend?"

"Yes, love. Nothing demonstrates the strength of a relationship like two lovebirds working side by side for days on end. See you both at the 0700 meeting. Do not be late."

"They were right about you, Paddington Sinclair. You are a real bastard."

"Flattery will not work with me, but you keep trying."

CHAPTER NINETEEN

TEN YEARS AGO

"A proper lady rewards a man as brave as you."

Flynn smiled. He liked the direction this was going. And yet, the violent destruction of the jumpship and the death of its crew, many of whom were his friends, still weighed heavily on his mind. Memories of the accident, only nine hours ago, were still fresh.

"Sorry, but I don't feel very brave," Flynn replied. "I almost wet myself when I saw those dead bodies."

At this age, Flynn was a scientist, a would-be technocrat, not a space infantryman like this girl or the other soldiers onboard that military shuttle. He had no aptitude for such things, and wasn't trained to cope with them. Besides, it had been one scary ride back up to the Space Station from the high-altitude site of the jumpship wreckage. Eighteen seconds of pure hell. Every human member of the crew had passed out on the way up due to the rapid acceleration. Only Flynn's pet robot, Claybotta, remained conscious and just after the boost stage, she took over the controls. Following the pulse-jump, the Z-bot had successfully slowed the craft and docked it with the umbilical at the station. Now, three hours had slipped by and the young woman who had been part of the recovery team sat before him in the Station pub.

The girl, Ouida Last-Name-Still-Unknown, had gorgeous red hair and an angular but pretty face. Her curves were much more evident now that she was out of her flightsuit and dressed in something more flattering and less military.

"Why so glum, chum?" she asked, stirring the cubes of ice in her drink.

"There's going to be an investigation," he said, "a months'-long investigation. You get that, right? People died onboard that test vehicle and someone must be made to pay."

"But not you. I have seen the bot's preliminary report. The fire started in the propellant compartment. You were never anywhere near that compartment."

"No, you are right. The fault isn't mine. But someone I know and probably worked alongside of for months on this project will likely be made to pay."

"All the same, my offer stands. A proper lady rewards a man as brave as you."

"And what sort of reward did you have in mind?" Flynn asked, clutching his drink.

The two sat across from one another, now, in the lounge of the tiny thousand-klom-high pub. The Night Cap Pub. Like all the eating establishments up here, the Night Cap was located in the one-g arm of the orbiting space station. Food stayed down better with a gravity-assist.

Space Station physics were remarkably simple. The Station spun slowly on its central tube. That slow spin generated pseudogravity in the outer rim where the living quarters and eateries were housed. The central tube was motionless and gravity-free. Specially machined elevators and stairways linked the two zones.

Flynn glanced rapidly about the Cap and felt a momentary unease. The only drinking establishment he felt comfortable in was the one on campus back home, the one he frequented on weekends with his drinking buddies, The Communion. As for women and relationships, there had been only two in his life thus far and neither had been consummated.

Flynn was intensely nervous about this woman as well. *What if one of her people reported her? What if her commanding officer saw the two of them together? What then?*

Ouida smiled her best smile, touched his hand from across the table. She had read his mind, seen his furtive looks.

"Don't worry about the colonel. He's probably upstairs getting laid himself. Besides, I have a seventy-two-hour leave. What say I offer you a reward of a turn in the sack?"

Flynn's jaw dropped. He was still a virgin.

"I am not very practiced," he admitted.

"And you think that I am?"

"I am saying nothing of the kind. I just don't want you to be disappointed."

"Why? You got a small willy?"

"Size isn't the issue. Experience is. Or in my case, the lack thereof."

"Do I look worried?" she cooed. "We are both adults. But neither one of us has ever done it in zero-g before. In that respect we are both still virgins."

That made eminent sense to Clay Flynn, and he smiled back. "Are you really still a virgin?"

"You are kidding me, right? I'm cute. I'm smart. I attract boys like steel to a magnet."

Flynn tried to screw up his courage. He looked across the table at this beautiful woman. Ouida's eyes were unlike any he had ever seen. As he sat there basking in her glow, he felt it happen. The line between love and lust blurred.

"My medical training has brought me here to the Station twice before," she said. "I wasn't posted here long on those occasions, three maybe four days tops. But I did stay long enough on one of those short hops to learn that there is a bank of zero-g sex rooms in the Station Hotel," she said breathlessly.

The pub was slowly filling with travelers. They were mostly couples on holiday from Earth, along with a squad of space travelers newly arrived from the outer planets seeking solace.

More people cracked up on the way home from Mars or the asteroid belt than from any other location. Thus, the Station housed one of the solar system's finest psych wards. Now, with the destruction of the lightcraft and the black box they recovered still under review, travel to and from the Station was restricted, at least until the debris field could be corralled. People were likely to be stranded here at the Station for days on end with no good way to get home. Everyone onboard was antsy and bored, and the Night Cap Pub was one of only three outlets on-station where the passengers could burn off that nervous energy. That wasn't counting, of course, the holo-bar one level up.

Within the smoky confines of the Night Cap, the usual antidote for boredom was a toxic blue-colored drink.

"Some sort of space hooch?" Flynn asked as a platter full of them went by riding on a waitress' arm. She was lanky and had nice breasts.

"Forget the hooch. And you can forget her as well. Let's go."

"Go? Go where?"

"To one of those rooms I told you about."

"Are you serious?"

"Do I look like I am kidding?"

"I like the way you think, woman."

"Then you are probably going to like some of the other things I can do."

"Are you talking dirty to me?" Flynn asked.

"You are an amateur, aren't you?" Ouida reached up and undid the top two buttons on her blouse. The crests of her firm breasts greeted his ravenous eyes.

"See anything you like?" she asked.

"Good God, yes." Flynn swallowed hard. "Yes, I do."

"Then let's get to it." Ouida leaned across the small table that separated the two and kissed him hard on the lips. Her red-hot tongue searched feverishly for his.

"We need a room." It was everything Flynn could do, now, not to lose control.

The Station had a central tube that ran for nearly one full klom from end to end. The tube was not wide — barely forty meters — but wide enough to house (among other things) a bank of zero-g rooms, the kind with beds, for having sex.

The two eager lovers moved quickly from the pub to the hotel registration desk. The clerk handed them each a keycard, a Tranquil patch to slap on their abdomen for nausea while in zero-g, and sent them on their way. They floated down the corridor to the zero-g room, threw open the door and literally flew in the room.

"I want you inside me," she panted. "Make love to me."

Things moved rapidly now. Ouida's passion had been ignited, and she would not be denied satisfaction. She braced herself against the closed door and pressed her body forward against his. Her nipples were hard, like polished stones. They etched out a message of love on his heaving chest.

Ouida reached down, below his belt, and touched his trousers. The burning heat of his lust was hard against her leg. At its touch, her heart began to race.

Flynn found himself swamped by a tremor of hot craving. He had imagined doing such things with a girl nearly every night of his adult life. The reality of being with a woman was something different from what he expected, something far more terrifying.

Locked now in a tight embrace, the two drifted across the room in zero-g. Like autumn leaves, they settled to the floor in slow motion, a jumble of arms and legs. Weightlessness cushioned their impact.

"This will never work," he panted breathlessly, hands caressing her bosom. "How can we possibly have sex without gravity? As soon as I move on top of you and begin to thrust, my every motion will only serve to push you further away."

"What can we do?" she asked, tearing off her clothes and begging him to hurry. "One of us needs to be fastened down."

"Check the bed. It must be equipped with sleeping tethers."

"Oh, that sounds downright pagan. I cannot remember the last time a man tied me to a bedpost and had his way with me."

"There was a first time?"

Ouida giggled. Then she tore off her clothes, stripped bare, and launched herself toward the waiting bed. Flynn followed in hot pursuit, launching himself along roughly the same trajectory.

The two landed laughing, a spaghetti bowl of arms and legs. "Okay, bub. Tie me up. I am all yours." She lay back, legs up, knees apart.

From where Flynn sat, it was a splendid view. Nothing could quite compare with a girl where the cuffs and links matched. Or, as some said, the carpet and drapes. Either way, her red hair and nakedness drove him wild. He didn't even notice her tattoo.

For her part, Ouida executed a quick survey of his nether regions and seemed properly impressed. "Mighty fine kickstand, if you get my meaning."

"Sex by metaphor, is it? Then what say we lengthen that kickstand of mine as far as it will go and see whether or not we can get that motor of yours running?"

"Oh, it is running hot already. Now find me those tethers."

Flynn fished around and found a set of elastic sleeping tethers attached to the underside of the bed on each side. At night, the tethers could be used to prevent a sleeping occupant from floating out of bed.

But at times like this the tethers had other, more interesting uses. Flynn found that by strapping one tether across Ouida's waist, well below her breasts, he could fix it so she would not float away yet would still have full range of motion with her legs. The idea was slowly forming in his head. Flynn was beginning to appreciate why certain adventuresome couples might make their way to the space station for purposes of having sex.

The two began to go at it enthusiastically. But no sooner had they begun, than they discovered something new. A lover could perform wondrous miracles of lovemaking for his mate when unburdened by the evil forces of "up" and "down."

The coupling lasted a surprisingly short time. Something about the setting or the ultra-low gravity or perhaps the fear of being discovered by one of her shipmates made them crest rapidly, almost too rapidly for their own good. Without ever meaning to, they both came almost immediately.

Flynn rolled off her, slid a tether across his chest and put a hand on her belly. "Tighten those muscles down there."

"You saying I'm flabby?"

"No, not at all. You have a body that just will not quit, I promise you."

"What then?"

"I'm worried about leakage."

"You cannot be serious."

"I am a space engineer by trade. Believe me when I tell you — everything floats in zero-g. Orange juice, barf, sperm, you name it. It all floats. If you don't want to be combing that stuff out of your hair two days from Sunday, I suggest you tighten those love-muscles of yours down there real soon."

"Oh, shut up and hand me that blanket. We will keep those floatie things under wraps one way or the other."

Shortly, Ouida closed her eyes and fell asleep. A satisfied smile was painted across her moistened lips. Flynn stared at her a moment, figured he had done pretty well his first time out.

Then, he dozed off himself.

•

•

Flynn woke three-quarters of an hour later with an enormous hard-on. At first, he was surprised. Then he remembered where he was and what his training had told him about his environment.

Ouida noticed his erection right off. "Still in need?"

"Ask a man that question and he will always say that, yes, he is still in need. But it isn't me. This place has an awful lot to do with it."

"Space makes you horny?"

"In a manner of speaking. Spacejockeys have a word for it. Extreme morning wood. In zero-g, excess fluids collect in a man's penis while he sleeps. He wakes up this way nearly every day."

"From the size of things, it looks to me more like morning lumber."

"I will take that as a compliment."

"Of course, you will. That is how it was given."

"If you think my wooden puppet friend swells with fluids in zero-g, giving me a hard-on, what do you think happens to that cute little button of yours?"

"Button?"

"Yes, you know exactly what button I am talking about, your love-button. Your member swells up just like mine does. — And with pretty much the same result."

"No wonder I am so damn horny," she said.

"That itch of yours is going to need to be scratched over and over again as long as we are here."

"Is that the voice of experience?"

"Not at all. Just stories around the campfire."

"Well, if the sex up here is so great, why ever leave and go home? Why not stay up here forever, live and make whoopie in a zero-g environment from now until the end of time?"

"Because weightlessness has its downsides," Flynn said. "Loss of bone mass. Constipation. Upset stomach. Spend too much time in a place without gravity and things will soon start to get dicey. Didn't they teach you anything in space infantry school? Long-term exposure to zero-g conditions is dangerous to one and all. That is why they spin the Station. To generate pseudogravity for the safety of its occupants."

"Just so we're clear, lover boy — I didn't enlist in the space infantry to become a soldier. The infantry has been my ticket to medical school. I worked once as a drill bit on an asteroid mining team. But that was dangerous work, a dead-end career, so I opted for something safer and a bit more respectful — medicine. I hope to one day be a medical officer here on the Station, maybe Venus; that is, if they finally cool the place down enough to allow in settlers."

"Then, my lady, you will learn the truth soon enough. Prolonged exposure to micro-g is invariably bad. It harms our immune system in the worst possible way. Our lymphocytes, which are our body's self-defense mechanism, can become seriously damaged by weightlessness. Without that army of white-blood cells to help the body fight disease, it doesn't take long before the immune system begins to break down. At the cellular level, certain elegant signaling systems do not function properly in zero gravity. Just one more reason why a woman must avoid getting pregnant at all cost while in space. Fetuses do not develop properly. Babies born in zero-g lack the strength to thrive once they are returned to a gravity well."

"I thought you were a budding space engineer? How does a jockstrap like yourself come to know so much about medicine and biology?"

"Mate a love for reading to a nerd with a love for science and mathematics and you get a big dumb know-it-all like me."

"And to think I just had sex with a man who loves science as much as biology. Maybe I should not have used protection. Come to think of it, your little wooden puppet friend looks so lonely, like he does not have a friend in the world. Should we do something about that?"

"I admit. The little fellow is lonely. He may need some handholding, maybe a kiss on the forehead for good luck."

"Oh, I just love it when you talk dirty. You simply must have your way with me again."

"If you insist."

"I surely do."

•

•

Flynn woke for a second time. He crawled out from beneath the sleeping tether and fairly glided across the room to a small aft alcove. There were windows back there, fairly large ones, where a person might look out into space, as well as handholds so a person could maintain their orientation.

The windows were darkly tinted now, to protect a looker's eyes from the unfiltered sun, but also to prevent voyeurs from catching a glimpse of couples having sex in the zero-g rooms. Voyeurism was a favorite pastime for visitors and staff alike in the lounges of the main part of the Station. The tinting had the added benefit of keeping the small rooms from overheating when the central tube swung into the sun.

Flynn steadied himself on the handhold, took a look around. Above him was the main part of the Station, all spokes and girders and struts. He could see it through the dark glass, but just barely. One thing stood out clearly, though — a trans-comet barreling its way through the ether toward its eventual rendezvous with the planet Venus.

The trans-comet was shiny — far out of proportion to its size. *And why was that?* The dirty ball of ice was wrapped in a giant manmade plastic liner. As always and forever, Man was fiddling with his environment, molding and reshaping it more to his liking, just as he had been doing since that morning long ago, when he first climbed down out of the trees, stood on two legs and stumbled out onto the African savanna. This constant fiddling is what made life interesting, after all. Shaping and reshaping the human experience, terraforming the ground under our feet. Those trans-comets, with all their millions of liters of briny water, would eventually cool Venus down, make it livable for mankind.

Ouida woke, saw him by the window. But she remained in bed buried beneath a pile of covers. She propped herself up on one elbow.

"Geez, my head hurts," she said, twice blinking her eyes to drive away the pain. "And boy am I hungry."

Flynn signaled for her to come join him at the window. She threw back the bedsheets and launched herself out of bed and in his direction. On the way over, she tangled herself up on his trousers still hanging in mid-air. By the time Ouida arrived on target, she was hurtling across the room in an out-of-control spin. She crashed into him then ricocheted into the wall.

"Damn. That hurt."

Ouida rubbed her head, shoved his trousers angrily away. "Didn't your mother ever tell you to hang up your clothes before bedding a girl?"

"Sweetheart, my mother would have a cow — or other sacred animal — if she knew I had bedded a girl."

Ouida was still spinning. Flynn laughed at her antics, grabbed onto her arm to steady her motion. He knew the score, courtesy of his experience working on the jumpship project.

"Girl, what catches most people off-guard in zero-g is how much rotational velocity they can acquire when they push off a wall or stationary object like a bed. A person can pick up a terrific amount of unintentional spin. Plus, you cannot just put anything down, not in a room where there is no gravity, not like you can on Earth."

Flynn continued. "There is always a certain amount of inertia remaining when you move about. Whatever you put down — be it a book or an empty milk glass — will inevitably float off, causing you all kinds of trouble later on. An hour afterward, you get bopped in the head — or your friend does — by the book you set down earlier. Air currents mainly. But also ship movements. They both cause objects to move off slowly from where you left them. That includes clothing you ripped off in the heat of passion."

"How dare you lecture me at a time like this. Do you have any idea how much my head is pounding? Ever since I woke up I have had this blinding headache."

"The techs call it grav-head. It comes courtesy of the laws of fluid dynamics in micro-g."

"Could you please stop spewing physics from some blinking textbook and tell me what the hell to do about my head?"

Flynn reached into his kit and handed her a pill. "When you spend too much time in zero-g, the fluids in your body try to redistribute themselves. The same thing happens to everyone when they are weightless. There is no escaping it. Clogged sinuses. Stuffy nose. Pounding headache. The symptoms can make you feel like you have a really bad head cold. At least until you become accustomed to it. Plus, you may find yourself needing to pee all the time."

"Yeah, now that you mention it. That is what first woke me. Then came the headache."

"The overwhelming need to pee will get you every time. That is just the body dumping what it considers to be excess fluid. You will be peeing constantly until your body establishes a new equilibrium. But get ready. You are just going to love that zero-g toilet."

Flynn pointed to a small alcove adjoining the bedroom. "It is really nothing but an inverted vacuum cleaner with cushioned straps to hold you down. Me? — I find the whole damn thing quite disturbing. It is the same old problem of containing free liquids. Remember what I told you about those little floatie things after we had sex?"

"Okay, nothing to drink, nothing to eat, can't take a pee. I still have a headache and I am still hungry. Can we please go back to the grav part of the Station already?" Ouida said.

"Yeah, I think we both have had enough zero-g for one day. Tranquil patches don't last more than an hour or two."

"That is why there is a two-hour limit on the room, isn't it? The life expectancy of a Tranquil patch. The hotel manager mentioned something about it when we checked in. But I just could not understand why."

"Yeah, most people don't need long. They just need time enough to get it on with their mate so they can brag about it to the folks back home, tell them of their achievement. But when they are done doing the deed, they all want to get back to grav as soon as they possibly can."

"It was fun though, wasn't it?" Ouida said.

"Could it ever be anything but?" Flynn asked.

"Now you are talking psychology, not biology."

"Well then, let's not talk either," he said. "Let's get our clothes back on and get the heck out of here."

Together, the two of them floated back to where their clothes hung. Some still dangled like spider webs in mid-air. Others had moved off to nearby locations. Then, with each other's help, the pair dressed and made their way back up to the restaurant level. All the eateries were in one of the outer spokes comprising the Ferris wheel portion of the Station.

The trip to the outer rim included a ride in one of the Station's infamous elevators. Their nasty reputation was well-deserved. As the elevator car journeyed outward from the central tube to the outer rim, the local gravity rose from zero to one-g. A ride in one of these elevators — even a short ride — was known to make people sick to their stomach. Fortunately for Flynn and Ouida, today the elevator was being used to move freight and its ascent speed was slowed to a crawl. So, no harm, no foul.

This second visit to the Night Cap bar was a Kodachrome replay of their earlier visit. Flynn was still quite the fish out of water. Men are creatures of habit, even young men. They do not care to have their routine disturbed. Men want their favorite chair, their favorite vid, their favorite woman, doing it to them their favorite way. The rest of the time, they preferred to be left alone.

"Boy, this place gives me the creeps," Flynn said. "Am I wrong? Everything about this place is off. Clean floors. Practically antiseptic. No rotten smells. No shady characters. Good lighting. Comfortable chairs. Blah."

"It is dreadful, isn't it?"

"You want to leave?" he asked.

Her hands were on the table, now, again reaching for his. "Let's eat something then fly back to that zero-g room to have another go at it. I think we may still have thirty minutes left on our room rental."

There was a small loaf of hot bread on the table. She hungrily broke off a portion. Her headache was already starting to melt away.

"I thought you had had enough of zero-g?"

"Can't a girl change her mind?"

"Honestly, had I known the Space Station would make a girl hungry for sex, I would have brought one here ages ago." Flynn squeezed out butter from the tube and spread it on a bread slice of his own. Then he signaled the waiter for a second time to come over.

A minute later, the waiter finally made his way to their table. He had an impertinent, unpleasant air about him.

"I will be with you in a minute," he said.

"What is wrong with right now?" Flynn snapped impatiently. "We have already been waiting five minutes for service."

"There is only one pub on this tub, Bub — and this be it. You don't like the service? Feel free to step off any time."

Flynn felt a flash of anger. He instinctively tightened the muscles in his jaw. "Feel free to step off? That is how you want to talk to me?"

"It's okay, Flynn. Let it go," Ouida pleaded. "We do not want a scene."

"Yeah, Flynn, let it go," the waiter parroted, staying just beyond Flynn's reach.

"But you said you were hungry." By then, Clay Flynn had decided that he wanted to be anywhere else but here.

"We will order in room service," she said.

"Yeah, you do that," the waiter scoffed as he walked haughtily away.

"Now who is stepping off?" Flynn shouted after him, fists clenched. But the waiter shrugged his shoulders and headed back to the kitchen.

"Let it go, Flynn. I would much rather have another taste of you than eat in this dump."

She grabbed what was left of the loaf of bread and stuffed it in her handbag. Flynn pocketed the tube of butter.

"If it is another taste you want, it is another taste you will get."

•

•

It was unhurried lovemaking at its best.

Rather than take another zero-g room, they went straightaway to the tourist hotel located upstairs from the pub in the one-g section.

The room was not much. Unstructured living space was at a premium onboard the Station. But the room did have a bed. One of those plump, oversized affairs with a brass headboard and a nightstand on either side. The floor was covered in a thick blue, faux carpet. The windows, which looked out on the verdant Earth below, were dressed only in auto-shades. The room lights were low.

She came to him at the window. He was watching North America go by. The sun had set. The coasts were aglow with light. So were the shores of the Great Lakes, as well as all the major rivers and their tributaries. Mankind loved his water. It made transport cheap and commerce possible. Every civilization, before or since, has set up shop along the shores of some lake or river.

Now came the less populated northern latitudes. Newfoundland. Greenland. Iceland. Such a strange little island, that one. A cold world stripped to its essence. Geography reduced to geometry. Glacial rivers. Lava fields. Sparse tundra vegetation. Black seas. Elemental landscape.

She pointed out Ireland on the western fringes of the approaching continent. Said it was her family's ancestral home a century or two back. Then a strip of water and more lights to the east.

Ouida wrapped her arms around his waist, pressed her head into the small of his back. The muscles of his abdomen rippled beneath his shirt. The tension in his chest brought forth memories of their first time together. She quivered, now, at the thought of the two of them joined again at the hips.

He turned in the circle of her arms to face her. He kissed her on the forehead. She sighed warmly in response.

He worked his lips down to her cheek, then to her neck.

Now Ouida took control, her hungry mouth devouring his lips and tongue.

Neither of them wanted to rush. It would be over soon enough in any event.

They undressed each other slowly, deliciously, button by button, clasp by clasp. Their clothes fell into two neat little piles on the floor. Gravity had its virtues. Panties and underwear remained unshorn.

Still standing, they kissed, tongue on lingering tongue. He pressed her to him, hands on her bottom. She moaned softly, feeling his hard, young body against hers.

They moved to the bed without saying a word. He peeled off his underwear and tossed them to the floor. She did the same.

Ouida lay back full-length on the sheets, inviting him in. Hips encircled hips, thighs pressed against thighs. It was instinctual lovemaking, the hallmark of inexperience.

A moan escaped her lips. His breath came faster, as did hers.

For several long minutes they were joined together, bodies pressed tightly, as if one.

Then it was over. In a warm explosion of energy, it was over.

Satiated at last, Flynn rolled off her and the two lay apart. Gradually, their heart rates returned to normal, and Ouida slid blissfully to sleep, a contented smile on her lips.

At that singular moment in time, ten years ago, life seemed awfully sweet.

CHAPTER TWENTY

Day Four, 0930 hours

Guy Cruz struggled to wrestle the refrigerator-sized piece of equipment loose from its restraints at the rear of the electric cart. The ground tracking laser device was not particularly heavy; indeed, at one-sixth-earth-normal gravity the thing weighed little more than a good-sized Thanksgiving Day turkey.

No, what stymied Cruz was the GTLD's overall size. With its collection of antennas, radios dishes, and pulse emitters, the GTLD had a circumference that easily exceeded the reach of his arms. His gloved hands made him clumsy.

Guy turned to his co-worker and steady girlfriend for help. But Neena was looking the other way. The woman was dressed as he was, in a cumbersome Mag 10 spacesuit. The two were on-station about three kloms from the habitat, at 0° East 0° North, working to properly position the large ground tracking laser device at this precise spot, then to securely anchor it for the critical job ahead. Once the settings were confirmed, the GTLD would immediately be powered up and set to work.

"Can you give me a hand with this?" he said into the headset.

She turned and made her way slowly in his direction employing that peculiar, skip-walking type gait a space traveler never quite becomes accustomed to, the Moon Dance as they called it.

"Positioning these telemetry devices is crucial to our efforts," she said, breathing heavily. "Our team's first job."

"What team? Where is our team anyway? I thought there were supposed to be four of us out here at any one time. This would go so much faster — and be a hell of a lot safer — if we had more hands on deck."

"Dick-head Sinclair thought it would be cute if it was just the two of us — you and me — working the first shift together."

"The man is an odd duck, isn't he?"

"Megalomaniac, more like," she said. "And he's probably listening in on our comm chatter as we speak."

"The man can go to blazes, for all I care. Three, four-man teams to set up three ground trackers. That was the deal. One team per tracker. The other two teams are at full strength; you and I are short-handed. That places the two of us at a disadvantage."

"Short-handed or not, it's our job. Three ground trackers to safely guide the elevator cable down from orbit to the surface platform. There's an incredible amount of cable to unreel from the space node, fifty thousand kloms in all."

Once the two of them were done anchoring the triangulation pod, the onboard programming would unfold the dishes and comm equipment and properly align them all by shooting a laser beam off an orbiting lunar-sync satellite, as well as the other two posts of the triangle, which were currently being set up by two other sets of team members.

Guy's companion, Neena Petronas, was a woman well-qualified for such work. "Are you even sure these LPS numbers are correct?" she asked, studying the lunar topographic map displayed on her handheld monitor.

Above their heads, a crescent Earth shone bright in all its glory. Oceans of blue, swirls of white clouds, continents of green and brown, ice caps of cold and ice tilted approximately twenty-three degrees off the vertical.

Guy answered. "I am not actually sure of anything yet, Nee." It was his pet name for her. "GPS, LPS, it's all Greek to me. These numbers we are working with came from Sinclair. He says what we are doing is a form of triangulation. Three ground tracking stations. They form an equilateral triangle, the center of which is located directly beneath the nearside libration point."

Neena shook her head. "See, that's the part that puzzles me. The libration point is not actually a single point at all. It moves up and down and from left to right from the lunar orbit eccentricity on a monthly basis. Sinclair knows this. The so-called point is more like a region, and not even a symmetrical region at that. More like an ornery pancake frying on the griddle — oddly shaped, not symmetrically smooth like a circle or an ellipse."

"I see your point, Nee, no pun intended. How can the center of a triangle lie beneath a point that isn't actually a point? Sinclair is guessing, isn't he?"

"I seriously doubt whether the man makes a habit of guessing. But even if he does, you and I aren't exactly in a position to argue with the man, are we? Look at what happened to Carl Rosen when he went up against Sinclair. Rosen got sent home for his trouble."

"Nah, you're wrong, Neena. That thing with Rosen in the conference room was about sex and nothing more."

"Sex?" She stopped what she was doing. "What are you talking about?" She unbundled the piton gun and set it to one side. They would use the gun to lock the big machine into place once it was properly positioned.

"Sinclair bats for the other team, you know that, right?" Guy said.

"No, I did not know that. But how does his orientation enter into the equation?"

Guy laughed, at least what sounded like a laugh through the miserable audio device called a comm. "Rosen made a pass at Sinclair, a pass that was incomplete and ended up out of bounds."

"Seriously? A sports metaphor? However, that would explain a lot. Jilted lover and all that."

"What did Sinclair want to see you about after our early morning meeting? I was intending to have breakfast with you."

"Oh, that. The goal was to intimidate."

"And did he succeed?"

"You know me better than that."

"Yeah, I do know you better than that," Cruz said as he paced off a short distance and bent to anchor a bolt. "But there is a great deal about our Paddington Sinclair that keeps me awake at night."

"Are you talking about how he danced around the static electricity grounding problem this morning in the meeting?" Neena asked.

"The man is making light of something extremely heavy," Guy said. "Those kinds of voltages can kill. Start fires. Cause explosions. Are we to assume from his attitude that every single one of us is expendable?"

"In Paddington Sinclair's world, everyone and everything is expendable. Except him, of course."

"Not to change the subject," Guy said, brushing his gloves against the lower section of his spacesuit. "But something must definitely be done about all this dust. How in the world are we supposed to make precise telemetric measurements if our instruments are gummed up with this crap?"

Neena agreed. "I read up on this stuff when I was in school, I suppose like every undergrad did. As far back as the first moon landings, the stickiness of lunar dust has been more than just an inconvenient nuisance. It was known from the get that lunar dust was a serious hazard, one that could really muck up a mission."

"Martian dust is worse," Guy said.

"You know this how?"

"I have been," he answered. "Six month stint with my father when he was in the service."

"Do tell. You are full of surprises lately, aren't you? Last night, for starters."

"The Clay Pots?"

"I never knew you played in a blues band back home," she said. "Bass guitar, no less."

"Nee, we haven't known each other long enough for you to know everything about me yet."

"Turnabout is fair play."

"Is it? What don't I know about you?" he asked quietly.

"The trombone player is my father."

"That guy I met last night? He is your father? Lou Santini? The trombonist? Shit. You both acted as if you hardly knew one another."

"We don't," she said.

"Oh, I see."

"Do you?"

"No, I really don't."

"Then let's leave it alone, shall we, and talk a bit more about the dust instead. I have it on good authority that Sinclair may have worked up a solution."

"Trust me," Guy said. "Martian dust is worse than anything we have ever seen here. Not only is there more of it, Mars has wind. The wind can propel the tiny particles at high speed across the Martian landscape. The dust blackens solar panels in a matter of hours. It often leaves settlers without a source of electricity until the panels can be cleaned. And dust isn't the only hazard. The Martian surface is laced with poisonous perchlorates. The stuff is toxic, poisonous even. Perchlorates mess with our thyroid. Their very presence would place a pregnant woman's fetus in extreme danger. Plus, the one-third gravity of Mars is too low for a woman to carry her baby to term. The low-g interferes with a young child's growth hormone, just as it does here on the Moon. No place for women or children, that much is for certain."

"I thought it was the guys, not the gals, who had to watch their step on the Red Planet, exposed testicles and all that," she said, briefly grabbing her crotch to make her meaning clear.

"That's true, but only to a point," Guy said. Together, the two of them had lowered the ground tracking laser device to the surface, lashed it to a dolly, and wheeled the thing to the anchoring spot, where they were now fastening it down. "The egg-producing organs of the female are buried deep within a woman's body. Her overlying muscle and skin make for something of a shield. A woman's ovaries are less impacted by radiation than a man's germ cells are. But the real problems begin only after her eggs are fertilized."

"Again — you know this how?" Neena said, catching her breath. Moving the GTLD had been hard, demanding work, even in low-g.

"I know this because no one is allowed onboard a ship bound for Mars without first receiving proper indoctrination. The instructors drill it into your head each and every day of the two-week-long training period. *Keep it in your pants. Always wear lead-lined undies.* That's what they would say to us day after day in class, boys and girls alike."

"How old were you at the time, Guy? You couldn't have been much more than a boy."

"Had my eleventh birthday on the outbound leg. Anyway, age isn't really the issue. Anyone who might be — or might become — sexually active had to know the facts. The trainers were quite insistent. Pregnancy had to be avoided at all cost. Fetuses would be aborted, with no chance for appeal."

"Just like that?"

"Nee, fetuses are the creatures at greatest risk. Prenatal radiation can trigger structural deformity. It can retard growth, cause sterility in the newborn, fuse abnormalities in the central nervous system. Bad stuff all the way around."

"Are you saying that the radiation risk on Mars is even greater than it is here on the Moon?" she asked.

"Oh, yes, I think there is general agreement on that. The Sun's bubble of solar wind deflects some of the most lethal cosmic rays. The Moon is closer to the Sun and thus better protected by the solar wind. But Mars is basted like a turkey in an oven by cosmic rays of every sort. The most lethal are highly energetic protons and heavier nuclei. Those bad boys zing through human tissue causing all kinds of damage, especially to the unborn. That's why the colony is built mostly in the mons, inside ancient volcanic lava tubes; for protection."

"Given all that, it's a wonder anyone would ever want to go to Mars," she grumbled.

"And let's not forget the gravity-related issues."

"There's more?"

"Oh, yes." Guy nodded. "Life on Earth evolved under the influence of a constant one-g pull. Cell structure. Cell shape. Genetic expression. All products of the g-forces they have been subjected to. Even inside a cell, or along the length of a DNA molecule, there is a gravitationally defined up and down. The microscopic architecture of a cell is gravity sensitive. It defines the very shape of a mitochondria."

"Yes, yes, all very interesting," she said. "But now, can we please circle back to our original conundrum?"

"Which was?"

"What to do about all this frigging dust? How are we supposed to cope with all the dust and crap we are kicking up out here with our boots?" Neena asked. "Working on the lunar surface must be every bit as messy as working on the surface of Mars, with boots and machinery kicking up a constant storm of dust. Just look at this stuff. It's like fine powder. We have been out here less than an hour, and just look at the two of us. We are covered from head to foot. So is the rover and the tracking laser."

Guy nodded. "There's the problem. Some of that angel dust sticks like glue to a man's spacesuit. Later, when the spacesuit is removed upon return to the hab, that powdery dust can spread like a pathogen throughout the living quarters. When the fine dust settles inside, it can contaminate and degrade surfaces, not to mention increase the risks of inhalation and skin damage."

"So, what's to be done?" she asked. "We didn't train for this back home."

"Numerous attempts have been made over the years to combat the dust problem. One early technique was to wash down the exterior of a suit before a spacejockey disrobed. But that was costly and time-consuming. In an emergency, it was all but impossible to do quickly."

"That's when they began to experiment with suitports, yes?" she intoned.

"Yes, Walter Hagerty. I did a paper on him when I was in graduate school. The Hagerty suitport. An idea harvested from science fiction. An innovative entry and exit system for exploration spacecraft. As the story goes, Hagerty was a compulsive tinkerer; a habitual user of 3-D printers for developing prototypes. One day he supposedly sat down at his drafting table and came up with the suitport. It was his solution to the Martian dust problem. The way he had it figured, a suitport would be a practical alternative to the traditional airlock."

"But that's not what we use here today."

"Oh, goodness no," Guy replied. "The damn things are far too expensive for everyday use, certainly far too expensive to hand out to lugnuts like ourselves. Plus, in the field they found that the seals began to fail after the fifth or sixth EVA. But the space agency did toy with them for a while. You have to admit: the design was pure genius. A rear-entry spacesuit was vacuum sealed and attached against the outside of the spacecraft. The spacewalking astronaut entered the suitport from inside the craft, then sealed up the suit mechanically and went on EVA. No need for an airlock. No need to de-pressurize the cabin of the spacecraft to exit it. When an astronaut returned from a spacewalk, he, in effect, left his spacesuit outside the ship — firmly attached once more to the exterior. His dust-covered spacesuit never actually entered the inside of the spacecraft."

"But, like you said, it is not the system we use today," she said.

"No, it certainly is not. The Mag 10 employs a micro-layer exosuit. It is like being shrink-wrapped in a thin plastic liner after you suit up. When you return to the airlock and before you unseal the inner hatch, a solvent wash dissolves the shrink-wrap and the whole thing, liner, dust, and everything else is washed down the drain and into a holding tank. But now you say that Sinclair has come up with something even better?"

Even as he spoke, a warning bell sounded in his helmet. They were down to fifteen minutes of air in their tanks. Neena heard it as well.

"Okay, Guy, let's finish this job before we run out of breathable."

"Roger that," he said. "Now for the last step, Nee. Line up that optical camera with the LPS tracking system."

Neena worked a few minutes with the touchpad and the rotors, and the cam unit slowly revolved and tilted skyward.

"Okay, done," she said.

Guy nodded. "Next, we shoot the sat with a laser pulse and measure the energy spike to see if we have the correct azimuth. The computer will shoot the azimuth over and over again, multiple times each second until it is exactly right."

"Yes, and I know the last step," Neena said. "We establish radio contact with the other two corners of the triangle. Once each of the other two corners shoot and set their own azimuths, we pulse-beam each other to check our angles vis à vis the other. Equilateral triangles have sixty-degree corners."

"Yes, Nee, I know what an equilateral triangle is."

"And let's not forget the final, final step. We have to lock down the pod legs using barbed spikes from the piton gun."

"And, Nee. Please do be careful. I don't want you to break your hand with that gun. The son of a bitch kicks back like a mule when it fires."

"Roger that," she said, clicking off the gun's safety.

CHAPTER TWENTY-ONE

Day Four, 1015 hours

"I have reports of toilets overflowing everywhere on the lower level," Administrator Winston Hanrahan said with detached amusement. He never came out from behind that great wooden desk of his unless he absolutely had to.

"I'm not a plumber," Flynn replied with great irritation.

"You are today," Hanrahan said. "Lasso that wop Santini and the two of you duckwalk your asses down to the lowest sub-basement and sort this damn thing out. I have been getting calls since 0800 this morning, and I am more than a little sick of listening to complaints."

"If you don't want to end the day with a black eye and a fat lip, I suggest you never let Santini hear you speak that way about him. Wop is not a word you will find in that man's vocabulary."

"I don't give a flying fig what you or Santini think of me. Do your job the way I tell you to do it or else I will find someone to take your place and do it the way I want it done."

"Yeah, good luck with that."

Flynn slammed the office door angrily as he left Hanrahan's cubicle. Under his breath he spewed, "Asshole." Then he walked rapidly down the corridor, turned left at the first pressure door and on to Lou Santini's tiny office. He knocked on the door.

"Come."

"Hello, Lou. Bossman Hanrahan says we got toilet problems down on the lower level."

"Yeah, the board is lit up like a blinking Christmas tree. Grab a towel and a wrench and follow me down. I have the grid coordinates in hand. All our systems seem to be stressed to the limit."

"And why is that?" Flynn wondered, still simmering from the confrontation with Hanrahan.

"It's these elevator people."

"I don't follow."

"Sinclair's lunar elevator people, the so-called Moon Beamers. We suddenly have a shitload of additional mouths to feed, and I don't have to tell you that what goes in the mouth eventually works its way out the other end. I hesitate to guess how many more liters of solid waste we now have to process on a daily basis. All our resources are stressed to the breaking point," Santini said. "It's Hanrahan's fault. I warned him weeks ago that there would be trouble with so many short-termers coming aboard. I told him we needed to have more replacement parts on hand. I told him to order spares months ago."

"This is more than just the toilets?" Flynn asked as the two hurried along from handhold to handhold.

"Oh, goodness yes," Santini answered. "We have problems all over the hab. Toilets stopped up, sewers that won't drain properly, air and water filters clogged, electrical failures everywhere."

"Are we short on spare parts?"

"Fewer on hand than you might think," Santini said.

"And you're only telling me this now?"

"It's that prick, Hanrahan. Plus, the re-supply ship has been delayed on account of some sort of mechanical failure at the launch site. Five days behind schedule, at last report."

Chief Flynn shook his head. "I thought we had 3-D printers on-station now that would solve all such out-of-stock problems? Didn't the honchos promise us that the printers would remedy our replacement part issues?"

"Additive manufacturing? Oh, yes we have the printers on-station, and they're good ones too. But, Chief, you are missing two critical parts of the equation."

"Yeah? Enlighten me."

Santini stopped, looked at his directional finder and then set off again at a good clip. "We turn left at the next T-junction."

"Yes, yes, yes. Quit screwing off. You said that I was missing two critical parts of the equation. What am I missing?"

"Chief, the tunnel sabotage led to a barrage of new requests for parts that needed replacing. Plus, the heightened security measures that you yourself put in place yesterday have boosted demand for sensors and small bots and the like."

"So?"

"So, we have run out of paste," Santini said, as if what he was saying ought to be obvious to the other man.

"Paste?"

"The stuff we feed into the printers to manufacture spare parts. Acrylonitrile butadiene styrene. The same oil-based gunk they use to make Lego toys out of. Shit, don't you read any of my reports?"

"Not if I can avoid it. Are you saying that the paste we need for the 3-D printers is on that same late re-supply ship?"

"Yep. No spare parts; no paste to make spare parts. We are buggered in the rear-end without Vaseline and things are breaking down everywhere and all at the same time." Santini broke off mid-sentence. "This way. I hear the sound of running water." He pointed.

"Yeah, I hear it too. Riddle me this, Batman."

"Seriously? Comic book references? Just how old school are you?"

"Yeah, like you didn't know I was a geek. What I don't understand, Lou, is this. We have been building nearly indestructible unmanned spacecraft for generations. So why can't we build a decent, long-lasting habitat with parts that don't constantly break down? I mean, it is no great shakes to build a semi-autonomous spacecraft of the greatest complexity. Ships of this sort have been built to such high standards they can endure space travel for decades, even explore an uncharted planet or moon for years on end without the slightest help from a human being."

"You mean except for the part where the human being is the one who actually assembles the blinking spacecraft and then later actually analyzes the data sent back for study. Doesn't sound very autonomous to me," Santini mocked.

"Yeah, except for that."

"But I do get what you mean. The challenges of building a long-lasting robotic spacecraft are worlds apart from the challenges of building a spacecraft or space facility that can accommodate a human being. The instant that a living, breathing human being enters the picture, machinery begins to break down."

"Yes, and why is that?" Flynn wanted to know.

"People sweat. They introduce moisture into any system they inhabit. Wet things gum up the works," Santini said. "And the passive dehumidifiers can only do so much."

"This place would be like a rain forest without those contraptions," Flynn observed, referring to the bright-green dehumidifier boxes that hung on the corridor walls at regularly spaced intervals, every ten meters or so. "We are constantly adding moisture to the air, just like you said — people steam up the shower, that kind of thing. There has to be a way to be rid of all that moisture."

"An interesting bit of history. The chemicals we use in the wall-mounts descend from desert survival gear and lifeboat technology."

"Not a story I have heard before."

"Tech originally developed for lifeboats, for stranded sailors, lost hikers, men trapped below ground in a mine. On the high seas, people in a lifeboat often used to perish from dehydration while waiting to be rescued. Ironic. Surrounded on all sides by water, basting in wet humid air, shipwreck survivors or downed pilots would expire from a lack of drinking water. But then came along this miracle powder. One klog of this stuff can absorb up to three liters of water every ten to twelve hours. The stuff doesn't wear out or get used up in the process."

"Exactly what sort of powder we talking about here?" Flynn asked.

"Highly absorbent," Santini said. "Zirconium-based. Organized in a metal organic framework."

"Sounds more like an underarm deodorant than a recipe for absorbing water."

"Truth is, deodorants of any sort are a problem for us here in the hab," Santini said.

"Particulates, yes?"

"Oh, my goodness, yes. In a self-contained system like this hab or the space station, deodorants can be a problem," Santini said. "Siloxanes are present in nearly every deodorant and antiperspirant people use. As these compounds dry, tiny particles become airborne. Try to keep a person's armpits dry with a roll-on or an aerosol deodorant and all you will get for your trouble are sticky particles added to the cabin air. Moisture and particulates are the kiss of death to space machinery."

"Lou, I am going to have to have more than just your word to accept that bit of folklore."

"Humans don't just sweat. They pee. They poop. They sneeze. They fart. They fuck. Think of all the wet stuff that comes out of us on a daily basis. Snot. Sweat. Urine. Spit. The air we exhale from our lungs. The tears we cry. The blood that drips from a wound. The contents of a sneeze. Saliva. Pus. Mucous. Poop. Menstrual blood. Ejaculated sperm . . . "

"Enough already. I get it. We pee a lot," Flynn exclaimed.

"Oh, it's not just the wet icky things, though there is plenty of that. There's also the not-so-wet stuff, the particulates, like I said. We shed dry skin off our bodies. Stray food particles fall from our lips when we talk or sneeze; they drop from our plates when we eat. Bits of fingernail cuticle. Strands of hair. Eyelashes. Grains of salt."

"So, what is the solution?" Flynn asked. They were methodically working their way down deeper into the lower levels of the hab, a place of unrelenting and constant machine noise, environmental systems mainly. "Do we stop sending people into space?"

"No, of course not. Giving up is never the correct answer. People like to explore."

"Then what is the answer? Humans are squishy, messy, and fragile, with little tolerance for radiation, and even less for vacuum."

"So far we don't have an answer; not a good one anyway," Santini said. "That is why you and I are down here in this hole fixing toilets the old-fashioned way, with a wrench, by hand. What we really need in the manned space program is a fundamental breakthrough in life support systems. Otherwise, there is no way for us to truly manage long-distance space travel. The simple truth is that our most modern and advanced life support systems are barely up to the task. They often break down and require nearly constant maintenance to be considered trustworthy for a long space mission. The urine pump is a case in point. Ditto for the carbon dioxide filter. Both indispensable. Yet, both nearly impossible to maintain."

"Those pumps are sketchy, I'll admit. Like you said, they have to be replaced on a regular cycle, every three to four months. But what of it? Machines and devices break down all the time at home too."

Santini chuckled. "Yeah, but your next-door neighbor doesn't drown if your toilet overflows or if it refuses to flush. Not so in a spacecraft. Roundtrips to Mars can take as much as three years to complete. To be certain that people can safely return home, every ship needs to carry a dozen or more spare urine pumps onboard. And that is just one type of spare part. There are dozens of other similar items. Think of the cost, not to mention the weight and the storage space devoted to warehousing such things."

"I get your point, Lou."

"Do you? Successful maintenance of a space vessel — or even this hab — requires more than just having the right spare part on hand. It also requires having the proper tools on hand to install them, along with suitably trained personnel. A space maintenance man must know where onboard his craft each spare part is stored, which storeroom, which locker, what the proper password is for the locker, etc. He must know how to install each replacement part because he will be called on to do so without any prior practice, maybe without having ever seen it done before. Even with RFID tags and the like, do you have any idea how easy it would be to lose track of a spare part or a tool or piece of equipment on a large spacecraft or facility as big as our moonbase? Do you have any idea how much valuable time can be wasted looking for a mislaid tool or through an improperly indexed supply room?"

Chief Flynn shrugged his shoulders in reply. Details could be boring, and he detested paperwork. Flynn was a man of action.

Santini continued. "There are hundreds, if not thousands of systems and subassemblies aboard a station like this. The number of sub-systems is simply too great for even a large crew to know them all in detail. Plus, the knowledge gets rusty when it is not regularly exercised. Months or even years may pass between training and application."

"But isn't that exactly what robots and computers are for? Machines don't forget; they don't lose track. They are programmed to know precisely where the parts are stored and exactly how to fix them when they bust."

Santini harrumphed. "Even small parts can matter, Chief. And sometimes no amount of tech can save a man when he is in trouble. Two years back, a man drowned in his own spacesuit on account of nothing."

"Space legend? Or space fact?" They started down the last set of stairs to the lowest sub-basement level.

"Fact. Raoul Pancato. Water leak in the cooling system of his spacesuit. It flooded his helmet during a spacewalk. He couldn't make it back inside the station in time. He drowned in no more than six inches of water."

"I had no idea."

"The leak was caused by a clogged filter. The piece cost all of two credits new, a pittance. There was a repair kit onboard. But fixing the spacesuit wasn't anything the astronauts had been trained to do. Sure, there was an instructional vid onboard. But who had the time? Pancato was already dead."

"You knew Pancato?"

"Raoul was my friend."

"Sorry, Lou." Chief Flynn said. "I guess what you're trying to say here is that our survival depends on simple things, like a more reliable urine pump."

"As in all things technologic, improvements are incremental, but yes. A redesigned gear train for the urine pumps. A more efficient Sabatier reaction system to recover pure water from exhaled carbon dioxide. An improved urine pre-treatment to reclaim more of the water in the life-support loop."

"Next time in English, please." By now they were sloshing through ankle deep water moving in the direction of what they thought was the source of the sewer blockage in the lowest sub-basement,

Santini explained. "The Sabatier. It's a chemical reaction. You need a reaction chamber of one sort or another. If you add hydrogen gas to the carbon dioxide we exhale in our breath, and if you do so under the right conditions, you can recover liters of pure water from the reaction, along with a quantity of methane gas. In the old days, the methane gas was considered a waste product and was vented from the ship into space. Nowadays we no longer discard it. The cost in terms of lost resources is too high. The Sabatier method requires that we constantly burn hydrogen gas. Newer systems use pyrolysis. They take the waste methane, add heat, and get back hydrogen gas, plus elemental carbon. The released hydrogen gas can then be recycled back into the Sabatier reactor, leaving an easily removed deposit of carbon in the form of pyrolytic graphite. The reactor is little more than a reinforced steel pipe. It can periodically be serviced by an astronaut where the carbon deposit is chiseled out and tossed away."

"Pyrolytic graphite?"

"The stuff has the consistency of mica. It forms a crystallized graphene sheet, pretty useful stuff in its own right to reinforce certain plastics and metals. Plus, it can be used as a thermal interface material, what techs call a heat spreader."

Suddenly Lou Santini became very quiet. He took a sharp breath, then said, "I think I may have found the source of our toilet clog."

"Finally."

"Chief, shine your light over here."

"Oh, my God. Is that a hand?" Flynn said as he knelt down beside the thing to examine it more closely. "This is an actual human hand."

"Not some fancy repro?"

Chief Flynn picked up the hand, but held it at arm's length as if the thing might bite him. "No, this is the real thing, including severed muscle, broken bone, and dried blood. I would say our disarticulated hand is fresh. It hasn't been floating in this water long, certainly no more than a day."

"Any reports of someone missing a hand?" Santini asked.

"Don't you mean, where is the rest of the body?"

"We both know the answer to that question."

"We do?"

"Further down the drain somewhere," Santini said. "The hand didn't clog the drains; the rest of the carcass did."

Chief Flynn threw up violently, dropping the severed hand in the process.

"Great! Now you have gone and soiled the crime scene," Santini mocked.

Flynn threw up for a second time.

"Okay, Chief, what say we get you home before you further clog up the drain?"

CHAPTER TWENTY-TWO

Day Four, 1145 hours

"A hand isn't much to go on," Winston Hanrahan observed without emotion.

After the severed hand was discovered and Chief Flynn had regained his composure, he and Santini had gone straight up to the administrator's office with the hand to deliver the terrible news. Hanrahan seemed nonplussed at the sight of the hand. They carried it in a bio-hazard container.

"It will be hours before we can fish out anything bigger than this hand from the sewer," Santini said, lifting the lid on the container. "In the meantime, you have to put out an all-points to everyone in the hab to conserve water. People need to stop flushing toilets until we can restore the sewer system to normal function."

"Edith is preparing the bulletin as we speak," Hanrahan said. "As for identifying the victim, if all we have to go on is a hand, I guess we go with what we got."

"Actually, what we have are two missing persons," Flynn said.

"What in blazes?" Hanrahan exclaimed. "Two missing persons? Who the hell has gone missing? And why am I just learning about this now?"

"Doyle tells me that he has been unable to reach Ouida for nearly one full day now, since sometime yesterday afternoon," Flynn said. "Doc Runyon says the same."

"How would Doyle know how long she has been missing?" Hanrahan retorted. "I thought you told him that contact with his wife was off-limits?"

"I said he couldn't visit. I never said he couldn't call. When she didn't answer her page, Doyle sent someone over to their place to check on her. Entry records show she hasn't been back to her flat since at least midday yesterday."

"Staying with a friend?" Hanrahan asked.

"We're checking."

"You said two people were missing. Who else has gone on walkabout?"

Flynn answered. "Lou reported to me on the way over here that Carl Rosen hasn't been seen since Sinclair fired him earlier this morning."

"But that was only a few hours ago. Did you check his room?" Hanrahan asked.

"Not personally. I haven't had the time. But I did send someone. Rosen's ID tracker shows him in his room. But there is no sign of him anywhere," Santini said.

"People cannot just up and disappear," Hanrahan said frustrated. "Not in a place like this. Do you think there is a connection between the two missing persons?"

"Well, that hand belongs to somebody, now doesn't it?" Flynn said.

"Are you mocking me?" Hanrahan asked.

"Why would I ever do that?"

"Because you don't like me."

"No, I do not," Flynn replied without emotion.

"Quit pissing for distance, boys," Santini said. "With all the dead ends, there is one thing I am absolutely sure of."

"And that is?"

"Our friend Mr. Hand does not belong to a woman. If Ouida is dead, this isn't her hand."

"You know this how?" Hanrahan asked.

"The hand is too large. I measured it with the spanner. Plus, there is no sign of her having ever worn a wedding band on her ring finger."

"So, you're saying the hand belongs to Carl Rosen?" Hanrahan asked.

"No, I'm not saying that at all. I have no idea who the hand belongs to," Santini replied, as he got up to leave Hanrahan's office. "All I'm willing to say with any degree of certainty is that the hand doesn't belong to a woman, not now, not ever. It may be possible to lift prints, maybe draw blood to determine blood type or make a DNA match from the database. It will take time, though."

"Where are you two cowbells going?" Hanrahan demanded to know, as they both headed for the door.

"The Chief and I have things to do. We have an appointment down in the control room to review security footage. As soon as we know something concrete, we'll report back to you with our findings."

Chief Flynn and Lou Santini left together. Once they were out of earshot, Santini said, "I always forget how much I detest that man."

"You and me both. Can you really lift prints or get a DNA match from a hand like that?"

"Maybe. But forensics isn't my strong suit. We'll need to call in a specialist."

"Doc Runyon?"

Santini shrugged his shoulders.

"Now what about those security tapes?" Flynn asked.

"We need to determine what has become of Carl Rosen and Ouida Baldwin. We have security cams in every corridor in and around crew quarters. If we roll back the digital record, we ought to be able to determine at what time Ouida last entered her flat. We can do the same thing on Carl Rosen. It is my understanding that earlier this morning Paddington Sinclair kicked him out of his orientation meeting. That would have been shortly after 0600. From what I gather, the boy was ordered to take the first ship back home. But, there haven't been any ships. Rosen never actually left the base. He must still be here in the hab somewhere."

"Who told you that?"

"My daughter."

"Since when do you have a daughter, Lou? And why haven't I ever heard anything about her before now?"

"The girl uses her mother's maiden name. Petronas. Neena Petronas. She is on the lunar elevator construction team. Neena gave me the down and the low on Rosen and Sinclair after her shift this morning. Neena had been topside with another crew member installing some sort of tracking device on the surface. I think the other crew member was that character Cruz from band practice last night. She tells me that both Rosen and Sinclair are queer as a four-sided coin. The two have been in some sort of on-again off-again love affair for the past six months."

"No shit. That gives us motive, doesn't it? Lover's quarrel."

"First, we need a body, Chief. Then we need a suspect. Only then do we need motive. Besides, there haven't been any ships in or out of here since the elevator team first arrived. Rosen couldn't possibly have left the habitat, even if he'd wanted to. The re-supply ship has been delayed arriving and nothing has departed here since, except for one Mars-bound freighter and that was a robot-ship. No humans onboard, no crew quarters."

"No place onboard that ship to hide a stowaway? No place onboard to stow a dead body?"

"I had not thought of stowing a dead body. But I will check the manifest. Launch weights are known and recorded down to the last ounce."

"In the meantime, I think we both know the truth, don't we?" Chief Flynn said.

"We do?"

"Both Ouida and Carl Rosen are still here in the hab. That's his body down there in the basement jammed in the sewer, and she has found a convenient place to hide out. The woman was already at the top of our suspect list for the tunnel bombing. Maybe Rosen fell upon the truth and paid for his curiosity with his life."

"You're saying she killed the man?" Santini shook his head.

"Now we have two suspects, don't we?"

"Enough fantasizing, Chief. We need to run those tapes and pin this thing down better."

•

•

Day Four, 1300 hours

"Chief, I have been studying these surveillance tapes for the past hour. I don't think our two missing persons ever crossed paths. Rosen left the early morning meeting, as we already know, and went straight to Hanrahan's office, probably to complain about being fired. After Rosen left Hanrahan's office, he stopped to make one or two calls on his comm and was next seen entering the men's exercise area. This was about 0700 this morning. But there are no cameras in there, none at all. Privacy issues. Naked guys showering and all that. But no hallway cam ever shows him leaving."

"Never?"

"Nope."

"Then he must still be in there," Flynn said.

"Had one of my people check the locker room. No sign of him. No sign of a struggle."

"Curious."

"Yes, and the only one to enter or leave the locker room after 0600 was a janitor, about two hours later. Near as I can tell, Ouida never goes into that part of the hab at any time. Yesterday afternoon, she is seen leaving her quarters about 2 p.m. wearing what looks to be a small backpack. She goes to see

Doyle in the bachelor wing. She leaves his pad about an hour later, *sans* backpack, and goes to the women's locker room, where she pulls the same disappearing act as Rosen. We never see her on tape again."

Chief Flynn was quiet for nearly half a minute, then he said, "We need to know more about that janitor. Maybe the janitor is our killer."

"Okay, I can have one of my people run that down for you. Also, I forgot to mention. My Neena talked to Carl Rosen not long after he left Hanrahan's office. She had just finished eating breakfast when she ran into the boy in the corridor."

"That was one of the calls he made?"

"No, they talked face to face before he went in the direction of the locker room. She asked him what he was doing. He said he was going to use some of his free time to investigate the sabotage."

Flynn spun around. "You are telling me that your daughter was one of the last people to see Carl Rosen alive?"

"Apparently."

"And the two of them talked about this week's bombing?"

"Chief, everyone in the hab is still talking about it. Nothing suspicious there. But maybe curiosity did kill the cat."

"Speaking of curiosities, here is one for you, Lou. Earlier, when you and I met with Hanrahan, he didn't say anything at all to us about Rosen having been in his office. Don't you find that a bit strange? Wilson Hanrahan might have been one of the last people to see Rosen alive."

"You mean if Rosen is actually dead. It's too soon to know that for sure. It'll be hours, perhaps days before we can lift prints or make a DNA match. And let's not forget that the torso has not yet been recovered."

"What say you and me go down to the men's locker room and see if there isn't another way out of there, one that Carl Rosen might have used to escape detection."

"Right behind you, Chief."

CHAPTER TWENTY-THREE

Day Four, 1330 hours

"It smells like dirty underwear in here," Flynn said as the two of them entered the men's locker room on the lower level. Towels everywhere, half-open lockers, dirty socks lying on the bench, a jockstrap hanging from a towel hook.

"You don't work out much, do you, Chief?" Santini said.

"Don't have to. I'm an Adonis."

"In your dreams, butt cheeks. If you did work out, you would know the truth. Locker rooms smell the same the world over."

"Okay, down to business," Flynn said. "Where would a man hide in a locker room if he didn't want to be found? More to the point — Does this place have a back door, a way for a man to leave without being noticed?"

"Several ways, actually. This is a locker room. Showers mean pipes, and pipes mean holes in the wall. Showers also mean drains. Drains mean holes in the floor. Both may be avenues for someone to enter or leave the room. Men work out. The room gets warm. The air conditioning system clicks on. There must be vents and fans, which mean more holes in the walls and the ceilings and floors."

"Okay. Point taken," Flynn said. "We have to consider air ducts, water pipes, service panels, sewer lines, ceiling fans, probably a garbage chute as well. Plus, there must be electrical panels, light fixtures, wall lockers, things like that. What we really need is a blueprint with a detailed layout of this part of the hab."

"Already got the blues up on my screen."

Santini handed Chief Flynn the small electronic device he always carried, usually in a satchel slung under one arm. A schematic of the hab was displayed on the screen. "Tab over to Level Three and you can expand the locker room area. Shows water lines, electrical lines, sewer, everything."

Chief Flynn immediately handed the device back to Santini without even looking at the screen. "Your device. You be the tourist guide. Any walls with empty passages behind?"

"Troglodyte."

"Excuse me?"

"Troglodyte. Someone who lives in a cave or belongs to a prehistoric community."

"So, I don't like computers. No need to call me names. Any walls with empty passages behind?" Flynn said again.

"Several. There is a false wall behind the row of sinks on the far wall. It gives a plumber access to all the waterworks — drains, sinks, shower heads, faucets, floor drains, everything. Plus, there is a service corridor that runs behind the far walls of both locker rooms. It can only be accessed via a locked panel door with outer corridor access. But the service corridor also offers access to the overhead crawl space. The crawl space is where the air ducts and other utilities are located."

"So, the janitorial staff has keys, yes?"

"Yes, and there is a freight elevator at the far end of the service corridor."

"Let me guess," Flynn said. "The elevator shaft runs down to the sub-basement where we found the hand, as well as all the way up to the crew quarters level. Any janitor with an access card would have free rein of the place."

"Not just janitors. Engineering, security, Hanrahan himself. A lot of people have access, including me and you — and I'm innocent."

"Which makes me what? — a Troglodyte and a murderer?"

"I didn't say that, Chief."

"Let's get back down to cases, shall we? So, the janitor comes into the locker room, whacks Rosen who is already there doing his workout, and dumps the body in the basement using the service corridor and the freight elevator? Is that what we are saying here?"

"The question is why?"

"Shouldn't the question be who?"

"You said it was the janitor," Santini replied.

"Or was it someone dressed up to look like a janitor?"

"I see where you are going with this. We figure out the who and we may be able to learn the why."

Santini reached into his pocket and pulled out a large set of punched keycards strung on a slender chain. He used his master key to open the door to the service corridor and proceeded inside. Flynn followed.

"The service elevator is about fifty meters down this corridor," Santini said glancing at the display on his small handheld device. "Let's go."

They had covered about half that distance when they first heard the sound.

"What was that noise?" Chief Flynn asked.

"I have no idea."

Then they both heard it again.

"We are not alone . . . someone is here in the corridor with us," Santini said quietly.

"Or something."

The same thought entered both their minds at the same moment.

They were being stalked, and not by a person, but by a mechanical device, a robot.

"If it's a bot, we can't outrun the thing, and we certainly can't whup it in a fair fight," Santini said quietly as before.

"Surrender is not really my thing."

"And dying is not really mine."

"Fair point."

Then suddenly the quiet was broken. "Gentlemen, no one is permitted in this corridor without written and time-stamped authorization from Administrator Hanrahan." It was the voice of Sentrybotta III, one of the hab's stripped down versions of the new class of Z-bot.

"We don't require written authorization to be down here," Flynn said firmly. "And you are only a robot. Your programming requires you to obey our orders. Step aside and allow us safe passage to continue our work."

"I do not answer to you," the Z-bot calmly replied.

"And to whom do you answer?"

"Administrator Winston Hanrahan. And he has instructed me to escort any unauthorized persons who enter this passageway up to him right away. Follow me, please. I have already scanned your ID badges, and I know who each of you are. Chief Engineer Clay Flynn. Senior Tech Officer Louis Santini. I see from your records that you go by the name of Lou, or simply by Santini."

"Why would Hanrahan post a sentry bot down here and not tell us anything about it?" Santini asked, expecting an answer from Chief Flynn. But before Flynn could reply, the robot again spoke.

"I have been waiting in this corridor since the morning of the bombing. My instructions are to block entrance to any intruders and to escort violators directly to the office of Administrator Winston Hanrahan."

"Sentrybotta III — Were your instructions to wait in this corridor for us specifically?" Chief Flynn asked.

"No, not you specifically. Any unauthorized persons. You have been the first to come by since the order was given."

Santini ignored the robot and turned to Flynn. "If Hanrahan parked this bot down here in the back corridor three days ago, he must have known that someone had been — or would be — up to no good back here."

"And yet, he didn't say a thing to us about it when we were in his office not one hour ago. We need to complete our investigation, sentry bot or no sentry bot."

"I agree," Santini said quietly, so that perhaps the bot wouldn't hear. "You know there is an override protocol, even for instructions from Hanrahan."

"I had forgotten."

"Luckily, I have not," Santini said before turning back to address the Z-bot still blocking their way. "Robot. This is Senior Tech Officer Louis Santini, badge number KK42HY. This is a command instruction. Protocol A15LKPQ25. Immediate override. Cease and desist all activities and communications until I reactivate you."

The robot came to attention, stood frozen like a toy soldier. "Awaiting instruction, Senior Tech Officer Louis Santini, badge number KK42HY."

"Robot. This is Senior Tech Officer Louis Santini, badge number KK42HY. This is a command instruction. Remain here. Make no report to Administrator Hanrahan. Allow no one beside Chief Flynn or myself up or down this corridor. Acknowledge."

"I acknowledge your instruction, Senior Tech Officer Louis Santini, badge number KK42HY. I will remain here. I will allow no one but you or Chief Engineer Clay Flynn to pass."

"Confirmed," Santini said to the bot before turning to his friend. "Let's go, Flynn."

"Where to now?"

Santini pointed into the darkness down the corridor. "Now we go figure out who killed Rosen and why. Follow me." Santini started off towards the freight elevator. "We need to follow this trail wherever it takes us."

"Hold that thought," Flynn said. "There is an urgent message coming in on my comm. Something about a solar flare."

CHAPTER TWENTY-FOUR

One Hour Earlier
Day Four, 1220 hours

"Dr. Sinclair, we have important news," Neena Petronas said, anxiety coloring her voice. "Guy tells me that we have just received a flash report from Los Alamos."

Guy Cruz crowded in next to her in the tiny control booth. "Los Alamos reports a high probability of an X-Class solar flare event to occur within the next eight to ten hours. Needles are off the chart."

At first, Paddington Sinclair did not react to the news. He was distracted and lost in his work. The readout before him said that his elevator team had just reached the two-thousand-klom mark on the down-reel and more than three times that number on the up-reel of the counterweight, some eight thousand kloms reeled out in all, damn good for half a day's work.

"What's that you say?" Sinclair looked up from his work. Guy Cruz stood before him along with Neena Petronas. Neena was easily his most able student, and though he would never admit it, Guy ranked high on his list too. Sinclair counted on their exacting expertise to help supervise the other students, most of whom he considered cretins.

Spirits were low, and with good reason. Rumors were flying. The grapevine was filled with disturbing news about Carl Rosen's apparent gruesome end. Although a positive ID had not yet been made, everything they'd heard pointed in that direction.

"Solar flares, Dr. Sinclair. Los Alamos reports that an X-Class solar flare event is imminent." Neena was never fully at ease when she spoke to Paddington Sinclair. It was in his nature to try and make those around him feel small and insignificant.

"Lord Almighty, the black swan event no one planned for," Sinclair mumbled, stepping back from his workstation.

"Sir?"

"Black swan event. The unexpected event that carries with it devastating consequences. Don't they teach you children anything in graduate school anymore?"

"Why black swan?" Neena asked.

"No time for that now."

"But I thought solar flares followed a set pattern," Guy Cruz said.

"They do . . . Except when they don't," Sinclair answered. "We chose this window to unreel the lunar cable precisely because solar flare activity was predicted to be at a minimum."

"Professor, I am sorry for being so thick," Neena said, beginning to question the man's intellect. "Why the flash report from New Mexico? Does something bad happen to the cable during a solar flare?"

"Don't exactly know for certain. Never done it before." Paddington Sinclair sat down with a sigh.

"Decades of planning and no one ran a sim?" Cruz asked in a sarcastic tone. He had come to despise Sinclair for the very reasons that Neena feared him, because of the man's staggering brilliance.

"Oh, we ran sims alright, hundreds of them, 'til we were blue in the face."

"And?"

"The three-body problem," Sinclair answered.

"I am going to need a little more than that," Guy replied.

"That's all the man ever talks about, the three-body problem," Neena grumbled.

"Yes, the three-body problem. Mathematics. Or is it geometry? How the energy and particles in a solar flare affect the cable depends on two things: where in its orbit the Moon is at the time the flood of energized particles arrive, and, secondly, the energy-equivalent of the event. If the Earth stands like a shield between us and the solar flare at the moment of impact, the effect on us will be minimized. The Earth's magnetosphere acts as a kind of shield or buffer. But . . . if our position is such that the Moon receives a thorough soaking — a full dose of radiation and the rest — all bets are off. There could be fireworks. Literally."

"Fireworks, as in a joyful Fourth of July? Or fireworks, as in a bolt of lightning strikes a dynamite manufacturing plant?" Neena asked.

"More like the latter, I am afraid. A solar flare can involve an energy release that is measured in joules, something on the order of 10 to the 25th power. This is roughly equivalent to igniting a billion megatons of TNT. The sims we did run told us several things. The line will become electrified along its entire length. Without a ground, there is no easy way to bleed off all that highly charged energy. The energy will flow upward along the cable until it collides with the counterweight. That's when the trouble begins. The counterweight will become superheated, then explode like a hydrogen bomb."

"Fireworks?"

"You bet."

"What is the risk to us personally?" Neena asked, beginning to worry for their safety.

Sinclair seemed not to understand the question.

"Professor, snap out of it," Neena exclaimed. "You seem more concerned about the safety of the cable than the safety of the people raising it. What about the risks to us, and to the hab?"

"No way to know. But yes, I see what you are driving at. That could be a problem."

"How large of a problem?" Cruz asked, stealing a nervous glance at his girlfriend.

Sinclair focused. "Solar flares can produce a very broad spectrum of emissions, magnificent streams of highly energetic particles in the solar wind, a so-called solar proton event. These particles can impact the Earth's magnetosphere, and they present a radiation hazard to spacecraft and astronauts and to us. Massive solar flares are sometimes accompanied by coronal mass ejections. Those evil mothers can trigger a fierce geomagnetic storm. Storms like that are so violent, they have been known to cripple satellites, even knock out electric power grids on Earth. High energy protons pass directly through the human body. They cause biochemical damage and present a significant hazard to any human being caught in its path. Some kind of physical or magnetic shielding will be required to protect us from the storm. We have to get indoors, preferably underground in the deepest sub-basement or volcanic tube."

"Are you ordering us to take cover?" Neena asked, thinking she should first talk to her father about the risk.

"Take cover? Oh, yes. Immediately. An X-Class event is the worst sort. From the moment of visual detection, proton storms like this require a minimum two hours to reach Earth orbit. We have to get everyone inside, behind shelter, preferably underground, to prevent radiation poisoning."

"Isn't there anything we can do to prevent the counterweight from exploding like a bomb?" Cruz asked, the pitch in his voice rising.

"Small things, sure. But not a great deal." Sinclair shook his head. "We could have as little as sixty minutes to prepare. It's not like we can just reel in 8,000 kloms of elevator cable in nothing flat. It's still being reeled out at a velocity of more than fifty meters per second. Plus, the stuff kinks when re-coiled. The cable's Zylon fiber core is wrapped in a mesh of Magellan M8, which can bunch up and kink if the cable is re-coiled. It will likely get tangled up and break."

"Jesus God," Cruz exclaimed. "Won't electrification of the line present as a regular problem throughout the life of the elevator?"

"Flares, yes. Overheating events, no, not at all. Once the tether is fully extended, the cable will reach the surface of the moon. Then it will be anchored to a conventional ground. In the future, such energy boosts can easily be shunted downward into the regolith instead of upward into the counterweight. Problem solved."

"But not today?" Neena said.

"Nope, not today. Today we will be lucky if the counterweight doesn't heat up and explode into a thousand million pieces and kill us all."

"You mean unless we die of radiation poisoning first."

"Yes, that is precisely what I mean," Sinclair said.

"Nice."

"Guy, do you really think sarcasm is appropriate here?" Sinclair barked.

"We better notify Flynn, Hanrahan, and the rest of the senior staff," Neena said.

"The sooner the better," Guy added. "Flynn first. He seems to be the only one around here who knows what he's doing."

CHAPTER TWENTY-FIVE

Six Hours Earlier
Day Four, 0620 hours

Carl Rosen never knew he had it within him to be this angry.

Paddington Sinclair had dismissed him from the team, and for what reason? *For no better reason than pure sexual discrimination.*

Such treatment enraged Rosen, and he was not about to let the matter lie. Only someone higher up the food chain than Paddington Sinclair could deal with a matter of such grave importance, someone like Administrator Winston Hanrahan. That's whose office Carl was headed for now.

Rosen burned inside with anger. Homosexuality was a certainty he had struggled with his entire adult life. His feelings were unnatural, some said, immoral, disgusting, abnormal. But not to Carl. This was the way he was and this was the way he had always been. Carl couldn't change it, even if he wanted to, which he did not. Certain types of men turned him on and that was that.

Rosen was a scientist first, a man with a keen mind. He observed the natural order of things and believed it to be orderly. But why would natural selection produce homosexuality if the genetic imperative was propagation of the species? *It made no sense!* And yet here he was.

Some people had a taste for chocolate ice cream; others loved raw fish; Rosen was attracted to handsome and powerful men. Civilization had come a long way since its birth in the ancient deltas and river valleys of the Mideast. But certain things had not changed as much as a liberal from another age might wish. Polite society tolerated homosexuality, but just barely. Polite society certainly did not endorse it, and polite society remained uncomfortable when it was practiced out in the open where others might see.

True, sexual orientation was no longer a deterrent to landing a good job, nor was it even much of a hindrance to advancement. But when your superior is a homosexual and a misconstrued sexual overture in the workplace leads to your dismissal, well, that was another matter. Rosen felt he was on solid ground if he moved to file a harassment complaint against Sinclair.

"Is Administrator Hanrahan in?" Carl asked the pretty secretary outside Hanrahan's office door. The wooden name plate on her desk said her name was Edith Wellsforth.

Edith looked up from her nails, glanced at the credentials he handed her. "He's in his office, Mr. Rosen. But Mr. Hanrahan is already running late for his breakfast meeting. I suggest you make an appointment and come back again at a later time."

"I promise to keep it short." Rosen didn't want to allow time for his anger to soften. It only made good sense to lodge his complaint while he was still pissed off and events still clear in his mind.

"It's Carl Rosen for you, sir." Edith buzzed in. "From Sinclair's Moon Beam contingent. I told him you were running late."

"Come in, Carl," a voice boomed from the inner office. "I can give you five minutes."

"I would like to file a formal complaint."

"And why doesn't that surprise me?" Hanrahan said in his usual haughty voice. "Against whom would you like to file a complaint this early in the morning? I haven't even had my morning coffee yet."

"Paddington Sinclair."

"And for what reason? I thought you folks were supposed to be in a meeting just now." Hanrahan looked at his chron.

"The reason?" Rosen said. "Sexual harassment. And yes, the rest of them are all still in that meeting."

"Sexual harassment, Carl? Against whom?"

"Against me."

Hanrahan paused to let that last statement sink in. "Sinclair made a pass at you?"

"No, I made a pass at him."

"I see. You made a pass at him — I assume uncompleted — and now you wish to file a complaint against him? I'm confused, Carl. On what grounds?"

"On the grounds that he just fired me," Rosen explained. "Fired me and ordered me home."

"Carl, I can have my secretary Edith take your statement. But I am not sure where we can go with this. Paddington Sinclair does not work for me, and I haven't any legal authority to discipline the man."

"But, the law."

"Earth-law doesn't have jurisdiction up here, Carl. This kind of thing is covered under the Moon Exploration Protocols."

"So, I'm screwed?"

"Is that even possible?" Hanrahan suppressed a nervous chuckle.

Rosen got red-faced. "Are you making some sort of crack about homosexuals? You think we cannot be screwed?"

"Now I suppose you will be wanting to file a complaint against me?"

"Fuck you, Hanrahan." Carl Rosen got up to leave. "When is the next ship home?"

"Not for two weeks; maybe longer. You will probably be going home on the very same ship and at the very same time as the rest of your team. How's them oats?"

Rosen shook his head angrily. "How the hell am I supposed to keep myself busy for two weeks on this frozen rock with nothing else to do?"

"We have an unsolved mystery you can work on," Hanrahan said as he gathered his things and rose to leave for his meeting.

"The tunnel bombing?" Rosen asked, following him out the door.

"Yes, the tunnel bombing. Go see Chief Flynn. Ask him if you can lend a hand in the investigation. It has only just begun. Edith can point the way."

"You're just trying to get rid of me."

"Indeed I am. Now go bother someone else. You have made me late for my meeting."

•

•

Carl Rosen left Hanrahan's office in a huff and descended to the ground level where the mess was located. Anger made his blood boil. It also made him hungry. He thought to stop and have a bite to eat before trying to connect with Chief Flynn.

But Rosen was self-conscious about his weight, so, as he approached the mess, he changed his mind about eating. *Work up a little hunger*, he thought. *Hit the weights first, then go eat.*

Rosen stopped to use his handheld to send a text, then again to map his location within the hab. As he stood in the brightly lit corridor studying the e-map of the hab's layout, a woman he knew walked up to him, Neena Petronas. She had just come from eating breakfast with Paddington Sinclair in the mess and was in a hurry.

"Eating breakfast with the enemy?" he asked in a caustic tone.

"Don't be like that, Carl," Neena said. "The man's my boss. I'm not a fan, but I do have to work with the buzzard on a daily basis. So cut me just a little slack, will you?"

"You have Cruz; who do I have?"

"Carl, I don't have time to fence with you right now. We'll take this up again at a later time, I promise."

"Now that I've been fired, I have nothing better to do with my time than go see if I can lend a hand in the bombing investigation."

"Good for you, Carl. Stay busy. That's a smart idea."

"Whatever."

Rosen turned on his heels, hell bent for the locker room and a solid workout. Neena tracked him with her eyes as he disappeared out of sight down the passageway.

The exercise paddock was down one level adjacent to the men's locker room. That is when he had a second chance encounter, this time with Ouida Baldwin in the lower corridor.

"Do you know where Chief Flynn's office is?" he asked.

Rosen asked the question as a means of striking up a conversation, not because he needed directions. Edith Wellsforth had already told him the way, and Rosen had already mapped out the route on his handheld.

"Who is asking?"

Ouida was suspicious of this face she did not recognize. The residents of the moonbase were a small community. *Was this unknown man an investigator up from Earth onboard the ship that brought the elevator team?* Scuttlebutt had it that an anti-terrorist specialist had been called in.

"Name is Carl Rosen. Administrator Hanrahan said I ought to look up Chief Flynn and see if I can help him solve the sabotage mystery."

Ouida's countenance stiffened. "And who are you again?"

Rosen lied. It made him feel important, something to boost his ego after his abrupt dismissal. "I am with the Marshal Service, the Space Marshal Service."

"A cop, eh?"

"Of a stripe."

"Can I see your badge?"

"Don't carry one. Don't need to."

"Some ID then."

"Don't carry any. If you want to check my credentials, feel free to do so with Hanrahan. He knows why I am here." It was a calculated gamble on Rosen's part, but she seemed like a busy woman and he doubted whether she would take the time to follow up his claim with the boss man.

She considered his answer, then asked, "You got any suspects?"

"This is not a subject I am at liberty to discuss. Who are you again?"

"Ouida Baldwin, medical officer."

"Glad to make your acquaintance, Ouida Baldwin, medical officer. Can you please direct me to Chief Flynn's office?"

"Yes, of course. It's this way." She pointed and started down the hall, her mind racing. She felt the walls beginning to close in around her.

"Are you the saboteur?" Rosen suddenly asked. The words were out of his mouth before he had thought through the possible consequences of his question.

"Why on Earth would you ask me such a thing?" she gasped, the color running from her face.

"Body language."

"I have a tell?" she asked.

"Don't know you well enough to say that with certainty," Rosen answered. "But I can read people."

"This way, Sherlock. Next hallway over is Chief Flynn's office."

That is when Carl Rosen knew he was in trouble. Edith Wellsforth had definitely said the Chief's office was upstairs and in the opposite wing. This woman was leading him into a trap of some sort.

"Are you sure?" he asked, his breath coming faster.

"Yes, of course I'm sure."

When they rounded the next corner, Ouida acted with furious dispatch. She was a doctor, a surgeon by trade, one with homicidal blood flowing through her veins. She knew how to kill a man quickly, if not quietly.

Ouida pulled the knife she always carried with her from its sheath. In one easy motion, she sliced him across the throat from left to right and a second time across the groin, severing the femoral artery.

Rosen staggered backward, clutching at his throat then stumbled to the floor, gasping for air and making gurgling sounds from his throat as he tried to speak.

"Just close your eyes and let it happen," she murmured quietly as she stood over him and watched the life drain out of his body. "See? All better now."

▲

Ouida's hands were dripping red with warm wet sticky blood, Carl Rosen's blood. The blood spatter was everywhere, on the floor, on the walls, on the ceiling. In one-sixth gravity, there was no way to contain that much blood. Anything liquid or viscous flew everywhere and took its time finding a new surface to settle upon.

Sweat poured off her brow, mixing with the blood and sinew. Taking apart a human body was hard, demanding work.

The corpse was fresh and she scolded herself. She should have thought this thing through better beforehand. *First drain out most of the blood; then cut the body apart.* She wouldn't make that same mistake the next time.

A frown formed on her face. *Would there even be a next time?*

Of course, there would be! This was delicious fun, killing someone, watching the life drain out of their body — way more fun than taking her own life as she had so often contemplated.

Now she finally had something to live for! Killing was pleasurable, a veritable pleasure that made good things twitch in a satisfying way between her legs.

Removing the limbs proved the most difficult. After she killed Rosen in the lower corridor, Ouida pinched a laundry cart from housekeeping and rolled the body onto the freight elevator and down to the basement. She came back half an hour later with a surgical laser and went to work on him, disassembling his limbs and torso.

The separation of head and limbs from the torso took time. Lots to cut through. Ball and socket joints. Tough, wiry ligaments. Strong white tendons. Cartilage. Bone. Major blood vessels. Bundles of nerves. Fibrous connective tissue.

The laser cutting tool sliced easily through muscle and skin. But, even with all its power, it was slower going with bone and cartilage and dense connective tissue. The blood spewed everywhere, warm and sticky and sweet smelling. *Ah, to be alive, to strip living tissue down to its dead essence! Could anything be better?*

Evil thoughts filled her brain. When she was done here at the moonbase — done killing everyone that called this place home — when the residents had suffered and all drowned in a soup of their own spew and vomit, when they had turned blue from a lack of oxygen and died an ugly death with swollen tongues protruding grotesquely from their open mouths, then she would return to Earth, to San Diego, and do what she should have done long ago, which was to end his life, kill him, her Jaxson, burn down the hospital that kept him on life support, take out her vengeance on all humanity around her in every place.

CHAPTER TWENTY-SIX

Day Four, 1400 hours

"Working alongside you has taken on a whole new meaning for me," Guy Cruz said with a broad smile on his face. The bed they shared was hardly wide enough for one person, let alone two. "I especially like the part where I am working my way down along your left side, which is, after all, your prettiest side."

"You saying I'm lopsided?"

"A tad asymmetrical. But hardly noticeable from this angle."

Neena returned Guy's smile from beneath the covers, but her face reddened in a blush. She threw back the sheets, got up, and glided slowly and nakedly across the small room to the narrow shower stall. Hot water was at a premium and she wasted no time washing the remnants of their love-making from her glistening white skin and down the drain.

Guy watched her shower through the narrow, translucent glass door and smiled. Neena was exactly what he wanted in a woman, smart, capable, and great in bed. Back home in New Mexico, they lived together and often shared a shower.

"All in all, Nee, I would say it has been a pretty good day."

"What's that?" she shouted from the confines of the shower stall. The water was metered and turned off on its own.

"I was saying that despite the solar flare scare, today turned out to be a pretty good day. First came the successful deployment of the triangulation pods. But then my day got even better."

"How so?" Neena asked as she stepped dripping wet from the shower. She reached for a towel, wrapped it around her chest and arms, then snuggled up close to the wall heater.

"You need ask?" Cruz said, his feelings hurt. "My day got even better when I had you."

"Had me?" she said, putting aside the towel and reaching for her clothes on a wall hook. "Not so sure I like the way that sounds."

"Hardly my intention to be crude," Guy said. "What say you let me have another go at it. My day got even better when a beautiful woman crawled into my bed and made sweet love to me."

"Much better," she said, slipping on her underthings. "But this is not your bed; it's mine, remember? Anyway, playtime has come to an end. There is much work to be done."

"Where you off to, girl?" Guy asked as he stepped into her shower stall.

"There won't be any hot water," she warned as he reached for the faucet handle.

"None? None whatsoever?"

"Nope. This ain't Santa Fe. Go shower in your own place. I'll not have you use up my entire water allotment. Go home and use your own damn water."

"Where you going, Nee?"

"I kind of promised my father last night at band practice that I would stop by and see him again sometime this afternoon. The two of us need to have a heart-to-heart."

"You and he on the outs?" Guy asked, slipping on his clothes. He was resigned to returning to his own flat for a shower.

"In a manner of speaking. He and Mom split up years ago. She pretty much raised me alone. I took her maiden name. Dad didn't like that. He and I were close when I was young, but not so much anymore. We haven't seen each other in a great long while. Having a chance at reconciliation was sort of on my mind when I interviewed to be on the Moon Beam team."

"Define 'a great long while'."

"Two years," Neena said. "Maybe three."

"So, I guess the two of you will have a lot to catch up on, plenty to talk about."

"Not as much as you may think. That's why, before I go see him, my first stop when I leave here will be on the rec level."

"The pub? Perdition's Cup?"

"I need a good stiff drink before I go see Father in his office. Maybe two good stiff drinks."

"Liquid courage?" Guy asked.

"I suppose."

Neena dressed in casual clothes and set out for the recreation level. Perdition's Cup had a reputation known even on Earth — game rooms of every stripe, holo bar, vid parlor, sim gallery, live ammo room.

"Care for company?" Guy shouted after her.

She shook her head. "Thanks, but no thanks. I'm afraid this is something I have got to do solo."

Neena left the room and strode with purpose along the corridor. In this wing someone had taken the time to paint a series of colorful murals on the concrete walls. They were illuminated in a warm, friendly way. Not so in other arms of the hab. Those other walls were drab, even unfriendly. To stare at them made people angry.

She reached the lift at the far end of the corridor and rode it up two levels. Then she proceeded through the connector tube between buildings and onto the rec level. It was noisy on this level, a bevy of activity and fun-making, bars, dancing, pastimes, dangers, and amusements.

Neena paused at the giant swinging doors to the Cup, hesitant to enter. This is where the Lunatics went when they wanted to get drunk; this is where they trolled to find a quick lay. Women, contraband, tobacco, Deludes, diversions of every sort.

Perdition's Cup had little to recommend it. Gaudy décor, unwholesome reputation, maelstrom of corruption and deceitful behavior. Like an oversized bug-light, it attracted every breed of pleasure-seeking vermin one could possibly suppose.

The air inside the Cup was stale. Neena coughed involuntarily. Too many bodies standing too closely together throwing off too much sweat and body heat. — wildcatters in or outbound; would-be miners, some looking for work, others just sacked; prostitutes; drunks; loons Venus-bound.

But this was where she needed to be for what she had to do. The holo bar was uncomfortably loud when she walked in, too loud for 2 p.m. in the afternoon, and far too crowded for her taste.

Don't these people have jobs? she wondered. *But, of course, they do.* Life on the Moon was colorless. It was regimented and stressful in the extreme, the sort of life that took its toll on the minds and bodies of lesser mortals. To escape from reality, even for one hour, was the only known prescription for retaining one's sanity.

Neena swallowed hard. The place smelled foul and the sense of unseen dangers ran deep. The sounds were unfamiliar and sinister. The people were base and disgusting.

Nor was the music any good, certainly not as good as what her father's band, the Clay Pots, played.

As Neena crossed the threshold into the jam-packed tavern, she was knocked back by a heavy nauseating odor. It hung like deadweight in the air. Smoldering tobacco. The distinctive sweet smell of cannabis. The deafening roar of cack music. Strobe lights. Holo people. Smoke. Commotion. Confusion. Mayhem and Chaos.

In the murky shadows, she could scarcely make out the expansive bar and counter that dominated the big room along one wall. Nor could she see the collection of gaming tables that were scattered here and there throughout the rest of the establishment.

Adjacent to the long bar was a row of tall barstools. They provided seating for a lucky few. The rest, drunken patrons all, had to be content to lean against the brass rail and bang on the tabletop for service. Behind the counter, half a dozen scantily clad bartenders and a few bots struggled feverishly to keep up with the incessant demands of the delirious crowd.

Neena recognized several familiar faces from the Moon Beam team. Most of the patrons, though, were complete strangers, probably on the staff of the hab. Some of them were not people at all, but holo images with lifelike attributes, and slave bots dressed up to look human.

A waiter bot approached. "What'll you have, sweet lady?" The bot seemed drunk himself. It was his programming.

"You have real alcohol in this place?" she asked.

"As real as it gets," the bot answered. "Ethyl alcohol. Or, as some say: ethanol. It is the same the world over. An ethyl group linked to a hydroxyl group. Chemical formula C_2H_6O — Yeah, we have alcohol."

"Yes, and make mine on the rocks," Neena replied.

"Coming right up, Missy."

Perdition's Cup. Neena sized up the place. Absolute pandemonium. Drunken rabble-rousers, probably with an hour or two of free time, sloshed tortan-ale everywhere. A few women masqueraded as bawdy bimbookers. They hustled the room like common whores trying to sell their bodies for a good price. The more drunken revelers shouted out gross obscenities at one another, making boisterous challenges.

Neena could barely make out a thing, the cigarette smoke was so thick. The mottled ceiling of the pub was high, easily twice the height of a man. It was splattered with restless shadows.

Then a woman approached, an older woman with red hair, older than Neena anyway. The woman wore a sleeveless blouse and held a blue colored drink in her hand. A colorful tattoo adorned her shoulder and upper arm.

"This seat taken?" the woman asked.

"Please sit," Neena answered, trying to speak over the racket.

It was difficult for the two of them to talk. Their eyes were repeatedly blinded by the annoying flash of a strobe. Then there was the mind-numbing blast of cack music from the speakers in the center of the room, plus the commotion caused by the throngs of holo-people. Conversation was a near impossibility.

The holo-people were the most distracting. Tech had come such a long way these past years, it was all but impossible to distinguish between a virtual image and an actual one. A man, eager for sex, might reach out to squeeze a cute woman's behind. A virtual woman might give him an electric shock; a real one, a sharp jab in the ribs. It was anybody's guess how many of which were blended like ingredients in this slumgullion soup of a crowd.

Ouida settled into the seat next to Neena, made herself comfortable. After Ouida had finished with Rosen, when she went to leave the service corridor behind the locker room, her exit had been blocked by Hanrahan's robot sentry. That's when she decided to double back to check on a possible witness, this witness, then go into hiding.

Ouida suspected that this girl Neena had seen her earlier in the day, when Ouida confronted Carl Rosen in the corridor, just before she killed and later dismembered him. Ouida wasn't taking any chances at being found out. She had come to the bar from the med unit prepared with a powerful rohypnol-like agent tucked in her purse. When the girl looked the other way, Ouida would drop the colorless tasteless drug into the younger woman's drink.

"Name's Ouida. What's yours?" She practically had to shout in order to make herself heard.

"Neena. Neena Petronas," she said as the drink arrived. "Have we met before? You look familiar somehow."

Ouida studied Neena's face, knowing she would have to act soon. "I don't think so. Where would we have met?"

"Forget I even brought it up," Neena said, suddenly uncomfortable.

"You here to meet someone?" Ouida probed.

"Later. But not here," Neena replied. "Excuse me. Nature calls." She got up and started for the woman's room.

"You coming back?" Ouida shouted after her, worried she had lost her chance.

"Why do you ask?"

"Place is crowded. Should I hold your seat?"

"I see what you're getting at," Neena replied. "Yes, if you wouldn't mind. Hold my seat. And while you're at it, order me another drink. They're small."

Ouida ordered her a second drink, dropped the colorless odorless chemical into the first drink the girl had barely touched. It wouldn't take much to incapacitate the younger girl. Then Ouida would have good cause to assist her out of the bar, no questions asked, just like happened here every day, ten times an hour. The rest of Ouida's plan would be easy.

CHAPTER TWENTY-SEVEN

Day Four, 1500 hours

"We're on the trail of a crazy woman, you know that, right?" Lou Santini asked. He and Flynn were in the #2 ready room suiting up. Even though the tunnels were pressurized and oxygenated with an Earth-normal atmospheric mix, the two men weren't taking any chances with a sudden decompression event.

"I lost my virginity to that crazy woman," Flynn said, adjusting his Snoopy cap before placing the helmet over his head. The cap had a built-in earphone and mic.

"This lost-my-virginity story is one I don't think I've ever heard before."

"And one you're not likely to hear today," Flynn said, verifying the pressure seal.

"Then why bother bringing it up at all?" Santini grinned, giving his partner the thumbs-up sign that he was good to go.

"To break the tension, I guess. Never in my wildest dreams did I ever imagine I'd be hunting down a woman I once slept with. She may be the mother of my son."

"You know she lied to you about that, don't you?"

"Did she?" Flynn asked.

"You're a gullible son-of-a-bitch, Chief. But could we please stick to a subject a bit more on point?"

"Shoot."

"Why would Hanrahan post a sentry bot down here in this back corridor on the locker room level?"

By now the two men had suited up, checked that all their systems were green-line and moved into the service corridor in the direction of the freight elevator.

"The same question had occurred to me," Flynn said as they approached the bot on which they had earlier run the override protocol. The Z-bot was still standing there, idle, in sentry mode. "Should we ask him?"

"The robot?"

"Why not?"

"Because robots lie."

"That is a logical impossibility," Flynn said. "Robots don't lie. They can't. They are programmed to tell the truth."

"Unless someone craftier than you or I have programmed them not to tell the truth."

"Now who is being paranoid?"

"Is it still paranoid if I am found to be correct?" Santini barked.

Chief Flynn shook his head as they passed the waiting sentry and reached the turn in the corridor that led to the freight elevator. "By the way, did you check the janitor logs?"

"I did. No one was on janitorial duty early this morning during the timeframe when we suppose Rosen was killed. What you and I saw on tape must have been someone impersonating a janitor. Probably the killer himself."

"Or herself."

"Yes, or herself."

"Who then do you suppose is the imposter?" Flynn asked. "Hanrahan? Ouida? Sinclair?"

"Or was it the bot?"

"Again with your paranoia?"

Santini pressed the call button for the elevator, and they heard the whine of machinery below them as the lift climbed the chain.

"Or maybe the tape was a sham. Maybe the original was altered," Flynn said. "Filmed earlier and spliced in to make it look like a janitor in the frame at the proper time sequence. Easy to do with digital files and the right computer."

"Maybe Rosen was spliced in as well. Maybe he was never there, never in that hallway, never in that locker room."

"You are talking about someone very smart, someone with access and computer skills."

The elevator arrived, and they descended to the basement level. Lou Santini studied the screen on his handheld device. "Every pressure suit has a tracker built into the lining. If these readings are correct, she is now outside the hab, maybe in the GAPS Crater, perhaps in the rail tunnel."

"What the hell would she be doing in either one of those places?"

"You said so yourself. The woman is crazy."

"But there's not much in that rail tunnel she can damage. It's all steel rails and flatcars. What can she possibly be up to?" Flynn asked.

"Let's go find out. There is a catwalk inside the tunnel system that runs alongside the track from rim to base. We can follow the tracks up from the bottom of the crater if we wish. Sooner or later we will catch up with her."

"But there are kloms of track, yes?"

"Oh, yes. We will run out of breathable long before we reach the top."

"Perhaps there is another way."

•

•

Ouida's lips parted in a wild and crazy smile. — The final act was close at hand.

Killing Carl Rosen had been a willful and stupid mistake; she knew that now. The murder had been done on impulse, a thing of the moment, unplanned and devastating in its consequences. The body would be found in short order, if it hadn't been already, of that she was certain. Plus, now she had a prisoner, Santini's daughter. The rohypnol in the girl's drink; the escort of the seemingly drunken Neena out the door; the laundry cart to the lower entrance of the tunnel, where she left the girl bound and gagged. But, Neena too would be missed before long.

What that meant was that Ouida would now have to move faster, certainly faster than she first planned. Any mistakes she now made in haste could not be helped. She had to strike while the solar flare event had everyone's mind focused on other things.

Ouida worked her way down the tunnel along the narrow catwalk. The catwalk ran like a metal ribbon alongside the railroad track its entire length, from the rim of the GAPS Crater to its base. Her knees hurt, and her breath came hard. She was physically tired and running short of air. The inside of a pressure suit was all knobs and rough edges, and she was becoming badly bruised along the extremities of her entire body, elbows, knees, and hips.

The tunnel that housed the track was barely wider or taller than the railcars themselves, including the height of their concrete block loads. When the sun was shining and electricity production was in surplus, the railroad cars climbed the concentric ring of track with their load, storing the excess power production at the top of the incline in the form of concrete blocks and gravitational potential. When the sun was near or below the horizon and electricity production ground to a halt, the cars descended the curved track with their load, their weight turning turbines to produce electrical power.

If Ouida could slice through the rails at the right spot with a laser cutting tool, she could derail a down-rushing train car, thus disabling the power storage system and plunging the entire facility into darkness and cold once the batteries ran dry. *Oh, wouldn't that be sweet!*

Her plan was to work herself down along the catwalk from the upper entrance of the tunnel to a place nearer the bottom of the concentric rings of track, where the down-rushing train car would have achieved maximum velocity. If she severed the rails with her cutting torch in the right spot — and in the proper way — the down-rushing car would jump the tracks and crash through the tunnel wall. Once the damage was done, it would no longer matter whether she lived or perished. Her revenge would be complete.

Ouida had thought long and hard how to do this, how to cripple the habitat, how to make people suffer as much as possible and in an extreme way. Then yesterday the solution dawned on her — disable the power storage system. Everyone would die a slow miserable death as they were poisoned by their own exhalations and the eventual loss of all environmental controls: air pressure, carbon dioxide scrubbing, temperature, filtration, everything.

Her weapon of choice was a laser cutting tool. A chemical laser was not a complicated device. Nor was it heavy or bulky. All it required was a source of energy, usually electricity, which could be provided by a battery, and a "gain" medium, a material with properties that allowed it to amplify light. The medium could be material in any state — gas, liquid, solid, or plasma. Carbon-dioxide lasers emitted in the thermal infrared, perfect for industrial uses, cutting and welding. A rather powerful one could be contained in a canister not much larger than an ordinary Thermos.

The real challenge lay in the target itself, the tunnel, gaining entrance, being certain of its destruction.

It had not occurred to Ouida that someone might follow her, that someone might ride the elevator up to the rim, then climb onboard one of the very same railcars she was trying to derail and ride that car slowly down the tracks until they found her.

•

•

Flynn and Santini had used the locator in Ouida's pressure suit to track her movements. But they had no idea what she was up to or why. So, while they had the element of surprise on their side when they came upon her in the tunnel, she had a laser cutting tool in her hand. Though outnumbered two to one, she still held the advantage.

"Well, what have we here?" Flynn asked.

Ouida stopped what she was doing when they approached, turned off her cutting tool, and looked up from her work. She had already cut through one of the two rails in two places and used a small hydraulic jack to hoist the excised section of rail out of position.

"You boys aren't very bright, are you?" she taunted.

"What makes you say that?" Santini asked, moving slowly to her left, trying to flank her position.

"You come upon a violent woman in a darkened tunnel holding no weapons in your hand and with no means of defending yourselves. How smart can you two lugnuts be?"

"The woman does have a point," Flynn agreed.

"Half a point, actually," Santini quipped. "Not a full point."

Chief Flynn turned to address his compatriot. "Perhaps we need to back up a bit, take cover behind these concrete blocks, and leave the woman to her work."

"Seriously?"

"Seriously."

The two men began to step backwards, seeking the relative safety afforded by the concrete blocks atop the flatcar they had ridden down on.

Chief Flynn was the first to speak. "Ouida, what exactly are you up to?"

"I am trying to bring down the power grid," she declared as she once again turned her back to them and resumed work making a laser cut diagonally across the track.

"But, sweetie, you will kill everyone," he said, trying to trigger an emotional response.

Ouida laughed a harsh crazy laugh. "That is the point, isn't it? To kill everyone? And don't you dare ever call me sweetie again."

"But why, for God's sake? Why kill everyone? Don't you care about me at all? We were once lovers. You said Adam was my son. Adam and I will both die, along with everyone else, Doyle too."

"Cannot be helped. Anyway, the 'why' stopped being relevant a long time ago," she sneered.

Flynn wasn't ready to give up. He saw that Santini was again trying to flank her and that she hadn't yet seemed to notice or care. "How do you expect this to end for all of us here today?" he asked.

She laughed another sick laugh. "I expect us to all die here today, you, me, him, his daughter, and everyone in the colony, Adam and Doyle included."

"And how exactly do you expect to make that happen? I mean there are two of us and only one of you. You can't kill us both at the same time, and by my calculation you are almost out of air. All we need do is wait you out until you stop breathing. Then this entire insane scheme of yours comes to an end."

"Brave talk for two unarmed men. Maybe I will just use your air supply when mine runs out."

Now it was Chief Flynn's turn to laugh. "And how do you intend to do that, Ouida?" Santini had almost flanked her on the right.

"Kill you and exchange air tanks," she answered crisply.

Now, suddenly, the two men acted. Flynn charged her from the left and Santini from the right.

She reached for the control panel on the laser, lit it up and slashed wildly at her attackers with the torch. But the beam took a moment to recharge and wasn't yet at full strength when they moved in on her.

She narrowly missed Flynn with the cutting edge of the torch but struck Santini obliquely in the PLSS. Escaping gas hissed from the leak in the life support pack, but not before Santini had tackled her to the ground and wrestled the torch out of her hand. His remaining air wouldn't last long.

"I am holding your daughter prisoner. Kill me and she dies too."

The devastating news shocked Santini long enough for him to loosen his grip. Ouida wriggled loose of his hold and got to her feet.

She jumped on the waiting railroad car and sped away, rolling down the track toward the base of the crater, where she had left Neena bound and gagged less than an hour ago. From there she could escape to any number of hiding places, including the tunnel housing the old cyclotron.

Flynn grabbed his friend with both hands, spun him around, disconnected his air hose and tied it into the T-valve of his own life support pack. Between them, they had about five minutes of air remaining, barely enough time to get beyond a pressure door and inside to a section of the hab that was oxygenated and pop off their gear.

"Come on, damn it! Move faster," Santini pleaded. "She's got my Neena!"

CHAPTER TWENTY-EIGHT

Day Four, 1700 hours

Administrator Winston Hanrahan's office was standing room only.

Chief Engineer Clay Flynn, Senior Tech Lou Santini, Professor Chandler Tattersall, Doyle Baldwin, Paddington Sinclair, Guy Cruz, Junior Mate Gunderson. They were all there.

Tensions were high. Flynn and Santini had just barely escaped with their lives from Ouida in the rail tunnel, but not without first learning that Ouida had taken Neena hostage. The captor and her prisoner were now holed up somewhere inside the cyclotron, precise location unknown.

"The slag whore took my daughter hostage," Santini said. "We can't go in there guns blazing. She will kill my Neena before we can even get in close enough to rescue her."

"We may have to sacrifice Neena's life in order to save the rest of us," Hanrahan said.

Lou Santini charged from his seat and grabbed Hanrahan by the throat, shoved him back against the bulkhead wall. "You heartless bastard," he screamed as Flynn and Tattersall tried to loosen Santini's grip. But Lou was strong, his body flush with adrenaline, and he wasn't going to give up easily.

"Give it a rest, Lou," Flynn exclaimed, pulling down hard on the other man's arm. "Nobody is sacrificing anybody. Hanrahan is being a jackass, as per usual."

"I resent you talking to me that way," Hanrahan said. "I am neither an idiot nor a jackass. For God's sake, man. I'm just being practical. One life for all our lives. That seems like a fair trade. We have to stop this crazy woman from destroying our acetylene supplies or else we will never be able to repair the track. Without that stored power, we all die a slow, cold, painful death. As the nights get longer, the hab will run low on electricity. There are more than two hundred lives at stake here."

"It's a big place, that cyclotron," Tattersall interrupted. "She won't find those acetylene tanks without some doing. Looking for them will take time. The tanks are well hidden and behind lock and key."

"And you, Hanrahan — you have a lot to answer for," Santini said.

"Me? Besides hurting your God damn feelings, what the hell did I do wrong?"

"Let me handle this, Lou." Flynn tightened his jaw. "What I want to know from you, Hanrahan, is why you had a sophisticated Z-bot stationed in the service corridor that runs behind the two locker rooms."

Hanrahan became white-faced. "It is all a bit embarrassing, I have to admit."

Flynn dug in his heels. "Tell me now or I will exercise Article 12 and have you relieved as Administrator before the day is out."

"Could I have a word with you in private?" Hanrahan asked quietly.

"No! Absolutely not!" Flynn exclaimed. "No more secrets."

"Okay, already." Hanrahan relented with a sigh. "Surveillance cams are not permitted in the locker rooms by statute." His face turned a lovely shade of crimson.

Lou Santini understood his meaning immediately. "What kind of pervert are you anyway?"

Chief Flynn was floored. "You're a peeping Tom?"

"I enjoy watching muscular women work out," Hanrahan said.

Santini lost it again and charged once more across the room. "You been looking at my naked daughter in the friggin' shower?" He started pummeling the man with his fists. This time, no one in the room made the slightest move to stop him. He knocked Hanrahan to the floor and broke his nose. Blood began to gush.

"Okay, Lou, that's enough," Flynn finally said, reaching down to pick him up along with Guy Cruz's help. "Hanrahan is finished here."

Santini hit the prone man once more for good measure then got to his feet. "Chief, as far as I am concerned, you are now the ranking officer onsite. Tell us what you want us to do."

Flynn nodded. "Here's our situation, gentlemen. Lou and I stopped Ouida before she could actually cause a moving railcar to jump the tracks. Had she succeeded with her plans, the tunnel would have been damaged, perhaps beyond repair, and along with it our electrical power storage system. We got there in the nick of time. The tunnel was spared. But our troubles are not over. Before we could stop her, Ouida did manage to excise a long section of track. The damage can be repaired, but there is a big but."

"Isn't there always?" Paddington Sinclair said.

"Yes, I suppose," Flynn said. "And here it is. To repair the track, we require acetylene for the torches. But, like Tattersall said, all the acetylene fuel for the welding torches is stored in the old cyclotron tunnel. There is a reason for this. The stuff is dangerous. We store it well away from the hab as a safety measure. We have to assume that Ouida also knows this. The woman is not stupid. She knows that we need those tanks of acetylene to repair the break. My guess is that her endgame will either be to destroy the tanks outright or else block our ability to access them. Doyle, you know her better than anyone. What do you think she will do?"

"I haven't a clue. I was married to the woman for years. But now it appears that I hardly knew her at all."

Santini interrupted. "We have to tread lightly. Acetylene gas is über volatile."

"Lay it out for us, Lou," Flynn said.

"An oxyacetylene welding torch has two pipes and two gas hoses. One hose carries the fuel and the other feeds oxygen to the flame. Acetylene gas is shipped upright in special containers designed to keep the gas dissolved. The cylinders are packed with a porous material, kapok fiber or diatomaceous earth. Acetylene gas is unstable. It decomposes explosively if put under too much pressure. One atmosphere, 15 pounds of pressure per square inch is okay. But get it up to two atmospheres, 29 psi, and it's good night _muchachos_. When acetylene gas combines with oxygen, it burns at more than 3,000 degrees Celsius."

Flynn looked at his friend, now, with deep feeling. "We are going to get her back, Lou. Don't you worry. You and me, we are going to get your Neena back. I promise."

Guy Cruz stepped forward. "How can I help? Neena is my friend."

"More than a friend, I'm told." Lou Santini looked at the younger man hard.

"Not today, Lou," Chief Flynn said as he took charge. "We need two teams, one to secure the canisters and a second to take down Ouida and grab up Neena."

"You mean three teams, don't you?" Paddington Sinclair intoned. "We need a third team to prepare the hab for this solar flare event that Los Alamos has been warning us about. They have issued a directive."

"Yes, I had nearly forgotten about that," Flynn admitted. "Doyle, why don't you and Guy try and secure the canisters? Take Gunderson and one or two others from the maintenance crew along with you. Be sure everyone is packing fire suppression gear."

"Roger that."

"Lou and I are going to go after his daughter. Sinclair, you and Tattersall should take charge of the hab. Get everyone in off the surface and downstairs to safety now, as soon as Los Alamos tells us to take cover. Annex B."

"What can I do?" Hanrahan asked.

"You can stay out of my fucking way."

"Don't speak to me that way."

"And why not? When there is ugly business at hand, it helps if a man is angry."

CHAPTER TWENTY-NINE

Day Four, 1830 hours

Chief Clay Flynn stood alone in the dark.

It wasn't supposed to work this way, he thought glumly.

They had split up, he and Santini, with Lou going counterclockwise around the giant circle of the cyclotron and Flynn going clockwise. Whoever found Ouida first was to call the other on his walkie and they would join forces to take her down together.

But that's when the playbook changed. The overhead lights in the cyclotron tunnel went out, something Clay Flynn had definitely not counted on. Except for the small miner's-style lamp on top of his space helmet, the darkness ahead was deep and penetrating. Flynn was finding it difficult to make his way along the tunnel floor alone in the dark.

The Universe is what it is. That's what his father would say. *It never forgives mistakes. Not even the stupid ones.*

Strictly speaking, Flynn had not made a mistake, not even a stupid one. What he had done, what they had both done, was not think the plan through to its logical conclusion. He and Santini had missed the obvious.

To conserve electrical power, the team of Paddington Sinclair and Chandler Tattersall, the team charged with getting everyone safely underground, had evidently cut the juice in other parts of the hab. It probably hadn't occurred to them that by cutting the power they would also be plunging the five men working inside the cyclotron into darkness. Flynn, Santini, Baldwin, Gunderson, and Cruz. Three of those men — Doyle, Gunderson, and Cruz — had gone ahead to try and locate the canisters of acetylene before Ouida could find and destroy them herself.

Flynn was not one to admit fear, especially not in front of another man. It simply wasn't his way. In a clutch, when it mattered most, Flynn was usually a rock. Just the thought of being scared, terrified him. But now he was cold, tired, and hungry. His reserves were practically at zero, and he was frightened. The pitch-black darkness made things worse. Without electrical power, the air inside the tunnel would grow cold and stale.

People believed in God or in ghosts or imps or fairy tales. This was human nature. People have believed in these spirits since before they began to measure time, since before they were even considered people, probably all the way back to that first afternoon when one of those early mortals clambered down out of the trees, scratched his head in wonder and began to work out a plan to see who or what was over yonder, beyond the next ridge.

People believed in these magical beings long before Clay Flynn arrived at the door of this black hole. And they would continue to believe in them long after he was dead and buried. Even now, after centuries of progress, science was still just a small voice in the dark. And skills, well, they were just luck in the right hands.

Cultivate your mastery. That's what his father would tell his son, when, as a boy, Clay became frightened. His father was not a particularly religious man. But he was practical and realistic, and he instinctively knew how to raise a boy.

Cultivate your mastery, son. Use your skills. Learn to adapt, survive, prosper. Everything else is just a big waste of time.

Flynn gathered his wits and pushed blindly forward in the dark. The walls were cold to the touch, and the air bitter. *What could he remember about this place?*

The lunar particle accelerator was built long after the dawn of the space age, about one hundred years after. Although its location was remote, the lunar cyclotron, as it was then known, was a hotbed of nuclear research until the funding ran out and the scientists packed it in. Then, the facility was shut down.

But all was not lost. The long curving tunnel was a valuable asset in its own right. Sections of it were eventually transformed into a subterranean city complete with hotels, shopping malls, and delicatessens.

But the economics of lunar shopping malls and tourist hotels were poor, and the development didn't last. Shortly thereafter, it became what it is today, an empty hulk of a former research center.

In its original design, the lunar cyclotron was employed to accelerate particles ranging in size from a single proton up to the heaviest elements on the periodic table and to cause them to collide with tremendous energy.

The heart of the cyclotron was a series of superconducting magnets. They lined the insides of the beam-tubes. The superconductors had the capacity to accelerate nuclear particles with energy equivalents in the range of 100,000 billion electron volts. That punch of energy made the accelerator a prohibitively dangerous piece of hardware, one that could not be safely housed anywhere on Earth. The Moon beckoned as the only sensible location for such an inherently dangerous device.

The operational risk arose when the gargantuan device was powered up. Large numbers of very-fast-moving nuclei circulated in opposite directions inside the two beam-tubes until they crashed violently into one another at a place called the COLLISION POINT. The larger the diameter of an accelerator, the higher the energy that could be imparted to the accelerated particles. The lunar cyclotron had a circumference approaching forty kloms, making it by far the largest ever built.

Specialized electronic detectors inside the tunnel recorded each collision event as it occurred. Every interaction left behind a signature, evidence of complex quantum mechanical phenomena, including sub-atomic specks like quarks, anti-quarks, gluon strings, and dark matter.

Almost from the first power-up, researchers made astounding discoveries. The search wasn't like looking for a needle in a haystack. It was more like staring through the eyepiece of a telescope at a pile of needles on a distant planet and trying to figure out which of those needles pointed north.

But the bizarre thing was what happened next. After using the lunar accelerator for little more than a decade, a decade in which physicists made a number of stunning breakthroughs in humankind's understanding of elemental forces, they lost interest in the project. Shortly afterwards, the cyclotron was abandoned.

But today the abandoned tunnels served a different purpose. Today the tunnels served as the perfect hideout for one crazy woman, Ouida Baldwin, and her terrified prisoner, Neena Petronas. They were the needle pointed north in a sea of needles, and Chief Flynn and Lou Santini had to find that one single needle and extract it from the pile before it was too late.

In the present endeavor, Lou Santini fared much worse than Chief Flynn. He too had been plunged into darkness when the lights went out. But then, when his eyes adjusted, he spied a speck of light in the distance, up the tunnel perhaps three hundred meters. Santini walked toward it. The light became brighter. He was drawing nearer. He heard cries of pain up ahead in the distance, his daughter's cries of pain. His pace quickened.

"Chief," he whispered into the comm. "I think I found her. If you can hear me, I see a light ahead. Reverse course as quickly as you can and come my way instead."

Then he flipped off his walkie so that it could not squawk and give away his position.

Santini took two more steps in the direction of the light, when all of a sudden, he was struck from behind by something round and hard. The blow knocked him to the concrete floor. The Mag 10 suit absorbed much of the energy of the blow, but not all.

He began to roll over when he was struck again. Santini saw it coming this time out of the corner of one eye, a piece of rebar across the side of his head. No suit could fully protect a man against that. Then his lights truly were out.

Lou Santini, like his daughter Neena, was now a prisoner of Ouida Baldwin.

CHAPTER THIRTY

Three-Quarters of an Hour Earlier
Day Four, 1745 hours

Ouida Baldwin stood inside the tunnel of the particle accelerator, proud of her handiwork. Though Neena was drugged and still drowsy, Ouida towered over the younger woman, holding her at gunpoint.

The subterranean tunnel curved gently away in both directions, its pair of slender beam-tubes sweeping quickly out of sight. The inner surfaces of each tube were softly lit in subtle grays, the grays of concrete, steel, and once-shiny insulation.

A scent of metal shavings lingered in the cool air. From a distance came the muffled rattle of a machine. The mech-bot was performing maintenance, checking the tubes for vacuum leaks. The scientists, when they abandoned the cyclotron years ago, had the good sense to leave behind a single monitoring machine to maintain the structural integrity of the place. The machine was self-repairing and ran twenty-four hours a day, 365 days a year.

Half an hour earlier, as Ouida and her young prisoner stumbled along the tunnel floor, the tunnel straightened out and, in due course, the narrow beam-tubes merged into a single wide channel. After climbing over a set of crisscrossing pipes, they emerged into a cavernous chamber glowing yellow in sodium floodlights.

In the middle of the floor was a black circle. The words COLLISION POINT were painted in gold letters next to the black circle. At one time, the paint was fresh and new; now it was crumbling and peeling. In close proximity were forklifts, winches, chains and pulleys, all used at one time or another to move supplies and heavy equipment into or out of the habitat.

Ouida spoke in her crazy detached way. "Torture has often been regarded as a method for punishing the guilty. That is a shame really, for physical torture has other, more interesting uses. Torture is best used as a device for extracting confessions. But for you, my sweet, it will be necessary to distinguish between the application of torture designed to bring about a confession, and the application of torture designed to bring about pain."

"You don't scare me," Neena said bravely. Her hands were bound tightly behind her back.

"I like a woman filled with resolve." Ouida smiled her evil smile. "It will be fun taking you apart."

"I would like to see you try."

"Let us not forget, little girl, that I am a surgeon by trade. I know how to disarticulate a limb. If you don't believe me, just ask Carl Rosen. On second thought, Carl isn't saying much these days."

"What did you do to him?"

"Sorry, but Carl won't be available to do an interview for the rest of his life."

"You killed him?"

Ouida shrugged. "The point is, little girl, I know how to hurt you. I know how to make you endure extreme pain, pain worse than you ever thought possible. And I know how to make you suffer a great deal without actually ending your life."

"I believe that."

"Good. Now, where was I? Oh, yes, torture. Torture has a long and bloody history. If you doubt it, you need only think back to the savage devices of primitive man. What early man lacked in brainpower he made up for in ingenuity. The Savage was not an unimaginative creature. Many of his tortures were clever and downright fiendish."

"The only savage I see around here is you."

Ouida brushed off the recrimination and coughed out a dry cackle. Then she looked Neena straight in the eye and hit her in the mouth with all the force her arms could muster. The blow sent blood spinning from the girl's mouth.

Neena was powerless to fight back. Her hands were still bound behind her back.

"What do you want from me?" Neena cried.

"Where in this shitcan of a facility do they store the tanks of acetylene?"

"How the hell should I know? Even a hag as butt ugly as you can't be that dumb, or are you? Surely you must know I landed in this insane asylum only a day and a half ago. I hardly know my way around. I cannot possibly tell you what I do not know."

"No one calls me dumb and lives to tell about it. I think we ought to begin with a simple torture, the strappado," Ouida said, checking Neena's wrists to be sure the binding had remained tight. "I draw you up by rope and pulley. Then, with your entire weight hanging on your hands and wrists, your shoulders will be wrenched from their sockets. I can do this without leaving so much as a single outward mark on your pretty little body."

Ouida grabbed for a chain, wrapped it around Neena's wrists, fed the chain through a pulley, and gave the free end a good tug. It was an easy pull. Moon gravity was low. The chain tightened. Neena's arms began to lift behind her.

Neena fought it with all her might, her triceps taut. But it was impossible. Nobody was that strong, not even at one-sixth-g.

Her arms lifted higher and higher. Her toes barely touched the ground now. She screamed out in pain. Her arms were nearly straight out behind her, horizontal to the ground. All her weight was pulling her down. The tightness across her chest made it difficult for her to breath. The inability to draw in air made her head pound.

Neena arched her back with all her might. But it was no use. Her arms would give out long before Ouida was done having her fun.

Ouida laughed. She loved to watch people suffer.

Neena was fighting the pain. But she was losing the fight. Ouida gave the chain another good yank.

Neena's arms went higher. Again, she screamed out in pain. But it was a muted scream. Her chest muscles were so constricted, she couldn't get a full measure of air into her lungs. The garbled sound echoed off the metal walls of the particle-beam tunnel.

Then came the sickening pop, as both shoulders broke free of their sockets. Her body fell limp as she passed out.

•

•

"Wakey, wakey," Ouida chanted, throwing cold water in Neena's face.

The prisoner had been out for more than thirty minutes. Her wrists were still bound together, but above her head now, as the strappado had pulled her arms all the way around in a complete half-circle. They were still attached to the chain, however, and the chain to the pulley.

But, while Neena was unconscious, Ouida had lowered the girl's body so that Neena's feet were now on the cold, concrete floor. Plus, Ouida had done one other thing while Neena was out cold — stripped her body naked to the waist, preparing the girl for possible indignities yet to come.

"Wakey, wakey," Ouida repeated, rubbing her hands against Neena's breasts. The girl's face was white, her breathing labored.

Ouida splashed her with water for a second time. Neena shivered as the cold water ran down her chest and across her legs.

"Yeah, you witch, I am still alive," Neena gasped, pain shooting across her abdomen from her shoulders.

"Good, because we have much, much more to do to you."

Ouida loosened the chain and Neena slumped into a heap on the floor of the tunnel. Her arms — still bound at the wrists — were again behind her, useless and lame.

Ouida dragged her broken prisoner across the room and propped her up in a chair she had set up for the purpose. A rope around Neena's abdomen held her snug against the back of the chair. Another one across her thighs held her tight to the seat. A third one ran from her bound wrists, underneath the chair, and to her ankles, now also bound. Her arms were black and blue, her teeth chattering in the cold.

"Water torture is next. Then mutilation."

"What exactly is it that you want from me?"

"I need to know where the space techs store the acetylene tanks."

"I told you once already. I do not know."

"But your father might. I looked you up. Lou Santini is your father. You two must have had a falling out somewhere along the line. But fathers cannot resist trying to protect their daughters, even daughters who have been God-awful mean to them. The longer I hold you prisoner, the more likely it is that he will show up. Daddy will almost certainly come and try to rescue his little girl. Once he sees what I have done to you, then he will tell me what I want to know."

"And if he doesn't?"

"Then the mutilation of your body will just be for my entertainment."

Neena shook her head in disbelief. "You stupid bitch. I'm warning you. If you ever hope to come out of this thing alive, you had better let me go. Because if you don't, my father and my boyfriend will make it their life's work to hunt down your sorry ass and put an end to you."

"Strong words from a woman in your position."

"Skank whore."

"You best get your head straight, girl. I don't care whether or not I come out of this thing alive. You see? Your threats are hollow. They mean nothing at all to me."

"Stupid whore bitch."

"Maybe it is about time we shut your filthy mouth for good."

Ouida picked up a cotton cloth, jammed it in the girl's mouth. "The way this works is a combination of water torture plus strangulation. But do not worry, little one. — What I am about to do to you will not kill you, at least not right away."

Neena's eyes were white with terror.

"Let me describe this splendid torture for you, little one. A piece of damp cloth is placed upon the tongue — like this — and a stream of water allowed to trickle onto it."

Ouida swung a flexible spigot over from the utility sink and positioned it over the cloth already jammed into Neena's mouth.

"In the process of normal breathing and swallowing, the cotton cloth will be drawn into the victim's throat and produce partial strangulation. After a time, the cloth will be pulled back out and the act repeated. Frequently, upon being pulled out of the victim's throat, the torturer will find the cloth saturated with the victim's blood and mucus. Shall we begin?"

Neena could not answer because the cloth was already down her throat and the water running.

Neena was scared. She was a young woman, too young to contemplate her own mortality.

Neena never imagined it would end this way for her. No one imagines such things when they are young. Her father had raised her to be brave. He wasn't often home when she was growing up — but often enough. He taught her to be brave, how to tell right from wrong, and most of all, how to keep her head above water in an imperfect world. In the fairy tales he read to her as a little girl, he taught her that monsters could be defeated, that she and he lived in a wonderful world peopled by wonderful people. But never once did he tell her about anything like this.

What she faced today was inhuman. Less than human. Subhuman.

If only someone — anyone — would come help her before it was too late.

But who?

In the next breath, the overhead lights blinked once and then they went out.

CHAPTER THIRTY-ONE

Day Four, 1915 hours

Ouida was in her element here, and she loved it.
Dominatrix. Torturer. Task Master. Deliverer of pain. *Could anything be more satisfying?*

The linear accelerator tunnel was the perfect laboratory for experimenting with elemental particles and, as it turned out, for torturing a helpless young woman. Ouida had before her a splendid specimen of womanhood on which to work.

Ouida stood in front of Neena, taunting her with her jibes. She had set up temporary lighting in the darkened tunnel, drawing power from a nearby battery. The young girl was naked, still strapped to the chair. Her face was pale. The bloody cloth was in her mouth, partway down her throat.

Something else had changed from before. Neena saw it out of the corner of one eye. Up until now, Neena had been held captive alone. Now her father was there beside her, also a prisoner of this crazy bitch.

"This ought to be great fun," Ouida snickered, pulling off her own shirt and admiring the rich lines of her glistening Phoenix tattoo on her upper torso. The colors fired the seething anger in her blood. "I get to kill the both of you. — And you each get to watch the other one die."

She yanked the bloody rag out of Neena's mouth, wetted it down, then shoved it back in again. Ouida's eyes were wild, her nipples hard. The woman was clearly deranged.

Ouida turned to Santini. After knocking him cold with the length of iron rebar, she had stripped him of his spacesuit and hogtied him. When she spoke, her voice possessed an animal quality.

"And for you, you big hunk of man, let us begin with a short round of stretching on the ladder, shall we?"

Ouida fastened Lou Santini's hands to the top of a utility ladder. She fastened his feet to the same pulley she had used earlier to break Neena's shoulders.

"I will ask you only once," she said. "Where in these tunnels do they store the tanks of acetylene gas?"

"Up yours," he spat, his head pounding from the earlier attack. Dried blood caked his hair on the back of his head where she had struck him.

"No, up yours."

Ouida tugged on the chain until it was snug. Then she stretched his body until it was possible to see his visceral organs. They were outlined against a utility light she held to his back.

Satisfied by her handiwork, she smiled a grisly smile. Santini would have screamed out in pain had he not lost consciousness first.

Neena looked on in horror. *The evil witch was killing her father!*

Ouida splashed water in Lou Santini's face. She needed him conscious for what she was about to do. *This was not going to be any fun if she couldn't see the terror in his eyes.*

Ouida turned and yanked the towel out of the girl's mouth. It was thick with blood and saliva.

"Slag Bitch," Neena croaked, her voice cracking.

"Still have a lot of spunk in you, eh? We will have to see about that."

Ouida laughed. Then she rolled up her hand into a fist and punched Neena hard in the face.

"Leave her alone!" Santini warned through clenched teeth.

"Or what, Daddy? You will hurt me? Hah!"

She tugged on the chain again, this time harder than before. One of his ankles gave way under the stress, a crippling injury. He might never walk again.

Santini was defiant despite the pain. "Kill me and you get nothing."

"Yes? Well, we will just have to see about that, won't we?" She hit Neena with her fist again. "I don't have to break you, old man. You will break on your own when I have hurt your daughter enough."

Chief Flynn moved quietly among the shadows. He had received Lou's earlier message on the walkie and had reversed course in the circular tunnel. Before long, he saw the dim light in the distance. Now he drew closer.

Neena was scared, though not as scared as she had been earlier. There was an upside — if a person wanted to call it that — to having a pair of dislocated shoulders. Wrists could be turned to almost any imaginable position, an injury that could now perhaps be turned to Neena's advantage. While her abuser was busy hurting her father, she too had been busy. Neena had succeeded in working her hands free.

Now all she needed was an opening.

Neena was still bound to the chair, a restraint stretched across her thighs and abdomen. Now, when Ouida turned to again torment her father, Neena made her move. She gripped the iron bar with both hands. Then, despite excruciating pain, she swung it at the woman with all her might.

The sound was horrifying, like the crack of dry, white pine. Ouida's skull split. Blood spurted everywhere.

Still naked, Neena limped over to where her father was lying on the tunnel floor out cold.

Neena's hands were nearly useless. But she had no choice. She slammed her shoulder against the tunnel wall to try and pop her shoulder back into place. The pain was staggering. She threw up.

Ouida stirred.

Neena had to move fast. *Time was running out!*

Neena tugged at her father to try and get him to his feet. He was groggy and could not walk. She flung his arms around her shoulder and the two of them limped off. In her free hand was the only weapon they had, the length of iron rebar.

Then Flynn shouted out to them from the dark. "Run! I got this."

Ouida got to her knees. She was hurt, but not mortally. It often takes more than a single blow to put someone down for good. Ouida Baldwin was no exception. She was down no more than half a minute before she got groggily to her feet and took off after them at a slow, unsteady pace.

Her quarry were two badly injured people with only a short head start. One of them, a woman, with arms that were black and blue and swollen from the shoulder down to the elbow and across the chest. The other, a man who was limping badly, his weight supported by a makeshift cane, the iron bar. Up to this point, she didn't realize that Chief Flynn had entered the frame.

Then a familiar voice spoke to her from out of the darkness.

"You haven't anywhere to go, Ouida," Flynn shouted, shocking her with his presence. "What say you surrender and we end this insanity right here and now?"

"Why would I surrender to you when I have already won?"

"In what possible way have you won?"

Ouida chortled. "You haven't recovered the acetylene tanks yourselves and without them your precious railroad track cannot be repaired. That means everyone in the hab will eventually perish. Like I said. I win."

"Not if I kill you first," Flynn said.

"And you are going to be the one to kill me?"

"If I have to."

"You haven't the stones."

"I didn't used to think so, Ouida. But things have radically changed. I'm not the man I was twenty-four hours ago. Bringing your life to an end is not something I want to do. It's something I have to do."

"Then quit jawing and simply do it already!"

Ouida charged him with visceral fury in her eyes and delivered a full body blow. She was an animal gone wild.

Flynn raised his arms and hands to protect himself.

But she was amped up on adrenaline, nostrils flaring, breath coming fast and furiously.

Ouida swung her bone-handled hunting knife wildly in front of her.

He stepped backward but she continued to advance.

Then, in an instant, she struck a blow.

She cut his air hose with her knife, then rammed the steel-hardened blade into his spacesuit at the height of his thigh and upper leg. The tip penetrated to within one suit-layer of his bare skin. Precious air began to leak out through the breach.

Then she turned and moved rapidly away.

CHAPTER THIRTY-TWO

Day Four, 2000 hours

Parked inside the tunnels of the accelerator ring were several high-speed electric carts. Bots performed most of the tunnel maintenance, but the occasional human crew used the electric carts to get quickly around the huge loop, which measured nearly forty kloms in circumference.

With head still oozing blood from the earlier blow, Ouida jumped in the nearest cart and took off to find Neena and Santini. They had disappeared on foot into the darkness. Without stopping to consider the odds, Flynn grabbed a second electric cart from the charging station and gave chase.

In a closed circular loop tunnel, even a large one, there is no actual way to "escape" a determined pursuer. With only one way in and one way out, going too fast around the circle meant eventually overtaking your pursuer. Going too slowly meant being overtaken yourself.

Do you even have a plan? Flynn asked himself, calculating his odds for success. Ouida had damaged his pressure suit with her knife. If she went for the airlock, he wouldn't be able to follow her outside. Then there was the matter of his bum leg.

On the other hand, now that he was hunkered down and seated in the electric cart, those odds improved markedly.

What Flynn needed, and none too soon, was a weapon. He searched the cart, looked in the back. There was a tool chest just behind the seat. He opened it. It had the usual stuff. Wrenches, pliers, wire cutters. But also, some more exotic tools. Rivet popper, acetylene torch, plasma gun for sealing the cooling coils for the cyclotron's superconductor.

Yeah, the plasma gun, Flynn thought, spinning the wheel on the electric cart and turning it around to face his adversary.

Ouida and Flynn came at each other now like jousters on a medieval battlefield, headlights blazing. With the butt of the plasma gun slung beneath his shoulder, Flynn held the business end out in front of him like a lance. Ouida had a lance of her own, an acetylene torch with half a bottle of gas.

Neither got off a clean shot first time out. They were too close to one another when he turned to face her. It became a game of chicken instead, a hazardous game played at short range and relatively high speed.

Flynn aimed his cart squarely at her headlights. His face was twisted into a snarl. *If a man had to do something dangerous, it helped to be angry.* — The anger was for his own protection.

And yet, the purpose of life is to remain alive. Observe any animal in the wild. The absolute only thing it tries to do is stay alive. The animal doesn't care about beliefs or philosophy; not capitalism, not communism, not religion; not right, not wrong. All it cares about is staying alive.

And whenever an animal's behavior puts it at odds with the realities of its existence, the animal becomes extinct. Flynn had no intention of joining the dinosaurs.

The two jousters struck one another practically head-on. The collision rolled their carts and threw them both to the concrete. Somewhere nearby were Neena and her father. But, the two of them were not going to be of much help to Flynn in the present circumstances.

How much of a fight can a naked woman with two useless arms put up? Or a battered man with one useless leg? — Not much.

The head-on collision put them both on the tunnel floor with a groan and the sound of flesh against metal. Crazy shadows played against the walls as the headlights of the electric carts lit up first the ceiling then the floor.

Flynn grabbed Ouida by the hair and rammed her head into the wall. She doubled over, and he slammed her head against his knee for good measure.

It made no difference. She came at him again, this time with a garrote-like cord in her hand. It must have been in her pocket or perhaps in the tool chest of her electric cart.

The woman was strong, all muscles and adrenaline. She tried to wrap the cord around his neck.

Flynn whipped around to face her. It was the only possible way to keep from being choked. Facing one's attacker sharply reduced the odds of being strangled. She would now be pulling against the muscles at the back of his neck.

Supporting himself, now, on his one good leg, Flynn brought up his other knee hard, striking her in the groin. Then, he boxed her in the ears with his hands. She screamed out in pain and let go of the garrote.

Flynn went promptly into a defensive posture, bringing his hands up to shield his face.

Ouida thought he was cowering in fear and laughed. But he was now in a fighting stance. He poked her in the throat with ferocious intensity. She choked, then stumbled backwards.

Flynn bent to look for Santini and his daughter. They were nearby. He could hear them moving about in the dark.

But Ouida came at him again, this time with her blade. She was still naked from the waist up. Her nipples were hard, like bullets, and pointed directly at him.

Flynn tried to pivot to avoid her. But his injured leg gave out from beneath him.

She knocked him to the ground, slashed at his torso with her blade. Sparks flew as the blade struck concrete.

He punched her in the throat for a second time, then rolled out from beneath her.

Flynn scrambled around on the floor, found the length of rebar, and swung it wildly. The bar connected with her arm below the elbow, splintering the bone. The blade fell from her grip. He heard it skitter across the floor into the shadows.

Ouida hit him low, in his bad leg, knocking him flat again. He still had hold of the iron bar. This time he swung it against her side. He heard ribs crack. She groaned. For the first time, Flynn had the upper hand.

Flynn was the animal now, hitting her over and over again. Twice on the head. Against the back. Upside the legs. This was a woman he used to make love to. Now he was killing her with grim determination.

On the fourth or fifth blow, Flynn heard a pop as her neck gave way. She gasped for breath in one long horrifying draw, then moved no further. It was like his father always said. *No one escapes from this life alive.*

Bloodied and near exhaustion, Flynn pulled himself across the floor. He had endured pain before, but never quite like this.

Somewhere, not close, were the sounds of moaning. It couldn't be Ouida. She was dead. He was certain of that. He had killed her himself. Broken her neck. Heard it pop.

No, the sounds of moaning had to be coming from one of the other two, either Santini or his daughter. But where were they? Near or far?

In the dark, it was hard to tell. Was he moving towards them or away? Were they mortally wounded or . . . ?

His leg was useless, might be forever. Flynn pulled himself into a sitting position. The room was dark, nearly black.

Red emergency lamps along the ceiling threw off a smattering of light, not much.

Flynn looked around. He thought he knew from which direction the sounds were coming.

He started to move in that direction, dragging the iron bar along with him, just in case.

Flynn called out.

No answer.

He called again.

This time, Neena answered.

"I'm here," she moaned.

He reached out to her in the dark. Neena reached back.

"Help us," she said.

"I am moving as fast as I can. But I have to tell you, this teensy-weensy leg wound of mine is slowing me down just a tad," a classic Flynn understatement.

"Oh, quit whining already and help me up," Santini said. "You damn near got yourself killed with that cart driving stunt of yours."

"What stunt?"

"Ramming that bloody witch with your electric cart."

"You can take out your wrath on me later on. Right now, we three have more pressing things to worry about."

"Yeah? What could be more pressing than what we have already been through?"

"Trust me, old friend. We are rather pressed for time," Flynn said, putting his arms around the other man's waist and raising him gently to his feet.

"Yeah, what's the rush?" Santini winced.

"Oh, I don't know," Flynn said with bubbles of tight sarcasm in his voice. "Little things. A solar flare that is going to destroy the counterweight on the lunar elevator. A power storage system that is about to fail, leaving us all cold, wet, and in the dark."

Lou Santini chuckled hoarsely. "Goodness, Chief. Everyone knows that you and I have been friends a good long time. But didn't anyone ever tell you that you worry too damn much?"

"Just say thank you, and we will be even."

"I thought I just did."

•

•

"Lord, these tanks are heavy," Guy complained, as he placed his gloved hands on one and tried to lift it from its harness. The tank wouldn't budge. "How can one of these tanks possibly be this heavy?" He and Doyle were in a different section of the cyclotron tunnel from Flynn and the others. The readout from the base manifest had given them the precise coordinates inside the tunnel where the tanks were stored.

"You're tired," Doyle said, trying to lift the tank himself. "Hell, we're both tired. We've got no bots on standby to help us, no lifting equipment, no electric carts for transport, nothing."

"We never should have let Gunderson go back to the hab ahead of us. That was clearly a mistake."

"No argument there. We could certainly use his help right about now."

"What do you think was so God damned important that Hanrahan had to order Gunderson back early?"

"Have not a clue. But bitching will not help."

"Are you sure?" Guy questioned. "Maybe we ought to call down to the Annex and get one or two of the others up here to help us move these mothers."

"And risk even more lives?" Doyle shook his head. "No, sir. Not going to happen. Besides, the only ones qualified for this sort of work are already busy elsewhere. We can do this, you and me together. Even an ordinary two-wheeled dolly would be of some help, though."

"Come to think of it, I do remember seeing one earlier."

"Where?"

"Back at the junction, where the master electronic controls are located."

"Geez, that's like half a klom from here."

"Like we have a choice here, Doyle. We have only two options — either we walk or we carry," Guy observed. "Either we walk half a klom back for the dolly or else we lug the two tanks twice that distance by hand. What'll it be?"

"You sure of what you saw, kid? You really saw a dolly back at the junction?"

"I know what I saw."

"Okay, but we go get it together."

"Why wear us both out walking all that way?" Guy asked. "Wouldn't it make more sense for one of us to stay behind and rest, while the other one makes the trek?"

"Because if you're wrong about the location of this dolly, kid, I want you standing right beside me where I can reach your skinny ass with my bare hands and beat the living daylights out of you. Plus, if you are right, we can take turns wheeling the damn thing back here together."

"Okay, I can live with that. Let's call it in."

•
•

Lou Santini had never felt pain like this before.

But it was not the agonizing pain that was at the forefront of his mind, it was the condition of his daughter. She had been badly tortured.

"Daddy," she cried.

"Pumpkin," he replied. "I'm going to get you to Doc Runyon just as fast as I can."

"Daddy, it hurts."

"I know it does, Pumpkin. We'll get you some pain meds soon as we can . . . Flynn! Don't we have anything to give her? The girl is hurting."

"There should be a med kit in the cart," Flynn said. "Hobble on over here and help me flip this damn thing over."

"You know I can barely walk, right?" Santini said, limping slowly in his direction. The lighting was poor, the air cold.

"Help me flip over the cart, God damnit. And quit your bellyaching. On three. One. Two. Three."

They both put their shoulders into it. But the two of them didn't have much shoulder to give, and the electric cart would not budge.

"Not happening," Santini said. "Too heavy."

"Okay, then we swallow our pain best we can and help each other back to the entrance of the cyclotron. How far can it be? Certainly, less than half a klom, fifteen minutes' walk, tops."

"Not at our speeds," Santini said. "We're looking at one hour minimum to cover five hundred meters."

"Think, man. There's bound to be at least one call box between here and the exit. Maybe we can get someone on the horn and then out here with a small vehicle to help us."

"By now, everyone in the hab is going to be bivouacked in the basement. No one will be upstairs in the Command Center waiting around to answer the phone."

"You really are a half-empty kind of guy, aren't you, Lou?"

"Just saying."

"Have some faith, will you?" Flynn said, as they trudged slowly forward, barely making any headway.

"Lost most of it today."

"Dad? How much further?"

Santini stopped, let his daughter take a breather, then said to Flynn, "Why don't you go ahead on your own, Clay? You'll make better time without the two of us along to slow you down. Leave us, go ahead, find a call box, get us some help."

"Are you okay with this, Neena?" Flynn asked.

"Dad's right. Go ahead. Get us some help. Fast as you can." Then she collapsed in a heap on the floor.

"Okay. I'm going for help."

CHAPTER THIRTY-THREE

Day Four, 2200 hours

"Is there any way that we come out of this thing alive?" Sarena Lopez asked her coworker and boyfriend *du jour*, Carson Phelps. Their carnal activity four days earlier nearly cost two children their lives. Now the two of them were at the indoor subterranean park trying to corral their dozen-plus charges.

"During the mandatory evac, our responsibilities are simple enough," Phelps said, pulling Sarena off to one side away from the others. "We collect the children; we see to it that they get safely below; then, we hold onto all the little bastards until their parents come reclaim their precious angels after they make their way below. See? Simple."

"I know what we're supposed to do, Carson. But what I'm asking you is something different. Is there any way we come out of this thing alive?" she asked again, tossing her head back in a provocative way.

"How the hell should I know?" Phelps said defensively. "I work full-time in the Equipment Department, not the childcare center. All they do in 'Quip is let me weld, help with inventory, and sweep floors. I don't know a stitch about physics or solar flares or electrical power or any of that other crap. My father made me come here. He said six months on this turd of a rock would take some of the wind out of my sails, whatever the hell that means. So, he exiled me here for half a year to get me out of the house, and out of his hair. I get into a lot of trouble back home, a lot of trouble. Only two months to go until I can return home to the real world. But who's counting?" he laughed.

"When you do go back home, are you going to behave like your father wants?"

"Yeah, like that's going to happen."

"I feel the same way," she said. "I'm tired of babysitting these bastard children. But what else can we do?"

"We could have sex," he said.

"Here? Now?"

"Why not?"

She was just about to answer in the affirmative, when a new voice could be heard.

"Heh, you, Lopez!" Hanrahan shouted from a dozen meters away. He stood on the center slat of the small wooden footbridge that traversed the manmade stream in the green space. The diminutive park was the current designated rally point for the fourteen children of all ages and races who called the hab home.

"Sir?"

"There's much too much commotion," Hanrahan whined. "Much too much noise. Can't you keep these children quiet?"

"Doing our best," Sarena replied, raising both hands to get the kids' attention. "They're children. You know that, right? Children are noisy."

"Don't care. Quiet them down or else."

Lopez looked to her boyfriend for help. But the young man just shrugged his shoulders and turned away.

"Sir, if I may," Sarena said, on the edge of sarcasm. "When children become quiet, that's when you should begin to worry, not when they are loud and obnoxious."

"Fiddlesticks," Hanrahan said. "All I know is that I want them quiet this instant. Do a headcount. Make sure we got them all. Then line them up single file and march their little butts and snotty noses toward the far stairwell. Time is running short to get below."

"It would be faster using the elevators to get down to the basement level," Carson Phelps said.

"No elevators. That's an order." Hanrahan snorted.

Sarena pulled out her clipboard and started reading off names. When she was done, one child was missing. "Kyra Goldman's not here," she announced.

Hanrahan flipped open his walkie and started to speak on an open mic. "Edith, where the hell is the Goldman girl? She's supposed to be down here at the park with the rest of them."

The walkie crackled in return with a reply. But Sarena couldn't make out the answer from where she stood on the far side of the bridge and park.

Hanrahan nodded his understanding at what was being said to him by Edith Wellsforth over the walkie. Then he shouted to them:

"My secretary says the Goldman girl is already down in the cellar. After the little girl's experience in the tunnel, she's afraid to be left alone. Nora took her down to the Annex herself an hour ago."

"Then let's move out, troops," Phelps said, sounding a single blast from his whistle to get the children's attention. "Line up! Single file. One behind the other. Move out!"

"Where we headed, Sarge?" one of the twelve-year-olds asked as if he were truly interested.

"Annex B, kid. To yon stairwell, down the stairs, Annex B." Phelps pointed.

•

•

"The latest Flash Report from Los Alamos is not encouraging," Paddington Sinclair said, dark circles under his eyes. The children had just arrived, and everyone was on edge.

"As always, you are a bit short on particulars," Professor Tattersall grumbled. Getting everyone underground in an orderly fashion and down into the basement annex had proven to be a monumental task, more like herding temperamental cats than organizing an evacuation of a staff of professional engineers and scientists.

"Our Venus observatory reports that a big one is imminent."

"How big is big?"

"Solar conditions are ripe for a major solar flare event," Sinclair said. "My specialty is not solar mechanics, mind you. But I do know a thing or two about the risks involved. If Los Alamos says we go into hiding deep underground, we go into hiding deep underground."

"This cannot be easy for you," Professor Tattersall remarked. He could see the strain in the other man's face. Sinclair's entire future was on the line here.

"What makes you say that?" Sinclair said, helping to direct people into the underground shelter where they would remain until the danger passed.

"This space elevator business is your baby, Sinclair. Your good name and everything you stand for are on the line here. Who you are and what you represent will forever after be associated with the success or failure of this project. Why lie to yourself, Sinclair? If that tether becomes electrified and goes boom, your lunatic Moon Beam project is toast and you, personally, are finished."

"Must you be so blunt?"

"Forgive me; I can't help myself. But know this: I've heard people say — smart people — that under the right conditions, that counterweight orbiting above our heads could explode like a bomb. Is that true?"

"You have been told right," Sinclair conceded. "Now may we please change the subject?"

"If you insist."

"Thank you," Sinclair said. "Has anyone heard from Flynn or Santini or Cruz or any of the others? It's been hours. And what about the girl, Neena Petronas? Is she okay? She is one of my brighter people."

"And one of ours," Tattersall remarked.

"Something I should know?"

"She is Lou Santini's daughter."

"Yes, so I learned earlier this evening."

"But to answer your question. No word yet from Flynn or Santini that I know of," Tattersall said. "We have, however, received one piece of good news via the wireless. The oxy tanks have been found and secured. Cruz and Baldwin located the tanks in the accelerator ring. They secured the tanks and, even as we speak, are bringing them out of the tunnel and up to the GAPS Crater."

"So, we will come out of this nightmare okay?" a young man from the Moon Beam team asked as he filed into the big, empty room along with the others.

"Repairs may take longer than we bargained for," Sinclair said. "Those tanks are brutally heavy. Transporting them will be no easy task. The electric carts seem to have all gone AWOL and the men have been reduced to wheeling the tanks out of the tunnel by hand on an ordinary dolly."

"Do we need to dispatch someone up there to help them wheel out the tanks? Gunderson was supposed to remain out there with them, but Hanrahan ordered the man back early to deal with some air filtration problem."

"Fact is, we can't send anyone else up there to help them."

"And why not?"

"At this point it's too damn dangerous. Tanks of breathable are bottled under pressure by machine. Pressurization requires pumps. Pumps require electricity. We have no juice to spare. Besides, we have no extra spacesuits to hand out. Cruz and Baldwin will have to manage on their own without anyone else's help."

"Okay," Tattersall finally said. "If we can't help them, then let's at least get everyone else settled. Even if the tracks are repaired in short order and power restored, detonation of the counterweight remains an ongoing threat."

Now, as the residents filed into the basement Annex in a not-at-all-orderly fashion, there was a lot of grumbling and long faces. The residents of the hab were a diverse bunch. Soldiers. Bureaucrats. Scientists. Technicians. Astronauts. Mothers. Fathers. Children. Not an easy bunch to control. Nor were the surroundings particularly pleasurable. Dry air. Stark walls. Concrete floors. Cold, ceramic fixtures. Fluorescent lights.

But whether they liked it or not, the innermost rooms of the lower habitat were about to become their home. Two hundred or more central staff, plus forty or so more from the Moon Beam team. The rail line was cut. Until it could be repaired, not even one watt of stored power could be consumed to keep the hab operational and its residents alive.

As a consequence, power usage had to now be kept to a minimum. The only way to accomplish that was to shut down entire sections of the hab and move as many people as possible to a secure central location. Plus, if the solar flare event collapsed the elevator cable, as expected, the risk to life and limb would be extensive.

•

•

"Oh, don't be such a baby. This won't hurt at all."

Santini knew Doc Runyon was lying. But he did appreciate the effort Runyon was making to calm him down. The white walls of the hab's medical emergency room and its antiseptic smells were unnerving. Frankly, Lou was more worried about his daughter's condition than he was about his own.

Doc Runyon gently touched a scanning probe to Santini's wounded leg. Santini jumped despite the light brush. "Man, that smarts!"

"Won't be but a sec before the pain goes away." Doc Runyon continued to apply slight pressure with the blunt instrument. "The anesthetic works almost immediately."

"Define almost." Santini gasped. An involuntary tear filled his eye and rolled down his cheek. His daughter, next to him on the examination table, reached for his hand but winced in pain herself.

"Oh, please do stop crying, Lou. How can a grown man be such a baby?" Runyon touched the sore spot on his patient's ankle for a second time without effect. This time, Santini didn't react. The area was completely numb.

"See?" Runyon said. "Ankle's numb. Like I said, the stuff works almost immediately."

Santini glared at Doc Runyon with crossed eyes. "I assume, Doc, that what you are about to do next would hurt like hell if my ankle wasn't already numb."

"You assume correctly. Now look the other way, Lou, and hold still. Things will go much smoother if you can't see what I'm about to do."

Santini turned his head as instructed. Doc Runyon pressed the steel surgical instrument against the man's broken ankle and touched his finger to the plunger. An indescribably thin titanium rod soaked in a bath of Acceleron shot from the mechanism into his leg at the point of the break.

Numb ankle or not, the pain was intense and Santini passed out. Doc Runyon caught him in his arms and gently laid him back on the examination table. He rolled Santini onto his side and shoved a pillow under his head.

Runyon turned to Neena, still white-faced and shaking. "Your turn."

"Are you going to lie to me, too, Doc?"

"You mean when I say it's not going to hurt?"

"Yes, that is exactly what I mean."

Doc Runyon's usually serious demeanor softened. "Truth is, girl, numbing agent or not, popping your shoulders back in place and trying to make you better is going to hurt like hell. The pain meds I already gave you should help. The Acceleron dose I am about to give you will speed the healing, days instead of weeks, hours instead of days. — But it's still going to hurt like a mother."

"Hurt me and make me better, Doc," Neena said bravely.

"Okay, here goes."

•

•

"How long are you Fascists going to keep us locked up down here in this dungeon?" one young person asked. Practically everyone was griping, Administrator Hanrahan included.

"It could be days," Sinclair said.

"Do we even have enough TP on hand? Two hundred people. Three days. That's a lot of poop, and a lot of flushing," another young person observed, as they filed into Annex B.

Professor Tattersall smirked. "That is what these Moon Beam kids are worried about, running out of toilet paper?"

"Be happy the women aren't complaining about a lack of sanitary napkins," Sinclair snickered back. It was a callous remark. He knew as well as anyone else that menstruation had to be chemically suppressed in all women of child-bearing age before they stepped aboard a spaceship and left Earth. Any embryo conceived on the Moon would be irretrievably doomed to a horrible end if carried to term.

Another student spoke up. "Do we have enough water in reserve to flush the toilets in this hole a couple hundred times?"

"Hah, the madness of crowds," Tattersall said.

"You got something to add?" Paddington Sinclair asked.

"Crowds can be foolish as well as wise," Professor Tattersall said in his most annoying professorial voice.

"And you know this how?"

"Economics," Tattersall said.

"I'm going to need a little more than that," Sinclair snapped.

"Negative externalities. That is what they call it. What is best for the individual is often disastrous for the group," Tattersall explained.

"Are we talking insufficient toilet paper here, or lack of water to flush our toilets?" Sinclair intoned.

"Both, in a way."

Paddington Sinclair thought a moment. "I suppose the classic case is that of commercial whalers hunting their prey to extinction in order to procure whale oil."

"Actually, you are not far off. If not constrained by law, individual whalers will fish more than is best for the group taken as a whole. Overfishing depletes fish stocks and all fishermen suffer as catches decline. Another example of this phenomenon is what we call the Paradox of Thrift. A person consumes less in order to save more. But if all persons in the nation consume less in order to save more, the economy will shrink, people will get laid off and no one will be able to save more."

The obnoxious kid, who had been hanging around listening to the exchange, spoke up. "Jesus Christ. What is wrong with you two? You realize we could all die down here, don't you?"

"Seriously? Two thousand two hundred years and counting, and you are still waiting for that bearded fisherman to make his grand reappearance, stairway to heaven and all that?" Tattersall said. "Give it up already, kid. He ain't coming back."

The kid was about to retort with some smart-alecky answer when there was a bustle of commotion at the top of the nearby stairway. Guy Cruz had just returned to the habitat in the company of Doyle Baldwin. The two were stumbling about with legs of concrete. They had just dropped the oxyacetylene tanks at the nearby entrance to the tunnel that led to the GAPS Crater and were about to collapse from dehydration and exhaustion.

"What is all the commotion?" Sinclair asked.

"Two of our people have come back with the tanks," someone reported.

"They made it," Tattersall said relieved. "By God, they made it."

"Word is spreading fast," Hanrahan reported. "They are all alive. Chief Flynn, Lou Santini, Neena Petronas. Hurt badly, but all alive. Doc Runyon is in with them now. He has had bones to set, Acceleron doses to administer, one or two bio-parts to manufacture. Once Runyon's done with them, the three will make their way down here. Probably within the hour, though a call has gone out for wheelchair drivers. Thank God, it is over."

"Over? Not by half," Tattersall snapped.

"What then?" Sinclair asked.

"Have you forgotten about the damage to the rail line?" Tattersall asked. "Repairs must be made. Until then, most of us are stuck down here."

"Most of us?" Sinclair said.

"I have to go topside."

"Why, for God's sake?" The color ran from Sinclair's face.

"The solar flare."

"What of it? Didn't Flynn ask us to sit out the storm down here with the rest of them? Isn't that our job? Get everyone down here and keep them here until it is safe to return to the hab?"

"The Moon Beam is your baby, Sinclair. But I want to be topside when that solar flare strikes the cable. I want to see the flipping thing explode with my own eyes firsthand."

"Have you lost your mind, Professor?"

"Not at all," Tattersall replied.

"What then?"

"Call it scientific curiosity. A teachable moment, if you are of that persuasion."

Sinclair thought about it for a long moment. "I know I'm going to regret this. But you really shouldn't leave the Annex alone. Buddy-system and all that. I really ought to go with you."

"Suit yourself. But we really must get a move on. It won't be long now before the flare hits."

CHAPTER THIRTY-FOUR

Day Five, 0100 hours

"We ought to be able to see it from here," Professor Chandler Tattersall said from a vantage point near the reinforced, acrylic glass window on the hab's Observation Deck. He stood beside one of several high-powered telescopes set up for recreational viewing by the previous administrator. Each telescope was anchored firmly to the floor and offered a different view of the surrounding landscape and sky.

"We are fools for even being up here," Paddington Sinclair declared. "I shouldn't have followed you up here; I really shouldn't have." The two had come up the back stairway from the basement Annex a few minutes earlier, after the final solar flare alert from Los Alamos.

"So go back downstairs, for all I care. I want to see the fireworks with my own eyes."

"The only thing that you are likely going to see with your own eyes is the two of us being cut to ribbons by flying glass, then dying a most horrible death when the air is sucked out of this room."

"You scared?" Tattersall asked. "Or just terrified?"

"Don't get your meaning," Sinclair said. The glass-enclosed Observation Deck was the highest point in the hab. From up here, a man had a 360-degree view of the surrounding lunar landscape. On any other day, it would be awe-inspiring.

"Are you frightened that your little science project is going to blow sky high in about eight minutes' time? When that field of highly charged particles makes contact with your ungrounded Zylon cable, watch out. Or are you afraid that your career is going to go up in flames when it becomes known that this disaster could have been prevented with a little forethought and any number of simple remedies?"

"You saying this fiasco could have been prevented? How? Do tell me how," Sinclair angrily replied. The lounge was home to several self-molding Comfy chairs. Sinclair selected one and settled in. Tattersall sat nearby, then cleared his throat to speak:

"I can think of three possible methods without even breaking a sweat."

"Okay, smart guy, what could we have done to prevent this outcome?"

Tattersall nodded knowingly. "Electromagnets, two of them. They would both have to be attached to the cable up near the counterweight. Then you could spin one magnet above the other, each going in the opposite direction. The electromagnetic forces generated by the two spinning magnets ought to be large enough to neutralize nearly any amount of static electricity build-up. Alternatively, you could first have dropped a few thousand kloms of copper wire or similar conductor down to the surface from the counterweight. That would have accomplished the same thing."

"Your magnet idea is intriguing. But what the hell good would it have been to drop down all that copper wire, except to blow the entire budget on copper?"

"The copper wire connection to the surface would have grounded the satellite electrically before you unreeled the expensive stuff."

"You're an idiot," Sinclair replied. "Nothing but a university professor with his head stuck up his ass, or worse — in the clouds. Copper wire is expensive. Very expensive. More expensive even than sheathed Zylon cord, which is what we actually use. Fifty thousand kloms of copper wire? There isn't enough money in the Northern Hemisphere to pay for that much copper wire."

"Perhaps not. But Zylon cord? The stuff's no good."

"What do you mean it's no good?"

"The stuff breaks. Longitudinal lacerations from micrometeoroid impacts. The little buggers will shred your Zylon cord in a matter of days, if not hours," Tattersall harrumphed.

"You sure about that?" Sinclair sighed. "That defect didn't show up on our sims."

"Pretty sure. High velocity, small size particles will inflict damage to the cable, even sheathed as you describe."

"But the manufacturer said . . ."

"Screw the manufacturer. The tether climbers will compress the M8 sheathing against the cable, then glancing blows from thousands of micrometeoroid hits will shred it. I give your grandiose cable under a year before it snaps."

Sinclair sighed heavily. "Now we've zipped from electrical conduction to physical failure. Isn't there anything besides copper wire that we could use to ground the assembly against static buildup?"

"There is at least one other option I can think of," Tattersall said, getting to his feet and strolling over to the food automat to buy himself a drink and a candy bar.

"What option?"

"Perhaps you have heard of a capacitor?" Tattersall asked, chomping down on the chewy peanut-chocolate-molasses bar.

"I have," Sinclair said. "Some sort of battery, yes?"

"In a manner of speaking," Tattersall replied, sipping his drink. "Well, meet the supercapacitor."

"I'll need a bit more than that."

"A capacitor is usually the size of a man's thumb. It can accept and deliver a charge much faster than an ordinary battery. For years, we have used larger ones to power particle accelerators and slapper detonators for nuclear weapons, even to fire an electromagnetic railgun. Now think of one eight to ten stories tall, a so-called supercapacitor. If a capacitor of that size were wired up to the counterweight, the charged particles from the solar flare would have a place to run once they collected on the cable. Instead of superheating the counterweight to the point of explosion, the sponge that is the supercapacitor could safely absorb the brunt."

"You know this for a fact?" Sinclair remarked, suddenly realizing that he had been defeated by his own blind drive for success.

"Not to an absolute certainty, no. But next time . . . "

"Next time?" Sinclair roared. "There isn't going to be a next time, not if we fail this time."

"Nonsense. Such arrogance. Of course, there will be a next time. There is always a next time. Human progress doesn't simply cease when an experiment goes awry or a project fails."

"You saying I'm going to fail?" Sinclair moaned.

"No, I'm not saying anything of the kind," Tattersall replied. "But who cares if you do? I think it was Samuel Beckett who said it best: *Ever tried. Ever failed. No matter. Try Again. Fail again. Fail better.*"

"I don't know what any of that means. Who is Samuel Beckett?"

"Playwright, poet, novelist. Twentieth century. What it means is that a man must learn from his mistakes. Face it, Paddington. Man cannot control his environment, not to the degree that he thinks, and certainly not every day all day long. Think of all the failures that have eventually led to success."

"I don't follow," Sinclair said, keeping a wary eye on the distant cable and counterweight. They had set up one of the Observation Deck telescopes to view both easily, with the image displayed on a nearby vid screen.

"The first Panama Canal was abandoned, unfinished for years. The first winged aircraft crashed. So did the second. The *Titanic* sunk. The *Vasa* capsized in its own harbor the day it was set afloat. The *Hindenburg* exploded in flames. Spaceship *Challenger* blew up before it could reach orbit. Newfoundland kicked the crap out of the first Vikings. It took four hundred more years before Europeans got to the Americas for a second time. Shall I go on?"

"No, you've made your point."

"Quiet!" Tattersall suddenly yelled as he accidentally knocked his drink to the floor and jumped to his feet staring hard at the vid screen. "Fireworks are about to begin."

"Shit! We're not safe here, like I said," Sinclair barked, starting to move away. "Stand back from the glass, man."

"The only smart thing you've said in recent memory," Tattersall replied, knocking over his chair as he too started to withdraw.

Light moves faster than sound. But the moon has no atmosphere, so there is never any sound ever. The detonation went unheard, making no distinctive sound whatsoever.

But a detonation is still a detonation, compressed energy driving an expanding concentric circle of destruction. A brilliant lightshow followed by a million bits of rock and another million shards of sheathed Zylon cord accelerated outward to great speed.

Since the counterweight was in orbit fifty-five thousand kloms above their heads, not all of the debris would come flying their way, at least not right away. Some of it would rain down later and for days afterward as gravity exerted its inexorable force and brought the bits and chunks down to the surface.

But now the lightshow began, as if in slow motion. Eight thousand kloms of cable sparkling bright and seemingly on fire, then the light collapsing upon an unseen point, the counterweight, about two-thirds of the way down from the upper tip of the light stick, then a horrendous explosion.

"Run!" Tattersall yelled. "Run fast! Away from the glass as fast as you can."

Sinclair was in motion even before Tattersall yelled out his instructions. It was only eight meters to the top of the stairway and they bounded down the stairs at high speed, tripping over one another as they descended.

When the shrapnel-filled debris field hit the dome enclosing the Observation Deck, the in-pressure initially compressed the air in the room before the pressure gradient could reverse course and begin to vent the cocoon of precious air out into space.

The sledgehammer of compressed air tossed them both down the stairs and across the threshold at the bottom, which is what saved their lives. A pressure door shut rapidly behind them. It was a safety feature, something the door was designed to do when the air pressure declined below acceptable limits.

Both men were badly bruised. But each helped the other to his feet.

"You crazy bastard," Tattersall said. "Tell me again why the hell we did that?"

"One of us said it might be a teachable moment."

"Well, whoever said that is a first-class idiot."

Sinclair laughed. "Who is crazier? The man who jumps off a cliff? Or the man who stands at the bottom of the cliff and tries to catch the jumper in his arms before he smacks into the ground?"

"I still say it's the man who jumps off a cliff."

"We can argue about this later. We need to get back below with the others, and I do mean right away."

CHAPTER THIRTY-FIVE

Day Five, 0245 hours

The three badly wounded heroes of the cyclotron battle limped into the underground Annex, two of them on crutches. Doc Runyon had just released the trio from his care — Clay Flynn, Lou Santini, and Neena Petronas.

When the three of them arrived, Doyle Baldwin and Guy Cruz were already inside, huddled off in one corner of the Annex, sketching out a plan to draft several volunteers, arm them with welding tools and acetylene cutting torches, and transport them all up into the GAPS Crater to try and repair the rail line Ouida had cut. As usual, Hanrahan was making a fuss and doing his best to interfere.

Neena worked her way slowly and painfully over to where Doyle, Guy and two other men she didn't know were gathered together, hunched over a table, discussing their options. Her father and Chief Flynn followed her over at a distance.

Guy looked up from the table as she approached. "Lord God, Nee. What the hell did that woman do to you? You look ghastly, worse than ghastly. Are you quite sure you should be up and about? Did Doc Runyon say it was okay?"

Guy got to his feet and reached out to his woman. Neena recoiled, afraid of being touched. Her hands and wrists were swollen and bruised from the torture. She was white and visibly shaken, but the Acceleron was beginning to work its wondrous healing magic.

"Are you in a lot of pain?" he gasped.

"Damn near everything hurts," she said. "Although, for the moment, nothing hurts. The pain meds Doc Runyon gave me have finally begun to kick in."

Doyle got to his feet as well. "Is she really dead?" he asked.

"Yeah, the bitch is really dead," Neena replied without regret.

"In case you have forgotten, that bitch you're talking about is my wife — or at least she was," Doyle said. "She and I shared a warm bed together for going on nine years."

"Forgive my lack of remorse," Neena replied angrily. "But your bitch of a woman hurt me very badly and she damn near killed every last one of us. So, excuse me for not caring. If I were you, Mr. Baldwin, I would consider myself lucky in the extreme."

"How so?"

"Chief Flynn did you a galaxy-sized favor."

"What favor?"

"He arranged things so that you could get a quickie divorce from that snake of a woman. No lawyers. No alimony. No child support to pay. You should be thanking the man, not crucifying him."

Doyle Baldwin lowered his head. "I take your meaning, young lady. Sorry. I meant nothing by it. The woman was an unrepentant snake, I see that now. And I am truly sorry for the pain you suffered at her hand. It's unforgiveable. But even a woman as evil as that one deserves a proper burial. Forgive me, but I haven't even recovered her body yet."

"Forgiveness is something you are unlikely to see from me any time soon," Neena said sternly.

"All I am asking is that you don't hold me personally responsible for what my wife did to you."

Santini raised his hand to interrupt. "Before you folks break out in a chorus of *Kumbaya*, do you mind letting me in on your plan for repairing the rail line? That has to be Priority One right now, and I can't be there myself, standing beside you to help. If we don't get the grid up and running again soon — and I mean hours, not days — our little homecoming reunion is going to be cut rather short by a sequence of unpleasant events, beginning with things getting awfully chilly down here."

"We can handle this, Lou," Guy said with some disparagement.

"It's Lou now, is it?" Santini grumbled. "When did we get on a first-name basis, you and me?"

"When I started sleeping in your daughter's bed. Now are you going to tell us how to fix the broken rail line or not?"

Santini clenched his jaw, swallowed his words, and nodded slowly at the other man. He bent to the table where the others were gathered and spun up his e-pad for all to see.

"You will need to place spot welds here and here," Santini said, pointing to a schematic on his e-pad. "These have to be high quality welds, spot on. Take Gunderson with you. He may be young, but at least he has some experience with such things. Take that boy Phelps too. He has some shop experience and may have done a bit of spot welding back home."

Santini continued to explain, but just then Paddington Sinclair and Chandler Tattersall walked over to join the group. They had entered the room only moments earlier looking disheveled and in great pain after their close brush with death upstairs as the Observation Deck collapsed around them.

"Lord," Flynn said. "The two of you look as if you've both seen a ghost. Where the hell have you two been off to anyway?"

"We came this close to being ghosts ourselves," Tattersall said putting his thumb and forefinger millimeters apart.

"Care to elaborate?" Santini asked.

"We were on the Observation Deck when the damn thing blew," Sinclair answered sheepishly.

"The solar flare?"

Sinclair nodded.

"What the hell possessed you two cretins to go up there at such an insanely dangerous moment?" Flynn asked flabbergasted. "Didn't I tell you both to remain down here with the others until the danger had passed?"

"Hah!" Tattersall chortled. "You actually expected us to sit on our hands and do nothing while you four went off and made heroes of yourselves? Not very damn likely."

"That's what you two are now? Heroes?" Flynn shook his head in anger and turned away.

"Not at all," Sinclair said. "What we did was plainly stupid. I told Chandler as much. We nearly tore off our testicles trying to get out of there alive. Glass was flying every which way. And what about you three? You people look like you have been on the losing end of a bullfight. What happened to you in that cyclotron tunnel?"

"A story for another day perhaps," Chief Flynn said breathlessly.

"No," Guy said irritated, leading Neena to a chair for her to sit down. "Make it a story for today. What did that slag witch do to you, Neena?"

"You have a soft spot for my daughter?" Santini asked again, watching how the two young people related. The two had arrived at band practice together, in each other's company, the night before last.

"Is having a soft spot for your daughter a bad thing?" Guy said exasperated.

"That is yet to be seen," Santini stammered. "But my Neena is a full-grown woman. Old enough to decide these things for herself."

"I thank you for that massive vote of confidence, Father," Neena said, her voice laced with sarcasm and twisted by as much pain as she could bear.

Santini began to scold his daughter. "You never should have come here, girl. The Moon is a much too dangerous place for a young woman to be."

She smiled. "Is that the voice of experience? Or just the voice of an annoying father?"

"Honestly," Guy said. "We're all safe now. The odds are rather long that we could ever face a repeat performance, wouldn't you agree? A second saboteur and solar flare incident at the same moment in time seems unlikely."

"Which reminds me," Neena said. "Just yesterday, our Paddington Sinclair was saying something along those lines. God, was it just yesterday? Seems like last week, if not last month."

"What are you saying?"

"The unexpected rare event," Neena said. "The orange parrot or something like that."

"Oh, of course," Santini said. "Let's all turn our attention to our newest resident know-it-all. The same man who nearly got every last one of us killed. Paddington Sinclair."

"Black Swan," Sinclair said, ignoring Santini's jibe and drawing closer to the group. "Not Orange Parrot. Black Swan."

"We have time now," Neena said. "Tell me about that Black Swan. Tell us all."

Paddington Sinclair was happy for the attention. He loved it when all eyes were on him. "It is a metaphor actually, a way of describing an unexpected event."

"Oh, stand aside, Paddington," Tattersall rudely interrupted. "You're not telling the story right."

"Excuse me. I am talking."

Tattersall ignored the other man. "Folks, the story actually goes like this: In Old World Europe, swans were known to come in only one color, white. A black swan was thought to be an impossibility, something that did not exist in nature. Then came the year 1697. Dutch explorers along the western coast of Australia. They became the first Europeans to see a black swan, and not just one of them, hundreds, thousands even. What was once seen as impossible was now seen to be real."

"So, it is more than a metaphor then?" Guy observed.

"Oh, my goodness, yes," Tattersall replied. "Capitalize the words and view the two words taken together as a philosophy, a way of thinking — a 'Black Swan.' The Black Swan has three attributes. The event is a surprise to the observer, something he did not expect, an outlier, as it were. Nothing in the observer's past would have — or could have — pointed to the event as anything more than a remote possibility, outside the realm of ordinary expectations."

"Now who's telling the story wrong?" Sinclair interrupted.

"Let the man finish," Flynn said. "Go on Chandler."

Tattersall nodded. "The second part of the triad is that the event has a major, sometimes extreme impact on other events and on people in general. It shocks them out of their complacency and into a new world they never thought could exist.

"Finally, after the truth sinks in and the first recorded instance of the event becomes more widely known, people and institutions begin to rationalize it by hindsight. *Of course, we saw it coming,* people will say. *How could you not?* In spite of the event's outlier status, human nature makes us concoct explanations for its occurrence after the fact, making it explainable and predictable, when it really is not."

"Okay, I have to admit. You did a pretty good job explaining," Sinclair declared.

"But I'm not quite finished," Tattersall observed. "I would venture to say that a small number of Black Swans explain almost everything in our confusing world, from the success of ideas and religions, to the dynamics of historical events, to elements of our own personal lives."

"Aren't you being overly dramatic?"

"Am I?" Tattersall snapped. "How else would you explain the events of the past few days? Sabotage. Power failure. Solar flare."

"What's to explain?" Sinclair said. "I have gained a new appreciation for the talents of the techs in our midst, the men who work with their hands as well as their minds. Lou, Guy, Doyle, Flynn. The next time a team begins construction on a space elevator, we will have all learned from our mistakes this time."

"So, have you finally come around to the idea that there will be a next time?" Tattersall chortled. "I call that great human growth."

Chief Flynn cleared his throat to speak. "Chandler, I'm not as smart as you and Sinclair, nor, perhaps, am I as well educated. But I have been around the block a few times and one thing had an impact on me when I was a young man. My father was a bit of a philosopher. Occasionally, he dabbled in the occult, that mysterious thing some call religion. He said we could always learn from the Ancients. There was this Jew. Hillel, The Elder. He was a first-century religious leader. Hillel was asked to summarize the Torah while standing on one leg. The Torah is the Bible of the Hebrews. Hillel answered: *That which is hateful to you, do not do to your fellow. That is the whole Torah; the rest is commentary.* I think we can all learn something from that."

"Yes, and what is it that we can learn?" Chandler asked. "All I know for certain is that I am damn happy to be alive. I think we ought to celebrate our good fortune with a party. Once power is restored, which ought to be sometime later today if these lugnuts get to work, we need to gather the band for a gig. It would be a huge morale booster."

"I don't suppose the dance will be held on the floor of the Observation Deck as originally planned," Santini said.

"Closed for repairs," Tattersall replied with flat irony. "I've been made to understand that a pair of foolish old men made a mess of things up there."

"If not the Observation Deck, then where?" Flynn asked.

"Why not right here in the Annex? We can send you upstairs with a work crew. They can help bring down all your equipment and musical instruments. What say you?"

Santini turned to his daughter. "Your mother tells me you can sing. Are you any good?"

"Why do you ask?" Neena replied.

"The Clay Pots could sure use a good female voice at the mic."

"I thought Chief Flynn was your vocalist," Neena replied.

"The man can barely hum, much less sing." Santini chuckled.

"I get my own mic?"

"Of course, you do," Santini replied. "Just as soon as your hand has healed enough to hold one."

"But won't that upset the formula?" she asked.

"Formula?"

"Four lasagnas, two bagels, and an American cheese."

"New formula," Santini replied. "Four lasagnas, two bagels, an American cheese, and a sweet pepper."

She smiled broadly. "Yes, I can see it now. Neena Petronas and the Clay Pots. I do like that name, don't you?"

"I'll tell you after the live audition."

ACKNOWLEDGEMENTS

Minds smarter than my own made valuable contributions to this book, helping me to better understand how a lunar space elevator might be built. Any remaining mistakes in physics or chemistry or related sciences belong solely to me and to no one else.

The International Space Elevator Consortium is an amazing hub of people, resources, and research dedicated to the future of space elevatorism. Some of the people who spearhead the ISEC volunteered their valuable time and extraordinary knowledge to help me write a realistic story that depicts a possible lunar outpost settlement. These include Dr. Peter Swan, Ph.D., Jerome Pearson, and Mr. Ted Semon. The tether climber depicted in my book is named for Jerome Pearson, or JP as his friends call him.

I read dozens of scientific articles on the subject, two of the more interesting being "Conceptual Design and Technology Roadmap for a Lunar Space Elevator" by Mr. Kaveh Razzaghi, an article I read with great interest; and "Dynamics Research of Initial Tether Deployment of Lunar Space Elevator" by Prof. Xiaohui Wang.

For an author like myself, being able to secure the assistance of highly intelligent and discriminating readers willing to make editorial suggestions and corrections is invaluable to crafting a compelling manuscript free of grammatical and other errors. I owe special thanks to these readers:

Loren Logsdon, Ph.D. Eureka College, a close friend, brilliant writer, and one of the smartest men I know. Craig Curtis, Professor of Political Science, Bradley University, Peoria, Illinois, a multi-talented professor with a love of music. Craig plays the guitar, the mandolin, and the 5-string banjo with gusto, all talents which helped me get my music right. Donald Sloan, a meticulous editor, talented and creative. Dave Broquard, a man with a keen scientific mind, perhaps one of the best readers I ever had the pleasure to edit my work. Fellow dreamer, Andy Hessler, another one of those guys who lies awake at night pondering the deep mysteries of the universe. And last but not least, my wife Debra, who puts up with all my many idiosyncrasies and still finds time to be the final editor of the completed work.

Cover Art By: Lin Li Hsiang